For Rory and Isobel,
and for Rollo

Winter kept us warm, covering
Earth in forgetful snow

T.S Eliot, *The Waste Land*

And even your lies were able to assert
Integrity of purpose

Louis Macneice, *Autumn Journal*

Prologue

This is what I can't forget: the icy pavement and snowflakes dancing around us. Clouds of your breath. The sky, vast, and violet-tinged. The plane, hopelessly, catastrophically delayed. You laughing, for no reason at all. *Brrr*, shivering, with exaggeration, and a merriness that bemused me given the approaching storm and problems with my flight. Then you blew on your fists and stamped hard, first on one foot and then the other, and said, *Maybe this is meant to be*, and I gazed at you, transfixed, and you snatched the croissant out of my hands, telling me, *You snooze, you lose*. You explained, with your mouth full, *No one is leaving today. Let's make the most of it. It's meant to be*.

Yes, this is what I can't stop thinking about, even though everything is different now, for all of us. I am still having these useless, one-sided conversations with the ghost of you. It's trying to snow at the moment in Edinburgh, and this morning, in the air that is turning grey with lazy sleet, I thought I saw you. I was on the bridge by your parents' house, and I even called your name. But whoever it was moved away, shrouded by the gloom, and covered his ears with his headphones. Like a mutinous child.

But it wasn't you, of course. You, with a magician's dexterity, had vanished long ago.

It was risky, standing there on the bridge for so long with the nearly-snow falling ineffectively around me, like

1

the blunt edge of something. But I was thinking of you and imagining that you might finally listen to me. I imagined that you could hear me. We could start at the beginning. You would remember the white mountains and the snowflakes, fast and alpine-sharp. When we went sledging under the chill of the pale sky, when I couldn't stop shivering. When you said, *I think I've been waiting all my life for you.*

But it's all pointless. It wouldn't matter any more if you remember the snowflakes or not. You aren't coming back, and you have certainly made sure that I can't follow you this time. It's over, whatever it was. Not a conventional ending for us (there was a time and a place for that opportunity, wasn't there? That sad but civilised goodbye, and putting it simply, you blew it) – but an ending nonetheless. I never could tell if you were ever sorry, about any of it. There was no trace of . . . anything when I saw you last and now, when I think of your face, it's still blank. Expressionless. All the intensity you once arranged on your features in artful display drained away. Nothing.

But there was Anna, and there was your mother. Ellen, who proved that your charm was not unique to you after all, and even your hateful father had a seductiveness to his stupidity and vanity that for a while at least, I couldn't ignore. I wish now, of course, that I had never got tangled up with them, that I hadn't lost myself pretending for so long, that I hadn't lied. I wish that I had been able to stay away – but the confusing fact remains: if I had, I would never have seen you again. And secondly . . . well, we would never have found you out and you might have got away with what you did.

1

Nine days in total. Nine days since Christmas Eve, and nine days since you disappeared. The realisation afresh, the fury and the confusion; a simultaneous, constant nine-day exhaustion. This is my merry-go-round. My unravelling.

I shake the little glass ornament on my desk. My precious fairy-tale snow globe, apparently filled with nothing more than water and bone fragments. As I put it down, I notice that my hands, still parched dry from the thin, cold air, are shaking slightly. The bottle of red wine is half empty. The thought that I probably need to eat something pricks at a corner of my mind. I remember at the same time that I don't have any food in the flat and so I pour another glass while I tell myself I will think what to do about that.

I don't think about supper. I think about Johnny, and after a while, turn my computer on. It's near the window so I sit with my back to the outside world, looking blankly into my world. I used to feel fondly about my flat. But when I came back from the Alps, I saw it through Johnny's non-seeing eyes and it altered for me. I'd cleaned it and bought flowers and champagne. I waited for him to come. I lay outfits on the bed, tried them all on and wondered if they would do. I rearranged ornaments and books. I threw away the tatty, and the dull; I replaced them with the gleaming and the enticing. The flat watched me wait

3

with Scottish sternness and shaking head and the flowers wilted. On day seven, when I got a message but not from him, I threw the champagne against the wall. And now, having witnessed both my anticipation and my humiliation, the flat mocks me. I wish the dust would materialise again, would resettle on the chest and the drabness re-establish itself. It is, after all, just me again: in my one-room apartment on a busy thoroughfare in Edinburgh, and the eager thought of Johnny just that. One shamed occupant and now, tiny glass shards lodged like slivers of glitter between the wooden floorboards.

When the phone rings, my eyes jerk to the screen. But it is Tamsin calling. My fingers spasm in anger. I clench my fist over the warm phone as though to crush it and then answer, jabbing at the speakerphone. 'Hi.'

'Skye. There you are. Happy New Year, finally.'

'And you. Happy New Year.' With my hands free, I can log into Facebook.

'Sorry we never saw you. Were you busy?'

'I was.' In one sense of the word. 'Hope you had fun.' Press search . . .

'It was brilliant. Best fireworks ever.'

I'm not interested in pyrotechnics. 'Someone at the door. I've got to go.'

'Wait, Skye,' she says, and then falters. 'What are you doing? Really?'

I hold my breath to control the irritation, thinking, I could tell her what I'm doing. Drinking, and thinking about Johnny. Looking everywhere for him. I could tell her but I don't want to, I'm busy doing these things. I want her to stop bothering me.

'Nothing.'

'And how's Nora?'

'OK, no better really. She doesn't remember things most of the time.'

'Poor Aunt Nora,' says Tam sympathetically.

'Yes. I've got to go, call you later.' With one eye on my computer screen, I just end the call. I acknowledge and dismiss my callousness at the same time, and drain my glass.

Sometimes — two or three times — I have found him active on Facebook at the same time as me. Or active two minutes ago. Of course, this is nothing other than what it says it is. It doesn't mean anything, other than he's still alive and this I know by now anyway. And after the burst of adrenalin, there's nothing, again.

I don't know why I do it. I haven't yet actually found anything out that's helpful, or comforting. I don't know — only that, like an addict without expectation of joy or enlightenment, I trawl social media constantly. There's a trickery to this sort of drug, not unlike the target himself: just the suggestion of information and a veneer of plausibility, enough to deceive, and tease me into another effort at cracking through. Tam can wait, and she can hear about my aunt's dementia another time — because nothing is so important as him, and I can't get near him any other way. I won't be interrupted. Knowing the worthless and invidious nature of the addiction doesn't stop me doing it.

He's not really there, even when the screen tells me otherwise — and I am led up various dead-ends in my frustrated search for him until well past midnight and well into the dregs of the Rioja.

2

Tuesday 3 January. First day back at work, on reception at a clinic on Alva Street which specialises in laser and plastic surgery. I consider not going, but know that I have to. I was away all of December and it would be impossible to keep my job if I don't return as promised. Before I leave for work, I deliver my neighbour's rabbit back to him and when I'm stroking her goodbye, tears start rolling down my face. Darcy's black eyes regard me solemnly.

The neighbour is desperately embarrassed.

'She's just been good company,' I explain. He looks unconvinced. 'She was company over New Year's Eve.'

At the clinic, another receptionist brings in flowers and I stare at the crimson petals on the table and answer the phones, my mobile cradled in my palm like a nut in its shell. It has become the symbol of how I have changed in so short a time. There used to be days or evenings out with Tam, or anyone else, when I would forget my phone, and leave it at home abandoned on a table and it wouldn't matter. Times when I had gone a whole day at work without checking it. I could have got home and gone out again without wondering where it was. I could have sat in the pub without it and nothing would have seemed out of the ordinary. Or, and this is staggering to recall, a message could bleep at me and it wouldn't mean anything, it wouldn't matter. I would get to the message when I got

6

to it, when I remembered about it again. A missed call would be just that.

But that was before. Everything is different now. I am different now.

At ten thirty, I leave the clinic and go out into the street for my coffee break. I walk to the usual café. Someone has left a paper on the table and I turn the pages robotically. The crossword at the back diverts my attention for half a second; I can't immediately solve the clue so, unable to sustain any concentration on it, I push the paper away. I start to walk back to Alva Street but on the corner, I realise I've forgotten to buy a sandwich. Tears pinch angrily at the back of my eyes. I go back, remove one from the pile, queue, buy it, and return to work. At lunchtime I eat it, chewing and scrolling through Instagram at the same time.

I always start with Johnny, just to check, but his own account has been stagnating unused for months, so I usually simply chop and divide through his followers and the accounts that he follows, through the threads and suggestions, and just see where I am led. This friend, that tag, (private accounts sometimes hamper the investigations but I circumvent them and carry on), who has liked what, who has started following who – and there is Anna. Johnny's best friend from the airport. There is always, very quickly, Anna, either with a picture of her own or a comment, an emoji, a new craze. Always something, as if she is frightened of being left out, or going unnoticed, even for a day.

Today, @anna_banana_xo has vomited yet another bad photo. It's typical Anna. It is a dramatic and self-absorbed boast about being chatted up; a brag veiled gossamer-thinly as a complaint about Edinburgh city transport. **#squashed #tooclose #tooearly.** A quick investigation of who likes this transparently attention-seeking picture (of a crowded bus), tells me Johnny doesn't – but that his mother, Ellen, does. I feel curiously disappointed by @ellen.strachan and her decision. Her own account – I know it well – is so much more nuanced, and cultured.

I return to it with a sense of gladness. I know things about Ellen now, some of which Johnny told me and some of which she offers up willingly, even to strangers. It's too hard to resist accumulating the knowledge. It's hard to stay away. And I'm aware how that sounds but there it is. There is the joint medical practice on Scotland Street, of course: Dr and Dr Strachan. It is a little twee, although undeniably ideal; it encapsulates what I have surmised about Ellen's and Andrew's civilised and middle-class approachability perfectly. But Johnny wasn't impressed by them. I know that he did not appreciate Dr and Dr Strachan and that although they lived in the same city, he stoically maintained his distance, adopting an air of disdain whenever they were mentioned.

I loathe Anna's bitchy and pointed Instagramming, but I love Ellen's. She obviously has an interesting and varied life outside her job and she's happy to share it. She goes to art galleries and new restaurants. She likes birds. And she's really pretty, if a little overweight. Anyone would want to follow her, to keep tabs on her, and because her account is public, anyone can. It's easy to infiltrate her life, to track her movements. Not for the first time, I note the difference between Anna's and Ellen's accounts. Both are wide open but Ellen's has a naivety that Anna's does not. Anna has a sly knowledge about the workings of social media; there is a self-awareness and insinuation to her captions and hashtags. Ellen, on the other hand, operates under the misplaced illusion of anonymity and trust. She seems utterly transparent.

I admit that I have probably allowed curiosity to become something else, something that I know is less wholesome, but there isn't any law against it and she does keep drawing me in; if Anna repels me, Ellen innocently beckons me forward with her photos. You can be involved in this, she seems to say. Join in with us. You'd like this picture of the ospreys too. Often, poring over the backlog of her enticing Instagram with an unsteady finger and held breath, I would add my own silent comment to the captions. *Andrew looks pissed. Where is your other nephew? I like the skirt you keep wearing. Sardinia?*

And beneath all the invisible, silent outpourings, the real question. Where are *you*?

Occasionally, on rare circumstance, you show yourself; when @johnny_strachan appears, deigning to like the picture, I stare into it, trying to gauge what it was that you had approved of. The reasons for your infrequent and indolent appreciation has always been a mystery to me.

I finish work at five and begin the walk home to Newington. Nothing on Instagram from the people in Johnny's life has given me any clue as to his movements. I feel as though I have spent the afternoon in an airless panic room, banging on soundproofed and blacked out windows.

Tomorrow, Wednesday, is my day off at the clinic and the day I am supposed to go to the university. I am studying part-time to qualify as an ice-technician. That was the idea, anyway, before ideas got sidelined. I'll see how I feel tomorrow. I'm not that interested in ice at the moment. It's been ten days now.

Weather used to affect my mood. All these clichés used to apply: that unexpected spring in the step, the involuntary lifting of the heart, the optimism that accompanies the dawning of a sunny day. Or the glumness of rain, like the rain on the night towards the end of November last year, the night before I left for France. 'Don't bother coming out,' I'd said to Tam on the phone at lunchtime, sadly. 'The weather is filthy.' I'd watched rivers of water cascade down Dalkeith Road after I'd packed up at work, and I felt miserable and nervous. 'Bollocks,' Tam had said, dismissing my defeatism. 'As if I wouldn't come to see you off. Don't you suggest such a thing,' and then the clouds had passed over and the afternoon light had been so fresh, like everything that had gone before was washed clean. We'd run, splashing through the puddles, to the pub on the corner. 'Look after yourself,' she'd told me. 'And say yes to things if you're asked. Make sure you don't hide yourself away in your room when you're not working. Make the most of the opportunity.'

Tam is one of the reasons I found the courage to come to Edinburgh. I latched on to her years ago when we lived in Fort William, I think partly because of her commitment to who she is (straightforwardly gay) and what she stands for (animal rights). She's a fitness instructor and there's no nonsense about her. I've always been in awe of her uncompromising take on life, and consequently how simple she finds it. She's the sort of person who has reminders on her phone, Buddhist ones that keep her inspired and kind, as well as insufferable occasionally. I remember a couple of her favourites. *Be passionate about something big.* Or: *Every day we are born again. What you do today matters most.* She's got that in common with Johnny; at least, he had pulled out similar little soundbites when he'd needed them, using the vagaries of cliché to hide his dispassion.

Weather, I see now, is just weather. Nothing more and nothing less. It has, and should have, no bearing on perception. It has, after all, never stopped me walking, working, eating, breathing. I don't miss the sun and I don't miss the snow. I miss the feel of his hand, warm and dry, in my palm.

This afternoon there isn't any sort of weather to speak of, none that my mood takes any notice of. I'm in the library and I have got myself and my files out of the flat and I am alternately staring at them, my bitten nails, and Instagram. Ellen has just posted a picture and today's photo is of a flyer for an event at Abbotsford House just outside Edinburgh at the weekend. It's an important lecture, culturally, historically and politically, and one that I know about already. It's been well-publicised. Gillian had mentioned it at work. I might have gone to it in another life, before other things began to take up my time.

Ellen only posted seventeen minutes ago. She's not far away. She could still be only 0.3 miles away. Bute House, Edinburgh. @ellen.strachan is always precise. She is reminded to post about the lecture because she has just walked past this #gorgeousbuilding #scottisharchitecture #scottishparliament. The forthcoming date is 7 January, this Saturday. Ellen finishes the caption: hoping to see some of you there ☺ and presumably has now walked on. I put my pen down. If I wanted to see her, perhaps I could guess the route she is walking. If I ran outside now and down this street and then that one, I might actually see her in the flesh. Has she left the surgery a little early? Could I bump into her, if she is going home to Stockbridge?

And who would I say I was? Ellen, I can be pretty sure, has never heard of me; her son does not confide in his parents but my name is not conventional. I'd need a new name, to be safe. I catch and stop myself. Then I think *No, I really need a new name*. And then I can do whatever I want.

I can follow her officially on Instagram. It'll be legitimate. I even look down at my text book and see a name, one I like. *She* could follow Ellen, and Skye could stop sneaking around in the shadows, terrified of pressing something that will give her away. I could become her friend. I could find out what happened. And then, embarrassed at myself, I put my head in my hands. The picture is still there, visible through my fingers.

Underneath it is the link to the lecture that she has helpfully provided. An idea, a better one than using guesswork to chase her down streets: knowing where she is going to be on Saturday. I can't let go of the knowledge. Then the thoughts begin to bat at me like wings. If there is some unease attached to my chaotic thinking, then I keep it at bay and I don't consciously decide then and there to do anything, or to do nothing. It just seems, at that point in the library, with Ellen's picture laid out as a boxed and alluring fact for me, that there could be something. For real: not in a dream and not in my imagination. That something might simply happen. Like the weather.

3

The French Alps, November 2016

There was an early flight from Scotland in the rain, full of students from Edinburgh. We were ice-technicians, French language students, winter sports athletes and more, all on an annual exchange with Grenoble University. There were the buses inching along a mountain pass into the sunlight and there were the Alps and their crystalline beauty. There were hostels and welcome drinks and the next day there were gloves to find and snow-boots to unpack and then there were one or two walks beneath a sky that was so piercingly bright and clear it seemed as though it trembled; there was a slight judder to its blueness, as though, stretching taut between the razor-sharp teeth of the mountains, it shook a little. There was the Aiguille du Midi cable car and the work to begin removing ice and snow from its cables. There was a morning snowshoeing. And one day, there was you.

How casually it starts. There were no words exchanged; you were involved with others, part of a loud group, and you were chatting and laughing as you passed through the doorway. I had to wait to the side of the entrance, like a doorman. The alpine air hovered alongside me as your boorish crowd pushed through. By virtue of the company you kept, you were nothing but an irritant – what an extraordinary thought this is – and then you glanced towards me, and your smile was apologetic and quick. Like a memory, something caught inside me.

Later in the day, when the sun had dropped behind the summit of Mont Blanc, you were in the foyer with friends. You were staring up at the jagged peaks, their sharp focus fading with the day into mistiness, and your face was inscrutable but I believed I sensed some intensity, some longing in you that set you apart from the others. I was mesmerised by your stillness. When you turned, you saw me looking at you. I watched you hesitate and then, propelled perhaps by the vague memory of a certain coolness from me that morning, you walked towards me. By the time you reached me, your boyish features had re-established themselves and your eyes were smiling.

'Look at that sunset. Every time. Wow.'

The sky was a flurry of purple-stained ribbons above the mountains. I concentrated on doing up my boots.

'*Parlez-vous Anglais*? Are you English?'

My shyness and lack of encouragement didn't bother you. It inspired you. In fact, everything in the Alps inspired you; there, you would lose the drag and ennui of your Edinburgh self. There, I fell in love with you.

'Actually, don't tell me. Let me guess . . .'

I tied the other lace and then I had nothing to do while you did your guessing so I stared at you. I looked at your eyes and your floppy blond hair and your face, not yet diffident, slightly reddened from the arctic temperature outside, and at your eyes again. They were not the same colour, they are not a pair.

'Maybe not English. Irish . . . definitely Celtic . . . with hair like that . . .'

You were being silly and I picked up my bag. But I couldn't help it, for some unfathomable reason I told you

14

before I got to the lift. 'Scottish,' I said, relenting. 'I'm Scottish.'

I was indulging you. And it was the beginning of the habit, a pattern of compulsions whereby satisfying you in every which way I could became the imperative of my life. I took on the universe to get it right with you. I tried to second-guess you all the time and give you the answers I thought you wanted. I tried to imagine what you would like me to be doing and pretended I'd done it. You told me once that sunlight suited me, and ever since I have tried to place myself in the most desirable light according to you. It was simply a matter of positioning. In this way, liars are easily made.

4

Before Johnny, though, before Chamonix. What was the point? To sum up: there was me, in my thirties and living in Edinburgh. There were some friends, although fewer than before as people got married, got busier, had babies. There was work, of course, four days a week at the clinic which didn't pay too badly and enabled me to live just as I needed, and there was the university day. Around this structure, there was the padding – purposefully placed and generally satisfactory – to mask the loneliness. There were takeaways and TV programmes and crosswords and films. There were themed evenings with a book club. There was the odd play. There was backgammon with the pub landlord, and tapas with my neighbour and occasionally there was Darcy, his rabbit. There were weekend walks along the coast. There were organised beach clean-ups and there was Tam's friend who made art out of the plastic rubbish we collected and there was her exhibition to help organise. The padding was OK, it was even good, I had made it so. There was loneliness, of a sort, but it was a manageable one and hushed, on the whole, by the efficient pursuit of routines and diversions.

The padding doesn't work any more.

Last night I dreamt that Johnny got in touch with me. Everything about the dream had been so real that when I woke up, I searched through my phone for the proof of what I had felt to be so incontrovertibly real. I had been in bed when he rang. My head, soft on my pillow, my room dark and still. The phone, for once not within reach, was charging on the other side of the room. I heard it start to ring and my eyes flew open. I remember the blankets had been heavy across my feet and I struggled for a second to rid them from my legs and then I had bolted across the room faster than I had ever moved in my life, barely touching the floor, hoping against all hope that it was him and also suddenly knowing beyond doubt that it must be. And the relief, the utterly overwhelming relief. It was like water to thirst, or air to suffocation. I wanted to cry with the blessed relief of it. And it stopped ringing just before I got to it and I sank to my knees on the floor, cradling the phone in my hands as if it were a tiny precious mouse. And there it was, glinting in green: missed call Johnny. And then in my dream it became crucial to me to try and get hold of him so I called him back and the number rang and rang without going to voicemail as it usually did and so a suspicion began to creep up on me and I couldn't bear this not to be real so I sent him a message.

Johnny. Are you there?

I sat with the phone in my hands, feeling my legs beginning to ache and the hope seeping from me and the pillow once again establishing itself soft against my head and the blankets heavier than before across me, and slowly coming to, in a murky pre-dawn light, with the realisation that there had been no missed call from Johnny and that he still hadn't been in touch.

I don't think I can go on like this. I need to do something. The kettle starts boiling and the steam burns my hand. After a second or two, when I can't stand it any more, I move away and look for the milk. I can't find it so I drink my coffee black. I'm too tired, drained by the dream, and drained by my anger. I've had enough. Johnny is not going to ring. Johnny has vanished and left me with nothing to go on, nothing except Anna who knows what I look like, and Ellen – who doesn't.

The thoughts begin to grow again, and beat. I open Ellen's Instagram picture of the First Minister's house, noticing that my hand is scarlet from the kettle steam. I could go to Abbotsford too. It seems as if I could wrench myself free from the boggy terrain in which I am so entrenched. It seems there might be another way to stay close to Johnny.

5

Chamonix is a deep valley that slices through the Rhône-Alpes region of France. The town is a frightened one at its heart, cowering as it does in the shade of the mountains that rear from it. It attracts the courageous, as well as the uninformed braggers and pretenders, but the gradients and the terrain will sort the one from the other. There is no margin for error.

There is something both compelling and frightening about the sharp scenery. It is like colouring between the lines but they are harsh, high lines with acute angles and deep drops. And one morning you were there, smudging the edge of them and encroaching on the landscape. You were everywhere, really, that morning. In the queue for the fruit salad, at the coffee machine. Suddenly rooms were defined by whether or not you were in them. Conversations began to be pointless unless you spoke up. There was, almost imperceptibly, a heightened sense of awareness of everything to do with you; I knew where you were that morning – just to the left of me and behind that man with the beard. I felt you watching me as I talked to the concierge and it's as if you cast a net and a corner of it snagged on me. I felt a tug every now and then.

Snowstorms had been forecast and we were huddled in the foyer in our groups, murmuring anxiously. Some were

19

more belligerent and determined to go out anyway. Some were relaxed and beginning to talk about going back to bed or going for hot chocolates. I felt as though I was waiting for you to decide.

In the end, the skiers left, some more reluctantly than others. There were a few extreme skiers with you, the posturing vagabonds who knew that this was a testing ground for them. I liked the way you seemed more humble and unsure of yourself. You trailed out behind them, head downcast, and I saw you bring out an inhaler to take a nervy puff on. And then, on the street, you looked back at me and mouthed *Help*, suddenly laughing and hoisting your skis on to your shoulder. *What am I doing?* I walked over to the doors and they swished open, the wind blasting in and sending my hair flying about my face.

'Will you be here if I make it back alive?'

'Yes,' I laughed back at you. 'I'll be here.'

'Wish me luck then. I may be some time,' and you strode away down the street.

The ice-technicians didn't like the high winds and we abandoned plans to go out. I spent the morning writing up some notes. I had lunch with two other younger girls on my course. They gossiped and giggled about the wider group. I listened for mentions of you. 'The good-looking guy who's skiing with Josh, what's his name?' *You?*

Perhaps you took the day on the mountains to consider your options. Of course, I did not assume that at the time but afterwards you swore that you had never been so taken with anyone and that I had been in your thoughts all the fast, icy day. And you arrived at the bar that evening before too long. Your *hello* – it sounded so natural and so innocently cheerful that my response was instinctive, it just fell out of my mouth.

'Hello again.'

And we grinned at each other because we'd been waiting for this all day.

'I'm Johnny Strachan. Can I . . .?'

'Yes,' I said, pulling the bar stool out. 'Of course.' And then, in an attempt to be cautious, to test you, I told you that I was only having one drink.

You were delighted. 'Stay,' you entreated, galvanised. 'Push the boat out. Let me buy you one more.' And before I could agree or refuse, others started to crowd the bar, to crowd us, and I felt ridiculously disappointed that we weren't alone any more but you managed to disconnect us slightly; I could hear the others and occasionally someone jostled my arm, but really, you had pulled a bubble around us and we were a little bit immune to the rest. The rest was incidental.

The wine went straight to my head. You were telling me, and maybe someone else who imagined themselves included, about your day which you hadn't enjoyed because you're such a crap skier and the slopes are crazy steep and now you're just relieved it's over. I couldn't stop looking at your eyes. Closer to you now than I had been before, I could see that one was hazel-green and the other one was brown, each as sincere and beguiling as the other. I didn't know which way to look because I couldn't stop staring at your eyes and everywhere was you again; your hand on the bar, pointing out the beer you want, just missing my shoulder. Your voice, low and absorbing, the shape of you on the stool, your legs in blue jeans, your arms in blue fleece and more than any of this, your eyes, fluttering towards mine and away again. At first our glances had been bashful – by the time you had to leave, it seemed to me that idle flirtation had drained away and been replaced with intent.

'Are you coming, Johnny?' someone shouted and you grimaced, indecision flitting across your face and then you stepped away.

'I'd better go. Ski team. Another time? We're here for the month.'

'The whole month?'

'Yes,' you said, 'really. Until Christmas.'

'But so am I. Or just about.'

'I know,' you said teasingly, and then in anticipation of my next question: 'I've been asking about you.'

My mouth closed, pursing with the pleasure of it.

'See you later then, alligator,' you offered and then sulky because you are still leaving, but dutiful, I half-answered.

'In a while.'

You made me jump when you touched my arm just five minutes later.

'I'm back,' you said, pleased with yourself.

'Why haven't you gone out with the others?'

You looked at me meaningfully but because I'm not sophisticated, I didn't allow the silence to speak for you and I repeated the question.

You laughed then, admiringly it seemed, and told me they weren't really your friends. That you were just on the same ski team and you'd had your night out with them this week and you didn't want another.

'How fickle you are,' I joked.

'No. Anyone can see that something,' you corrected yourself, 'someone. Someone far better has come along.'

You had been drinking, we all had. 'Oh please.'

You blithely deflected my derision. 'Don't bite my head off.' You weren't remotely bothered by it. It was no sort of defence against you. 'You're too gorgeous to be so cross all the time. I can't put my finger on what it is about you. You're very striking, my mother would call you striking, but there's something else.' You allowed yourself to look slightly shamefaced. 'You're like what I used to imagine a mermaid to look like. A green-eyed mermaid, like the one in the film.'

'How old are you?' but I was enjoying myself. 'Honestly. Isn't it past your bedtime?'

'Twenty-seven,' you said. I hoped that you weren't going to ask me how old I was and of course you didn't and then that irked me, so I told you.

'I'm thirty-one,' and you didn't say anything, your expression never wavered. 'Well, it may not be past your bedtime but it is past mine.' I got up and tried to slide off my chair and ended up wedged, ungainly, between the stools. You put your hand on my arm. They were cool, your fingers. Your touch was light.

'Don't go.'

I shook my head. I had to pick my stool up and move it so I could get out. Once I was free, I moved away. 'Good night.'

'You haven't finished your wine.'

'Good night.'

When I was waiting for the lift, you joined me there.

'Stay with me.' I used to hear you in my mind saying that, long after you'd gone.

The lift pinged open.

I remember that you put your head on one side, in a hopeful manner. I expect you thought that I was making a decision but no; I was awestruck. I was realising, *this is happening to me*, and I was wondering what on earth to do with the fact that it was happening to me. While you supposed I was considering whether or not to go to bed with you, I was thinking about the wine and the tealights along the bar. I was marvelling at my handful of moments. They would have been enough for me.

Just as the lift doors were about to close, I stepped through them and they shut with me safe on the inside and you on the outside. I expect I ought to have thought to myself, phew. Lucky escape. I ought to have been relieved, and thought: men being charming on holiday, I know men like that. But the truth is, I didn't and I'd certainly never met anyone like you. I was in awe of you and your confidence from the start and the easy way you handled things, the easy way you handled me which felt both absurdly exciting and absolutely steady at the same time. I ought to have thought, I know men like you, but I didn't.

Upstairs, I googled Johnny Strachan. Not much came up apart from a private Facebook page, but plenty, as it turned out, about a Dr and Dr Strachan from Edinburgh. Edinburgh?

The irony, of course, only struck me later that when looking for you, I find your parents.

6

You snooze, you lose. That banal phrase you used comes back to me again now as I stand in my kitchen, blowing softly on my scarlet hand and thinking about Abbotsford. I don't know why I always thought I had to flatter you by laughing in response to your dead-end clichés. Nothing ever went anywhere with you and I suppose that the exchange of humour was just a way of concealing this fact. There were just layers and layers of childish, diverting nonsense. I had always assumed there was a man somewhere, a man who might emerge.

I go into my messages and look under Johnny's name. There are rows and rows of my texts to him like the blue and green blocks of a wall, and there are none from him to me. None since a food order on 20 December last year in Chamonix anyway, and that hadn't given me anything to go on. As a dead man's final words, they were pretty unremarkable.

Can you order me the pasta.

That was it. That was what Johnny had left me with, a text about carbohydrates on my mobile. Except, now I see that wasn't just it. He made mistakes. There was Anna, fleetingly introduced at the airport and constantly online since, and there was Ellen, inviting and friendly, letting me know where she is going to be on Saturday. Johnny won't be there, I can be sure of that at least. He wouldn't deign to go with his mother to something like this, and I'm not sure he would even go without her. Politics, the grubbiness of any conviction, is slightly beneath him. And he hasn't liked the picture. I think if he was going with Ellen, she would have said so in the caption.

Actions not words, Johnny was fond of saying that. Indeed. At last, something we can agree on again. I click on the link and buy a ticket to the lecture at Abbotsford on Saturday. I'm done with snoozing.

7

The French Alps, November 2016

'Excuse me. Johnny.'

You'd dropped your phone. You were struggling to take off your layers and whilst you were hidden from my gaze by your fleece, with your head stuck in its depths, your mobile had tumbled from a pocket.

'You dropped your phone,' I said again.

Your head emerged from the fleece.

'Hello. Thanks. I'd have walked off without it. I'm always losing my phone.'

'Me too.' It was a lie, I don't tend to lose mine.

'How are things?' and you walked towards me. 'Have you got time for a coffee?'

We sat on the terrace of our hostel, and you were quieter then, watching the skiers with the same palpable longing I had recognised the day before in the foyer. Mont Blanc and the north face of the Aiguille du Midi glistened above us. You ordered espressos and I felt curiously happy watching you (not as surreptitiously as I'd believed, you later teased) with the tables and chairs between us, and a smattering of red-nosed guests.

'Where are you from exactly? I'm Scottish too, you see . . .'

I started to interrupt but you rode over my disbelief.

'. . .I only sound English because I went to school there. I live in Edinburgh.'

Long after you had gone, the streets of Edinburgh would be littered with this throwaway remark. 'You won't believe it. I live in Edinburgh as well.'

Incredulous but looking at your coffee: 'No. Really?' And then you looked up smiling. 'That's very good news.'

I felt myself blush.

'And what exactly are you doing here? I noticed you last week, but you never have any skis.'

'I'm here as part of a degree course. I've taken December off to study, a mini-sabbatical. How have you managed it? What do you do?'

'Something I mainly wish I didn't. I'm supposed to be a solicitor but I just push pens around the office.' And you didn't elaborate further but instead told me about your first ski trip, which your parents had taken you on when you were only seven. I remember that you never mentioned your father even though he had been with you, and so for me, Andrew was notable on this trip by his absence from your story.

'What's your mother called?'

'Ellen,' you said, 'short for Eleanor. I don't see her much,' even though, you added, your parents also lived in Edinburgh (they were indeed the ones that had surfaced on my Google search) so it was Edinburgh that loomed over the conversation, all of Edinburgh was sprawled out on the table in front of us, with three varying locations like pinpoints on a map. Your flat and mine furthest apart, and your parents between us. I wondered out loud about your siblings.

'I don't have any brothers or sisters. I'm a self-centred only child. You?'

You're like me, I thought at first, and only afterwards that it was an interesting choice of adjective. There are so many others to choose from to describe an only child. At the time, I assumed that you were being self-deprecating. 'The same. Sort of.'

I didn't say anything further, lost for a moment in my thoughts, and after a polite pause you asked if I was enjoying the conditions.

'I am – but I'm not a skier. I've never tried.'

You waited again, and then waited some more.

'This is the part where you tell me what it is you are doing here. Apart from studying.' But you sounded approving. You were enjoying me, I think, without really knowing what it was that you were appreciating. Teasing things out of me, perhaps, just drawing me in? I didn't know, I never did. If I had, I could have been that person, done that thing, surely, had I ever had the slightest clue?

'Walking,' I told you. 'Snowshoeing.'

'That's impressive.'

'Snowshoeing is very demanding here,' I say defensively, wondering if I had picked up on some uncertainty about this middle-aged sounding activity. 'It's not always easy.'

'I mean it,' you protested. 'I've never done it.' There was silence for a second as you sat back, contemplating me. 'Will you take me one day?'

'Yes,' and I really did mean it. 'It's so good to be here. Out of the city. Walking, and in the fresh air.'

'Agreed,' you said emphatically and then, 'I've got a feeling that you're full of surprises.' You said it wonderingly, as if you were almost surprised. 'There's something about you,' and I watched you rub your strangely coloured eyes and quite out of the blue you cleared your throat and said, 'Can I ask, can I get this out of the way? Are you with anyone? Sorry. I'd just like to know if you're married.'

I shook my head, shy again. 'No.' With all the necessary questions that had gone before about who did what and where we lived, this seemed to be the nub of the matter, the point of the coffee. 'No,' I reiterated, unnecessarily.

'Good,' and your eyes crinkled against the sun. 'Are you free this evening?'

Yes yes yes yes yes. 'I'm supposed to be seeing my tutor . . .'

'Do something with me instead?'

'Yes.'

'The two-metre rule will of course apply,' and I looked at you quizzically, and you were embarrassed because of course I wasn't sure at this point what you meant although I think I did. I think I always understood and of course it was much too soon for metric rules of distance but on the other hand, of course it wasn't.

We didn't separate at all that day. I ought to have been doing other things but being with you was intoxicating. I think we were both aware of the unavoidable harmony of it, of the exact and perfect pause; bracketed in some sort of haven that didn't take any account of anything else. At one point you said, 'I must have done something good in a past life,' and you finished the hot chocolate and ordered a crêpe for us to share, forks and fingers brushing against each other. For the whole of that day, no one else existed for either of us. I slept like the dead that night, exhausted by the blinkered and committed time we had spent with our heads bent towards each other.

'Is something happening here?' you asked, before we said goodbye, genuinely confused – and I couldn't answer. We'd no idea what was happening. We were only sure that it was.

8

I've been thinking about what I am going to take to the Borders with me and what clothes I should wear and when I get home on Thursday night, I make myself a gin and tonic and open my cupboard. I am looking at my wardrobe when my aunt rings the landline. No one else ever does.

'Hello?'

'It's me. It's Nora.'

'I know. Is everything all right?' Green skirt or black skirt?

'We've had an awful lot of rain up here,' Nora tells me. 'Too much.'

'Is the river high?'

'Getting higher.' She hates that, she is frightened by the ease and steadiness by which the river can reveal its power.

'You're OK though?'

She doesn't answer me directly. 'It's cold up here. Is it cold down south, in that queer town of yours?'

Nora always talks about Edinburgh as though it's in England, as though Torcastle in the Highlands is a different country away to the north. Although sometimes I know what she means and I don't bother to correct her. 'It's not too bad.'

'Will you come and see me soon? Before your birthday, mind.'

It's not till April but she has remembered and I feel a prick of relief, and fondness for her.

'Thirty-something,' she adds, 'clock's ticking,' and the affection wanes but I promise that I will come and hang up after a few minutes. She won't remember anyway.

And as for her views on Edinburgh, 'that queer town', well, they aren't only Nora's. Highlanders have always viewed Edinburgh with suspicion, and I carried that scepticism south with me when I first left Torcastle with Tam. I remember drifting through the Old Town and finding it puzzling, not only in contrast to the symmetry and haughtiness of New Town, but in contrast to the grandiose version I had in my head of it. No, the Old Town is mediaeval, steeped in grime and Gothic mystery. I didn't trust it at first, every instinct warned against the whole city. I remember leaning over the castle battlements towards the Scott Monument one day and overhearing a tour guide describing how women found guilty of witchcraft had been drowned in what used to be a river of sewage below. The story frightened me at the time, but I lost my wariness soon after. Perhaps living here dulled my suspicions, cultivated after years of being alone with Nora. I became too comfortable, making friends, finding my course and my job. I was made ordinary and now I am come to a standstill, deceived and undone by common heartbreak.

I have been too long away from the Highlands, from the deep and fast-flowing river. I used to believe, after I'd met Johnny, that I had somehow ended up in Edinburgh in order to be near him, that the universe had contrived to make it so – and now, without him, there's no point to the city. I see it for what it is now; artful, and defunct.

I make myself another gin and this time I don't bother with the tonic. It's day twelve but I'm going to leave Edinburgh and go to Abbotsford in my green skirt and if I meet Ellen, who knows what I might find out? Who knows what might happen?

9

The French Alps, November 2016

We met again on the veranda the next morning, as if we had planned it. You did not want to ski with your friends. You never gave a reason. You didn't ask why I wasn't walking (avalanche risk) or studying (the incentive was lost). We talked about you.

You said that you weren't a bad skier, technically. It was your fear, you said, self-loathing filling your features – it was your fear of heights that stood between you and success. If only you could conquer this, you could deal with the famed Mallory route on the north face. It was fear that prevented anyone from doing anything, you concluded. You talked about your obsession with the Swedish extreme skier, Tomas Holmberg, to whom you said the verb 'fearless' should belong. Only two or three years had passed since Holmberg had broken his neck, but survived, in an avalanche in the Chamonix region. This had not proved to be an obstacle to his ambition. *Feel the fear and do it anyway*, you insisted, the light of the zealot shining in your eyes.

That day, to me, your admiration and envy were more memorable than Holmberg's superhuman achievements. Your glorious, ordinary human jealousy and your drive is what I remember – as well as this knack you had of knocking yourself out of your gloom, and cheering yourself out of the misery of your averageness with a *vin chaud* and a joke. You could very quickly find the humour in yourself, as well as everything else. I had never met anyone like you. I was still scrabbling around the fact of fear (I had thought guilt was what stopped people doing anything) when you leapt up and started searching for your jacket and gloves. You had decided that we should take the cable car all the way to the top.

A mini test of your fear, I suppose, and you jogged impatiently at the top of the steps whilst I pulled on my coat. We walked into town and queued for our pass and we joined the slow-moving throng that was crawling like an arachnid towards the station. When the doors slid open I saw that you were still and your face was growing pale.

Disaster never occurred to me. But you filled me in, you told me, didn't you, as the cable car began to heave and pull back up the mountain, what had happened last time.

In May 2013, an engine in the Chamonix cable car caught fire. Two hundred and fifty-one tourists had to be evacuated by helicopter.

'Shush. Everyone's looking. Be quiet.'

'No, worse, listen to this.' You had committed these shocking facts to memory. *In 1999, a cable car near Gap (that's only three hours south of here, by the way) plunged eighty metres to the valley below. The hook had detached from its cables. Twenty people died.*

Everyone in the cable car had gone silent. You stood next to me and unexpectedly picked up my hand and closed it between the two of yours and I'd like to say how safe I made you feel, how I consoled and comforted. Instead I began to feel as if your terror was attaching itself to me, or that I was latching on to your terror.

'That is not going to happen,' I said firmly, and with a confidence that I suddenly felt none of.

'How do you know it's not going to happen?' You were looking at our hands wrapped together.

'I don't know that, of course. Just don't look down.'

'OK. OK,' you said, looking at me now, not taking your eyes off me.

I scoffed a little and swallowed the tension rising in my chest and I pressed my nose to the window and tried to identify landmarks, to hold onto the security of the early morning. You asked me if I knew what Aiguille du Midi means and you told me before I could reply, and reminded me that at 3,842 metres it is the highest vertical ascent cable car in the world. You told me that the upper section runs without any support pillar. You spotted the Vallée Blanche ski run nearby and half-looked. I felt the wind shake the cabin and the magnificence of the mountains surrounding us but I was also feeling your fear and inexplicably when I commented, 'Look, nearly there,' I found that my teeth were chattering. The closer we drew to the top, the more relieved and off-hand you became.

We exited the cable car and while you were finding your feet, I lost mine. Triumphant, you took the elevator up the final sixty-five metres to the summit, while I waited for you, at a loss. It seemed to me, as it often would, that you had deliberately left me behind but also that this was entirely my own fault. I don't know why I didn't go with you. Perhaps you had let me know that it was something that you needed to do alone. You reappeared after you had only been gone a short while, but I felt as though there had been the possibility of you totally vanishing on the ice-capped peak. You dragged a telescope round towards us and peered into the lens searching for something. I think you sighed slightly, half in awe and perhaps half in despair. Were you looking at the summit of Mont Blanc and

35

feeling its unattainability? Were you revelling in beating your cable car phobia? Or maybe in what you knew to be a potential conquest of a different kind, imminent and knock-kneed by your side?

You weren't bothered by the return journey – you had been irrational, you admitted, and I would learn that this was how it went sometimes – it grabbed you unawares, your insane, stultifying fear, and then you laughed it off as though it hadn't meant anything at all. You were fine now. I shut my eyes and tried to salvage my splintered self, scattering like shards of ice over the mountain.

10

I wish now that we could have left it there. The story up until now could have been the whole story. The bits that had gone before – the interest, the civility, the gradual descent into wanting . . . and stop. Stop before the wanting became the having enough. I wish we could have remained in the bit between the wanting and the gratification. The bit where, mysterious and unknown, *I* was unreal to *you*.

There is life between the gratification and the having enough, you know. We could have had life, real life. But you were just playing at it and playing at being a grown-up, and a defining and careless characteristic was that you were always losing things. I ought to have noticed; you lost things and found it amusing rather than exasperating because you didn't care about them. Just as I ought to have listened to your lack of interest in me but you were an expert in whimsicality and avoidance. You fooled me, anyway, and I never saw what you were doing because you were doing all those other things too: you were texting me all the time, even when I was next to you – gorgeous, by the way – and you were telling me how good I made you feel and enveloping me in your arms as the cable car stopped, and raising your eyebrows and making me laugh. Making me happy.

Heterochromia, is that what you have? I once asked but there was no answer even to this. You made some self-deprecating joke, a witticism that as usual I found hard to follow up on but was content to just admire. And then, later, you gave in and told me that your eyes were different colours because of what was called genetic mosaicism and that ambiguity became a metaphor for you in my mind: that you had assembled yourself beautifully but randomly; that you were a puzzle to everyone but possibly not yourself. Why did I search for some secret in you? Why was I so sure that there was a pattern to your mosaic, when all you were was decorative?

And even now I suspect you were not always just texting me - that those unnecessary missives, (greeted by my silly, ridiculous face opposite yours), may have camouflaged who else you were texting - I carry on searching, refusing to believe that your flaws, the cracks, are really just that. Refusing to believe, in between the anger and the scheming, that you really did leave the way you did. I don't understand it. I want to understand you, to unlock this secret, and I wonder if your mother will provide any answers — any at all — to questions that I still don't know how to ask.

I travel south on Friday evening. I am going by train to the Borders to listen to the lecture being given by a famous Scottish historian on the long-term implications of the most important political debate of our lifetime. It just so happens that Ellen Strachan is doing the same thing. When she heard I was planning on going, Gillian, who has been eyeing me with badly concealed concern since I got back from France, encouraged me to go early. 'Go to the countryside, why not. Get some colour in those cheeks of yours.' She knows that there are rooms in the area and lots of B&Bs. She even telephones Abbotsford House to ask where I might stay that night and she is told that they themselves have a single room available. She gave me the thumbs up and passed me the phone to book it. It's expensive, but not prohibitively so because of a last-minute cancellation and anyway, the night away in the countryside, suggested and endorsed by Gillian, is another justification for going.

Gillian surprises me when I leave by clasping me to her for a quick second, and then tutting disapprovingly. 'You're too thin. Here, pop your scarf on.'

Everything falls into place so smoothly. I only need a small overnight bag and that takes me five minutes to pack. The train is waiting at the station. I find a seat straight away, the train leaves on time. It is only an hour away.

And it is beautiful. I walk from the station in the dusk, breathing in the soft, clean air. A pair of buzzards are mewling high above me, high above the pine trees. The house, visible for the last mile, was once Walter Scott's. It is on the banks of the River Tweed, and the gentle slopes nudged up against it are like molehills. It's a large, Gothic house, but it isn't too grand. It's the sort of place that was on Johnny's list, the sort of thing we might have done together.

The scene, dropping into a velvet darkness, is a world away from the rugged peaks of Torcastle and the north, and I'm glad to be out of Edinburgh. Yesterday morning, when I had stood in my kitchen, scalding my hand, dry-eyed and numb, seems an age ago. I have made it here.

After I've checked in, I order a bowl of soup with some bread and cheese to eat in my room. I listen to the hotel fill with its visitors and wonder about the one that is missing – or the two that are missing, rather, because I suspect that Johnny's parents might be the sort of couple that go everywhere together. Dr and Dr Strachan. I drink a glass of wine and eat some chocolate from the minibar and try not to dwell on them too much. I try to stay away from the reality of what being here means, namely that the energy it has provided me with is an unhealthy and negative one. It just doesn't feel like that. It feels proactive and important. It feels a blessed relief. The insane decision to come here in search of some answers feels as though it might just have saved my sanity.

11

The French Alps, December 2016

We were inseparable from then on, and that night you announced the two-metre rule again. You took my hand and positioning it 'this far' from yours, you issued your edict. You told me that I wasn't allowed further from you than two metres. Stay close to me, you said, it's the rule. And you weren't to know this but for me, who had felt abandoned, thrust from people, who had learned to defensively position myself at a distance from them . . . can you imagine the unfamiliar feeling this order ignited, and then can you imagine disobeying it? A yearning I didn't even know I had was satisfied then, by you.

You took my hand as if we were shaking on something and I gave in to you completely, any remaining shreds of common sense and self-preservation destroyed. Buried beneath the devastating weight of the two-metre rule.

After supper we took the stairs to the first floor, your hands on the small of my back, nudging me along the corridor. When you had fitted the key into the lock and pushed the door open (it was stiff and you had to use your shoulder), you stayed leaning against the doorway and ushered me through. I looked at you and you folded your arms, smiling, one leg was bent and your confusing eyes, one hazel-green and the other brown, were unreadable. I stepped into the room and you did not shut the door behind you; you hesitated, so that I, marooned in the centre was forced to turn to you.

I opened my arms, more as an expression of submission than an invitation and your uncertainty (was it that?) vanished as you moved forward, kicking the troublesome door shut with your back-stretched foot.

You had recently shaved and your skin was smooth. And this, I remember this, the smell of your moisturiser. Not aftershave, you never wore aftershave. It was just a moisturiser like Nivea, one that I felt I should have known, but didn't. It was an almost-remembered smell, a throwback to the innocence and the intimacy of someone's childhood. I collapsed into this. I remember that you put so much emphasis into every touch, and that your eyes were wide as you stared into mine. I remember that you stroked my hair, over and over. You kissed the side of my neck. You couldn't put enough meaning into your kiss and both your eyes darkened so the green became more like the brown, or the other way round, and you navigated our way across the floor so that finally we were standing by the bed.

I put my palms against your chest, and then my head. I asked you to stop. You said, 'What's the matter? Is everything OK? Why are you fighting this?' And then, regretfully: 'It's too much, too soon, isn't it?' You were wrong but I still couldn't speak, so you nodded in agreement with yourself and said, 'There isn't any rush. Not if you're not ready. We've lots of time now.'

It wasn't what I meant, Johnny. It wasn't too quick or too soon. It was too slow. Too late, even. I wanted to play catch-up, to fast forward to this point and at the same time gather all the lonely years gone before, and add you to them. It turns out I had been waiting for you, for ever, and that everything else was just inadequate preparation. I wasn't 'not ready', I had been ready all my life without even knowing it. You were the answer to the question. Quivering in your arms, not with indecision but with awareness, I recognised myself. Something turned over and unfurled, like a lake blinking at a spectacular sunrise. I couldn't speak in the face of this overwhelming affirmation of myself, which occurred in the same moment as you ruefully examined me and then moved away.

I don't remember what words I finally found, I only remember the desperate feeling as you began to turn away and I couldn't bear it. Everything had surely been leading up to this moment and I would never have forgiven myself if I had let you go then.

I think I simply said, 'Johnny,' and you stopped, and hesitated (grappling with something? Anything?), and you said 'Yes. No more talking,' and you pulled me towards you and held me, and I was half-trembling and half-paralysed and then you began to tug and pull my clothes from me and you said things like, 'You are the most beautiful thing I've ever seen. I will never get enough of you.'

Relaxing, I sunk like a stone falling through clear water into you. When it was good, it was out of this world, wasn't it? Isn't that the sort of expression you used, to flatter and reward? But it was, then. Your ambition to succeed, at anything, and my newfound longing and willingness made us good together. The combination made me good enough for you.

You kissed me so much that my chin became raw. I used to touch it sometimes, its blistering damp the proof of you. And I used to watch you sleep, feeling that I had walked off the precipice. I knew that's what I'd done and I didn't yet care or truly believe how calamitous the walk was. Despite – perhaps because of – the intensity of the happiness with

43

you, I felt the warning undercurrents of fear very close. And yet. . . within the swirling eddy of nerves there swum silvery fish, quick and tentative feelings of optimism. You were so good at it, you see. So good at the focus. I believed that you had absolutely nothing else going on in your life. You never kept your phone close, you never went off to make private calls. You mentioned your friend Anna and it always sounded natural and unthreatening. You talked about Ellen, and gave me snippets of tantalising information; the unspoken proviso always being that I would find out more for myself one day soon. I discovered she loves Sauvignon Blanc, which she drinks by the bucket, daily. That she loves birds and architecture. The subtext seemed to be that she loved you more than anything. I liked the idea of your mother's adoration. You talked about her as though I would meet her imminently, as if we would be friends. You talked about a future.

You found cheap half bottles of champagne at the supermarket and we drank one every night to toast each other. There was an old-fashioned way you chinked my glass – *happy days*. It seemed to me that you began to open up. (How subtle you were, how proficiently you gave the impression of a complicated honesty and a cautious trust in me.) But with the exception of your mother, and the odd dig about your father, you didn't refer to anything that might have made up some emotional terrain. At the time, I thought I had simply eclipsed everything else for now and we would resume a more realistic and temperate way of life together in Edinburgh.

In sleep, your face lost its clownish unpredictability and caught in your dreams; with furrowed brow, you looked almost vulnerable. I touched my finger to my chin to check that it hurt.

'Hey. Where do you think you're going?' You caught my hand as I passed.

'Hello,' and I bent to kiss you; tried to pull away but you held on.

'Come and sit here.'

I thought to perch at the edge of your knee, but this wasn't how you did things. You pulled me back into your arms, not caring that everyone could see us, and you said into my ear, 'Hello, gorgeous. Josh is getting a round in, you want something?'

I nodded. 'Gin please,' and you asked for the drink, and I lay curled up in your lap and felt the tonic water fizzing at the back of my throat and your heartbeat against my cheek.

Later, when everyone else had dispersed, you presented me with a souvenir, a mini Aiguille du Midi. One of those glass frosty things that you shake. I shook it, and snow cascaded over the miniature figures at the top of the mountain. A snow globe.

'Thank you,' you said, seriously. 'It's only a small thing. To say thank you, for coming with me in the cable car. It was good to have a sympathetic ear in it for once.'

'You didn't have to get me anything,' I told you, equally serious. 'It was nothing.'

'It was,' you were insistent. 'Anyway, just wanted to say thanks.' You hesitated. 'Thanks.'

I looked at the two figures encased in the glass ornament and shook it again, liking the smooth weight of it in my palm. The snowy scene made me smile and you misinterpreted it.

'OK, it's not the most elegant or glamorous of gifts. But it's the best the co-op down the road could do.'

'You went far then.'

'Would have gone to Italy for one of these. I've got about eight, Mum used to give them to me in my stocking every year.' You put on a warning look of mock severity. 'So don't knock them.'

'I won't,' I assured you. 'I won't. I'll treasure it for ever.'

'No idea how lucky you are. I've never seen this one, it's probably a collector's item.'

'I love it,' I said. 'You get them at the gift shop in Fort William. Not Alpine ones, obviously.'

You asked about Torcastle then, and seemed enthralled by the myths from the Highlands that I told you. Like the Cat Pool legend.

'Cat Pool? Strange name.'

'There's a reason for everything up there. It's to do with an old clan chief who was one day filled with remorse for all his past wrongdoings and overcome with the urge to atone for them. He asked the witch of Moy, called Gormshuil, what he should do and she told him to come to Torcastle with a cat. He was to run a spit through the non-vital parts of the cat and roast the creature over a fire. He did this and waited to be told what to do next.'

'Poor cat. What clan?' and I told him their name. 'I was at school with a Cameron,' he mused. 'Anyway, go on.'

'The wild and terrified screeches of the roasting cat attracted all the cats in Lochaber. The leader, a large and black cat called Cam Dubh, asked the clan chief why he was torturing the cat and the chief replied that he would release the creature when he was told how to obtain forgiveness for his past misdeeds. The black cat immediately told him that he knew the answer and that the chief must build seven churches. The chief released the burning cat, which dashed from the scene and threw itself over a cliff and into a deep pool. All the other cats, following their leader, jumped in as well and later dispersed, returning to their homes. Ever since, the pool has been known as the Cat Pool, or *Poll a'chait* in Gallic.'

'A gruesome tale,' said Johnny. 'My mother has a cat, it's even called Witchy.'

'But you're allergic.'

'Not allergic as such, just not good for asthma. What's the moral of the story then?'

I leant across Johnny to pick up my drink. 'I'm not sure there is one. Does there have to be one?'

'Of course. Without, it's just a nasty story.'

'OK then, it's just a nasty story of how the Cat Pool got its name. But we believe in the witch of Moy up there. When they built the Caledonian Canal, they refused to dig through the spot where legend has it that she was buried. They went round it.'

'Your Gorm . . . whatever she's called . . . you, Skye, are an endless source of information. You green-eyed witch. Seven churches, hey? I think you deserve another drink for that.'

'Nonsense,' I said, flushing. 'Just a story.' Stupidly pleased.

'And then I'd better get building.'

You had done that thing, that thing you do when you're sounding serious but you're joking and you crinkle your eyes, one brown and one hazel-green and really, you were leaving it up to me to decide what to do with your dual offering. Often, I had no idea but as the days passed I became more used to you, and you became clearer − as if the extreme obviousness and clarity of our situation did not require any pretext or game-playing. There was no shame and no coquettishness attached to your blatant and consistent pursuit of me and it made it feel honest. I did not suspect at the start that the motivation for the attention might have come from within and may not have been anything to do with me at all.

You made sure that you were everywhere, so sure that I became used to finding you waiting for me at the bottom of the lift, outside the ski room, on the terrace. You were reliable, and steadfast – unfailingly. I had never met anyone who seemed so naturally open and warm; and yet I had this permanently tantalising feeling that there was more to you for me to discover. That despite your candour, there was something more concealed beneath it; someone for me to connect to. I thought that sometimes you let things slip and I allowed myself to believe you had let your guard down. That you were learning to trust me, as much as I you. We talked, all the time, about a lot of things but perhaps it's true in the end to say that you often ended intimate discussions with a cliché or a joke. You never really did let me in. Your opacity was a tool; it was going to be easier for you this way.

12

The sky is a fluttering blue hanky, and I have been up since seven o'clock walking on the mossy riverbank, nudged downstream by a quick wind and following the sun as it rises. I'm nervous. Feeling rattled, I don't look where I am going and I stumble into a rabbit hole. My ankle twists awkwardly and the pain shoots up my leg, making me gasp.

I limp back to the house and, worrying about my ankle and what I've done, I hobble into the dining room. And there she is, alone at a table amongst just a handful of other guests. Ellen. She isn't supposed to arrive till later today, is she? But I know it is her and I feel tricked, or at a disadvantage somehow. I feel unprepared, as though I've been caught out. But realising she will not even give me a second glance, my confusion is quickly followed by the bitter awareness of my anonymity and the injustice of her complete ignorance of me. My sore ankle throbs alongside this knowledge and I get to the nearest table and sit down.

Still, she is something of a revelation. I can't say for sure *how* exactly. She is certainly just as glamorous as @ellen. strachan promises; the pictures do her justice. But something else – she doesn't seem as comfortable as she ought, or as careless as I had assumed. She sits alone, on the edge of the dining room chair, as if poised for something. She has the expression of someone who minds. I remember it very clearly, because it was never an expression I found on you.

The pain in my ankle is receding. She really is pretty, but in an unobtrusive way. Not much make-up, or none that is discernible anyway. Just lip gloss. Her hair shines with blonde highlights but the casual bob isn't overtly styled. Two butterfly clips hold it away from her face. She is wearing a navy suit, although not one that makes her look efficient. It is an off-duty suit that complements her; it's fashionable, if a bit short for someone in her late forties. She seems a little unsure about the length anyway. She glances occasionally at the daring hem and flexes her fingers pensively. She is sitting with one leg slung over the other, flicking her foot backwards and forwards. One arm is tentatively – uselessly – trying to attract the waiter's attention.

She is self-conscious. Perhaps she doesn't like to be on her own; the swing of her leg is a nervous one. She is looking for the waiter, not with impatience but with apology. And then she gives up, her back rounding in defeat. She lowers her hand, graciously, and as she does so, she catches my eye. She smiles, quick and shy. It is merely the polite response, I know. She reveals a furiously crooked bottom row of teeth that she has hitherto kept hidden from me. And I haven't consciously thought about this before but as we exchange glances I realise how important it is to me that I present a good, even the best, impression of myself. I wish that I had checked my appearance before blundering into breakfast.

She looks away again and takes some papers from the briefcase on the floor and straightens them. She laces her hands above her head, yawns and stretches; the jacket falls open and the buttons (incorrectly fastened) on her white shirt strain a little.

'Darling,' I hear, and both she and I look towards the voice.

'Andrew,' she says, softly spoken and lilting; conciliatory.

'Darling,' Andrew says, again. 'You haven't managed to even order.' He strolls across the room, looks at the empty table and spreads his arms in frustrated enquiry. 'What have you been doing down here all this time?' He flags down the waiter who instantly appears before him and all of a sudden Ellen is now at the centre of a flurry of activity; a white tablecloth billows around her, a pot of coffee is placed in front of her, a basket of pastries appears, and she is someone else entirely. She has become someone else with Andrew's arrival. I sink back into my chair, invisible to them both. The sort of couple who go everywhere together.

My first thought about Andrew is that he is a large man. Your father is bulkier than I imagine you will ever be. And older than I thought; he looks at least sixty-five. His hair is very white, but very thick. His bulk causes him to stoop slightly. He tosses his tweed jacket onto his chair and then takes another chair from a nearby table. The waiter comes back and Andrew gives him his order, and I can hear, the whole dining room can hear, what he wants for breakfast. Ellen shakes her head and points at the pastry basket when Andrew gestures questioningly at her, then she begins to scroll through something on her phone. He runs his hands through his luxuriant hair and picks up the newspaper and she checks her watch and sips the orange juice that has materialised and it is as though they are doing ten different things all at the same time with busy smiles and emphatic hand gestures. It's like they started a conversation at the halfway point, they don't need preliminaries, they are already there, ahead of the rest of us, powering through their meal, their morning, the entire day, with a united and breezy air of nonchalance.

Listening to their conversation closely, I wonder if Andrew is short-tempered. He sounds brusque sometimes. Ellen asks him something, I can't hear what, and he snaps, 'Don't be so bossy.' I feel rather taken aback. Perhaps they hadn't slept well, perhaps, like you, Johnny, he is peevish if he doesn't sleep. I, for one, had not slept because my last-minute single room was airless, and I couldn't open the window. I longed for a sharp highland wind. But I never sleep well, do I, Johnny – unlike you. Your toddler-like ability to nod off anywhere amazed me, the way you could just turn away and be asleep, with your arms sweetly crossed above your forehead and face. I remember the agony of your peaceful nights once you had barred me from your life; pressed up against my bedhead with my knees to my chest watching the headlights from Dalkeith Road probe around the unhappiness in the room. Tormented by not knowing where you were or what you were doing.

The hotel room faced out onto the back, and late into the evening I had to listen to the chef arguing with the waitress, their invective and cigarette smoke swirling outside my window. I started to pick at the skin around my finger-nails. Eventually, as the night approached a misty dawn, I drifted off and dreamed I was a little girl again, playing in Torcastle, but you were in the dream and I woke disorientated, cowering against the iron bedhead, with my knees bent against my chest and my sore fingers clutching them, and a lorry roaring outside.

I'm sure that if Andrew's sleep was disturbed it wasn't anything to do with the location of their room, which I now know (the volume of Andrew's voice seems purposefully to include me) is a suite on the first floor with a view of the formal gardens and a balcony from which to enjoy it.

The Strachans have finished their breakfast. Ellen folds her napkin and helps the waiter collect saucers and jugs and put them on his tray, and Andrew does his bit, which is to clap the man around the shoulders.

'Have a good day, sir,' the waiter says. 'See you tomorrow.'

'No, sadly not,' Ellen said over her shoulder. 'We're not staying tonight,' and she thinks of something and nudges Andrew who has moved on. Andrew pats his pockets ostentatiously and finds a bank note for the waiter. I'm sure the waiter was pleased enough but I'm thinking, he's not your personal butler for the weekend. So I'm not looking, I'm not concentrating when Andrew comes back towards the door and passes me. His voice, deep and benign, makes me jump.

'You don't want to miss the start.'

I just gaze stupidly at him.

'Ten a.m., in the imaginatively named Walter Scott Room. The warm-up act. Darling, where on earth do you suppose the Walter Scott Room is?'

I look for Ellen. Ellen has gone. He raises his eyebrows. I tell him I don't know where it is, or anything about the warm-up act. He smiles, with a touch of the conspirator – 'I'd better find out' – and strides away into the corridor. But he turns to appraise me once more.

I look at my hands. I have to sit on them to stop them shaking.

I am the only one left in the dining room and the waiter begins to hover impatiently near my table. But I am paralysed with a sort of horror. There is enough of Johnny in his father to have shocked me and I sit there trembling and supposing that I am finally coming to my senses. What on earth am I doing? Finally, I get to my feet and move slowly down the passage, more in amazement at myself than pain from my ankle. I have spent money that I don't have in a hotel that's more like a castle, on the off-chance I see Johnny's parents, imagining that if I do . . . what? They haven't anything to offer me, they can't make it better. And I limp past the Walter Scott Room, red-faced, not anticipating that I will stop outside this badly publicised pre-lecture event – but I find myself pausing at the entrance.

The last person in hasn't shut the door properly so I can hear the murmurings of a projector and the sounds of a room full of people, the shuffling, the coughing and then the speaker's voice. I nudge the door open a little more . . . I push further in, the memory of Ellen's fleeting smile fresh in my thoughts, and then jump as someone, a steward, gestures into the room. Andrew, on a bench near the door, looks up, grins and motions silently towards a spare seat with a satisfied nod.

I limp to the seat and sit down. I don't think it is because I want to listen (although I do, in another life I do), and I don't think it is because it would have been rude and disruptive to just back out again, nor even because I have nothing else to do. I think it is because I am fed up – *fed up* – with being back on the wrong side of a closed door. Fed up with feeling marginalised. Of passively succumbing to intolerable situations; with listening in on conversations and not being part of them, of not being part of anything at all. I refuse to be shut out. I've got this far, I'm here, after all. I stay where I am, insulated by sporadic murmurs and sighs, in the Strachans' world.

13

I was still fussing with the foundation that refused to blot out my freckles, but knowing it was you knocking, I didn't completely give up. I rubbed away at my face as if I could make them disappear, and then, sighing, smeared a dark lip balm over my mouth. I pulled all the gloves and scarves I had out of my drawer and onto the floor. I found the red ones I wanted and opened the door. You were leaning against the wall with one leg bent and one hand in your pocket.

'Hello, green-eyed witch,' you said, not moving. 'I don't much like nights on my own. Let's not do any more of those.' And your arms swung open and in I went.

We went snowshoeing that day and I remember the eye-rolling we met with from my fellow ice-technicians as we left. Everyone seemed happy for us, and my tolerant tutor, turning away benignly, proved to be more of a romantic than a university professor. 'Let's see what all the fuss is about,' you had challenged, and I was instantly anxious that you would not enjoy the activity. We started walking in silence.

It was almost totally deserted. Some bad weather was blowing in from the east and the wind was icy, and the snow was thick either side of the path. I remember thinking that the clouds were like the waves on the Forth, thick and grey. But we kept walking and I directed you over one horizon and towards another, snow beginning to fall heavily into the views behind us. You strode out ahead, one hand reaching back for me. I grabbed it and held on. By now it was too windy for conversation so we just walked, you rapt by the summit, concentrating on reaching the top and me concentrating on following your tracks. (When we turned back, not even an hour later, I couldn't find them. We might never have been there.)

At the top, you turned to me, fumbling for your phone.

'Stay there,' was the instruction, and you pointed your mobile at me.

'No,' I said, laughing, and put my hand in front of my face.

'Yes,' you insisted and then I turned around so my back was facing your camera lens.

'No,' and this time I was sharp.

You were curious. 'Why not? No press, please? It's just for me, for us.'

I don't like my photograph being taken. I never have. I always think of the Native American tribe that believes a photograph of them would steal their soul when people ask me why not. It isn't because I believe the same and I don't really know why I think of it. I said firmly to you: 'Memories are better in the mind.'

'Yes,' you agreed, putting the phone away and wiping the snow from your eyes. 'That explains why I couldn't find you amongst the hills and Scottish emblems on your Facebook page. Or your Instagram. @scottish_skyegrant.'

'I made the account during the referendum. I don't really use Facebook.'

'Is that why you haven't accepted my friend request?'

'Ah,' I said. 'Well, I'm still thinking about that,' and you darted towards me, catching hold of my gloved hands. You thought I was teasing; the truth was I liked having it there. The request would stay until it was accepted.

Far below, Chamonix was lighting itself up for us like a distant fairy-tale city and the hills around us were white and silent.

'I feel like a million dollars.' Your cheeks were flushed and your eyes were shining. 'We should do this all the time.' You added, 'You make me feel like a million dollars. I can't get enough of you. What have you done to me?'

'You're daft,' I told him, the warm glow spreading. 'We've only come for a walk.'

'I don't know where you've discovered. I had no idea you could go this far here.'

'We can walk at home. Can't we?'

'I won't stop you,' and you had a lopsided grin on your face.

'We'll go north,' I told you, 'to the beaches on the west coast, maybe even Skye, do proper walks there. My mum was from Skye.' The mention of Mum slipped out.

'I'll go to Skye with you,' you agreed. 'My red-haired mermaid.'

'I can't even swim, you know. Don't call me that.'

But you brushed the confession aside. 'Don't be silly, everyone can swim,' and in the end, I just frowned and pulled my hat further over my head.

On the bus back to the hotel, you started counting my freckles.

'Are you going to stay the night with me tonight? Ten, eleven, twelve.'

'Do you want me to?'

'Erm,' you started saying, 'might need to think about that,' and then you saw my face. 'I'm joking. I'm joking. Sixteen, seventeen, eighteen, nineteen . . .' You declared yourself defeated by them.

I began to love you here, when you were red-cheeked and complimentary. I felt lucky, more than anything. I couldn't think what had happened and couldn't explain it either, only that it seemed as though the universe, once set on course, had shifted ever so slightly and things that had been static had gathered some energy and momentum. It was irrational, and it was thrilling. It was because of you.

14

Andrew is waiting outside in the corridor and when he sees me, he approaches.

'You snuck in just in time,' he says, 'I think you owe me one.' He folds his arms, amused by something. Himself, I think. I look at him and think about you and lodged somewhere between panic and longing, I turn to your mother.

'How do you do? Ellen Strachan. That was interesting.' And she extends her hand with a friendly smile.

'It was. I wasn't aware it was happening. I think I have you both to thank for it.'

'Not me,' she says, her head on one side.

'Me,' Andrew says, and for some reason I blush.

Ellen, unflinching, doesn't lose her smile. 'But what did you think?' She smooths her navy suit, slightly crumpled, over her hips.

'Fascinating,' is the only thing I can think of to say, and I say it again. 'Fascinating.'

'Have you come far?' asks Ellen, and then, 'Oh!' on hearing the answer, 'We're from Edinburgh too. Hardly surprising, I suppose many here are.'

And it's weird; even though I know this, it still feels like a coincidence and hearing her say it gives me a prickle of worry. Much like the revelation that Johnny came from Edinburgh had felt fateful. I had a calm sense of inevitability about it, one that would later help trick me into believing that we were meant to be. But it also gave me a sinking feeling, as if I was being warned. I feel this dissonance now too. I feel the anxiety again.

And then it turns out that we are on the same train back. 'Are you on the four thirty?' Ellen asks, and I say, 'I think so,' meaning, I could be, should I be?

'Excellent,' says Andrew, and then I know I would be. Andrew says, more than once: 'What a coincidence.'

And we find ourselves walking together along the corridor towards the large sweeping staircase and it is here again, the limp is returned. Ellen slows to match my pace, Andrew saunters on ahead.

'Oh, no. What have you done?'

'I'm not sure, to be honest.' I pull a wince onto my face. 'It was a stupid thing. And probably nothing, but it's sore.'

Ellen frowns. 'Poor you.'

'I hope it's not a sprain. I walk everywhere. It'd be a disaster.'

'Hmm,' says Ellen and then Andrew turns at the staircase. 'Dear me. What did you do?'

'I put my foot in a rabbit hole,' and to my discomfort, he starts laughing.

'Like Alice. Down a rabbit hole.'

'Andrew,' says Ellen, sounding embarrassed. 'It's not funny. I was about to offer to take a look at it.'

'Oh no,' I say, 'please don't worry.'

'She's a doctor,' drawls Andrew. 'Even trained in ortho-paedics. It's no problem for her.'

'In which case, definitely not. I wouldn't dream of asking for your professional advice.' And I put my hand out, as if to draw our meeting to an end. Ellen takes it, uncertainly, but Andrew bats it away when I turn to him.

'Might I suggest you join us for an early lunch before the lecture? Wouldn't that be the thing? And we can see what that ankle is doing if it's no better.'

I look at Ellen helplessly but she is nodding. 'Good idea, Andrew.'

'Well . . .' I hesitate. 'Well . . . OK. Thank you. If you're sure.' They look sure and their warmth and friendly normalcy is persuasive. It ensures it keeps happening. Opportunities keep presenting themselves – the ankle, the train, the lunch – and it all keeps happening, as if the situation decides it has a mind of his own.

Andrew chooses the club sandwich. He eats using cutlery, slicing away at the layers of toasted bread with a feminine delicacy. Ellen picks at a salad with her fingers as though they are tweezers, little gold tweezers. She pushes around the bed of greenery and extracts the bits she likes. She drinks white wine, Andrew has beer. I have water, and I eat – well, guess, Johnny. I would always have scallops if they were on the menu. You used to call me a Scottish gourmand, didn't you, joking that you weren't sure such a thing existed. *A mermaid's meal.* They are expensive, but I didn't resist. Ellen, a little embarrassed, accepts payment for them.

They aren't very good ones, not like the ones harvested from Loch Levan and which I used to eat with Aunt Nora by the bridge at Ballachulish on her birthday every year. Andrew says it's not the month for shellfish, dissecting the second half of his club sandwich, and Ellen tells him nonsense, what do you know, and her fingers scuttle into the salad. What's that rhyme, he insists indignantly, and she shrugs. I don't say anything. I hardly say anything at all and later, hardly remember what we talked about because it was difficult to hear, it was always difficult to hear what they were saying because my head was always

61

so full of you. Still ostensibly unknown to each other, we are polite, but nothing else, with me adopting the gratitude of the scooped-up, injured loner. I manage to avoid the subject of me and I sense that Andrew, enjoying his largesse, appreciates this. Quiet, grateful, and in a little pain: both your parents show varying degrees of concern and sympathy. Your mother orders another glass of wine and pats my arm at some point halfway through it. And when my foot begins to throb again, it is easy, it is not in the least bit difficult to agree to be ushered to the Ladies, to take my sock off there and cry a little in front of Ellen, whose cool, professional fingers sweep over the ankle and whose advice as a GP is to rest it up with ice and whose compassion as a woman and mother urges me to make sure I am looked after by someone later. 'Poor you,' she says, again, her brown eyes warm. 'It's horrid being on your own and away from home if you hurt yourself.'

I can see how you tapped into this as well. I guess people on their own can be easy targets. But it's really hard to accept this. To admit that I had been vulnerable and this was in part what you were attracted to. And to admit that I had been grateful.

The four thirty is a slow link to the north. We aren't stopping at any stations, we just keep chugging through the countryside towards Edinburgh. Ellen and Andrew and me.

Nobody asks if they can sit at our table and so it is just us. I am by the window and Ellen is opposite me, and Andrew – because of his troublesomely long legs – is in the aisle seat next to her. The pesky legs are stretched out across the corridor. Mine are bent backwards under the seat and I don't dare to move them in case I touch one of Ellen's, presumably within inches of mine.

'I'm sorry I was so pathetic at Abbotsford.'

Ellen rolls her eyes. 'No more apologies. Promise, please.'

I look out of the window. 'I promise. I'm very grateful.'

'Nonsense. Now. Have either of you got Wi-Fi?' and she pulls her phone out.

I begin to reach into my bag, eager to please, but she's done that thing that you used to do. She answers her own question. 'It doesn't look like it,' and she sighs. I let my phone drop back into its hiding place. My lock screen is still a picture of you. In your black puffa jacket, in the mountains, on a sledge. I have captured you serious for once. Unsmiling, you are staring directly at me and the sun is softening your gaze.

Andrew is looking at a magazine but when the trolley comes up the aisle, it is forced to stop in front of Andrew's legs.

'What are we having?' Andrew throws the magazine onto the table. 'Vodka? Wine for you, darling?' As though it is perfectly normal to drink together in the afternoon, companionably and unremarkably like this. 'We should drink to this,' he confirms. 'Drink to having found each other. To coincidences.'

But Ellen knows that he is not being serious about the vodka, she knows long before the lady offering the drinks and I do. 'No. Thank you,' Ellen says. Andrew lifts his legs away from the aisle and places them diagonally under the table.

The trolley moves on. I may be imagining it but Andrew's gaze seems to linger a little longer than necessary on the stewardess's departing rear. Every time the train jerks, his calves roll against mine.

'I must say, I'm terribly impressed that you've been so . . . um, what's the word, darling, when you're young and

63

intellectual, when you're curious . . .' He acts as though he is the pivotal point to our triangle.

'Curious,' says Ellen in her soft way.

'Well, you've been jolly something, diligent, that's the word. Diligent. Coming to Abbotsbury to what, let's face it, turned out to be a rather dull conference.' Andrew becomes expansive approaching a station, like the countryside.

'Dull? Did you think so?'

'Weeeell. More of a waste of time. They'll never pull it off, these separatists. The union is for good now.'

Ellen looks at me warily, sipping from her bottle of water. 'Andrew. No politics.'

'Didn't want to come with a friend? Family? Boyfriend?'

'Don't be so nosy,' Ellen chides impatiently.

I look at my lap. Andrew is the opposite of you in this respect. You only ever asked about me up to the point of civility. You didn't want to know any more than was politely necessary and your courteous afterthoughts are in stark contrast to Andrew's interrogation.

'No politics and no personal business,' he grumbles, 'so what's a man to talk about?'

'It's all right,' I assure Ellen, smiling understandingly and then turn to Andrew. 'It's fine. I'm on my own, perfectly happy.' When I've said this, which I have done before, I have believed it. I know it is no longer true. These days, I endure loneliness – before Johnny, I had conquered it. I see this with such clarity now that I'm amazed Andrew believes me. He raises his eyebrows at me, as if he's impressed, as if my isolation is a self-imposed lifestyle choice.

Ellen looks more doubtful. 'I suppose you have some freedom.'

'Exactly.'

'Think of the places you could travel, the things you could achieve.'

Ellen is torn between sympathy and envy and she is also sort of smug. There is nothing to prevent her travelling anywhere but married people only ever really imagine that sort of lifestyle as a consolation prize for single women. They don't imagine it for themselves.

'Well, I'm not going anywhere,' I tell her. 'Scotland is my home.'

Andrew says, 'I won't ask which way you voted in the referendum.' They are sparse, those white eyebrows, in comparison to his extravagant hair. His eyes are small and disc-like, a flickering, vacant blue. Even Ellen's brown eyes don't seem to be the same colour as your brown one, Johnny. Where do you get your mahogany eye? And your hazel-green eye? 'Which way did you vote in the referendum?'

'Andrew! Don't you dare,' says Ellen and turns to me. 'It was an awful time, wasn't it? Everyone took against each other, took everything to heart. One could hardly go out for dinner.'

Everyone should have taken it to heart.

'I'm glad I came,' I say to Ellen, changing the subject. 'Are you?' and she inclines her head in agreement whilst rummaging in her bag. Bizarrely, I think, *Eleanor of Aquitaine*.

She leans forward suddenly. 'Oh, I'm cold. It's cold in this compartment, isn't it?' and she starts trying to struggle into her coat. 'Andrew, do you want to find someone to ask about heating?' Then her phone starts to ring but she can't get to it with her arms stuck, so it shakes and buzzes on the table face down until she gets to it. Her face alters immediately. I recognise the softening, the gladness instantly. It's not like she starts grinning, or even that she smiles. I know what she is feeling. It's you.

'Sweetheart,' she says and now she is smiling, looking out of the window, fanning herself. 'It's you.'

'Proverbial apple of,' says Andrew, not altogether indulgently. 'Johnny, the son and heir.'

Your name sounds strange the way Andrew says it. Still, I want to hear it again. Say it again, I think, talk to me about him. But no words come out. My mouth is dry.

'How are you?' Ellen is asking him. Are you happy? I want to add. Do you think about me at all? I miss you. And then I hear myself out loud. 'Is he happy?'

Andrew looks taken aback. 'Well, it's rather hard to tell, isn't it?' It is the wrong question. I bite my lip in embarrassment but Andrew never notices.

'Tell me more about yourself,' he says.

But I haven't told him anything about myself at all. He has assumed everything he thinks he knows.

'Yes, on our way back. We're on the train now,' says Ellen. My palms prickle a little. There's no reason she should mention me and strangely, they haven't asked for my name yet. But it's too close to the bone. The colour of my hair makes me easy to describe and possibly identify. 'Fascinating, a great success.'

'Any children yourself?'

'No,' I reply to Andrew. 'It's just me.'

He pronounces mine as a state of bliss and asks what it is I do with myself then, how does Edinburgh amuse me, do I like going to the theatre? – Ellen does, he doesn't, there's some play that's either on or coming soon to Edinburgh and whilst I am watching his lips move, I am hearing Ellen's voice.

'I am sorry,' she is saying, and then there is a pause. 'What a bore. Have you asked Anna?' Ellen gesticulates at Andrew, making a small pumping action with her fingers.

My smile feels strained. Anna. Andrew ignores Ellen.

'Well, I said' – Andrew's lips are still moving. Ellen makes the movement again – 'I said to her, as long as it's not Shakespeare in a car park. Can't bear all that NCP business. If it's on a moor, it's on a moor. And you know what? It's in space!' His mouth falls open in hysteria and then Ellen is saying, sharply:

'Sorry, sweetheart, hang on. Andrew. I need my inhaler.' So Ellen is an asthmatic too – an imperious one. Johnny was always leaving his inhalers lying around, like his phone. I still have one of them.

'*Macbeth* in space!' He has the inhaler in the pocket of his jacket and he hands it over without looking at his wife. 'You ought to go along with Ellen to see it, if you like that sort of thing. Girls' night out for you both.'

'Oh no, darling. How bad? If you need a doctor, of course I'll take a look. Who was this hooligan? I'll take a look anyway.'

I can't help it. 'Doctor?' I ask Andrew.

'Doctor?' he repeats to Ellen, irritation fast following his unconcern as Ellen puts two tetchy fingers to her lips, listening intently. But then she repeats the news – that you had tripped playing football, and hurt your arm. It is not clear how severe your injury is, but there is no need to worry too much. Apparently Anna was with you.

How fluid, how deft the switch from anxiety to jealousy.

'He's an absolute hypochondriac,' says Andrew.

'Well, I'm going to come over as soon as the train gets in,' says Ellen into the phone.

Andrew rolls his eyes. 'It's not necessary, Ellen,' and you seem to have said the same thing.

'Yes, well I'm sure you're not alone. Still.'

The picture I have of Anna at your bedside is very fucking touching. The picture of her touchline loyalty.

67

'I'm sure it is just sore now. But I'd like to see you. All these injuries,' and then my heart stops. 'We're with someone who hurt—'

Andrew interrupts. 'Was it a foul? Ask him.'

Ellen sighs, and asks. I exhale too. 'He thinks so,' she confirms. I expect the answer was more aggressive than the one she passed back.

Johnny says a few more things and she doesn't repeat what. She nods and then hangs up, telling us sadly, 'Well he won't be playing football for a few weeks. If it makes you feel better, Andrew.'

'Why should it make me feel better?' he protests and she rather scowls at him.

It makes me feel better. It really does.

'You will have a chance to be more sympathetic at dinner tonight,' she tells him sternly but then quite without warning, she sticks her phone under my nose. 'Here's a picture of him.'

I have to stop myself from putting my hand over my mouth. Here you are. Positioned by the sea, a turquoise sea, very close-up and smiling tolerantly at the photographer, at me. Your eyes, very close to me, saying so many different things. I start to push the phone away and then immediately try and hold on to it, my fingers curling around it.

I had almost – not really – begun to stop obsessing about where you were and what you were doing as Ellen took over at the forefront of my sleuthing, and it is both a familiar and frightening sensation to return to the guessing, the eliminating and the likelihoods. Where are you here? Sardinia? Did you go on that holiday with your mother in September? Or are you somewhere else, with someone else? Your Instagram, so frustratingly out of use, does so much more than suggest you do nothing at all, it actively conspires to keep things from me. I haven't really known anything about you at all. My mind picks up the buzz of you like electricity. 'Isn't it a lovely snap?' your mother says. 'Can I have my phone back now?'

Ellen pulls her phone and the picture of you away from me. Then she and Andrew begin to shut me out and talk between themselves, so I open up my book and pretend to read. But I refuse to be shut out and I think about your arm too, and about Anna, joining in the conversation in my head. Listening, my jealousy of this woman increases. I hate your friend because she is there and I am not, and I hate hearing from Ellen how much she is a part of your life. I gather that she has a habit of dropping in to your flat. On Brunswick Street. No, I didn't know that she had a spare key to it in her possession and that she organises dinner parties for you there. I hadn't known some of this, Johnny. You kept more from me than I have so far managed to discover. I hardly knew you, just as you (deliberately) never knew me.

I can't listen any more. 'Excuse me,' I say and I push Andrew's legs aside and clumsily step over Ellen's. 'Excuse me,' falling blindly into the aisle.

In the toilet, I hold on to the sticky rail and let the motion of the train make me feel sick. It wasn't the injury, or even the mentions of Anna. It's more that the connection with you has taken on meaning that it didn't have before you called your mother. I couldn't hear your voice; it was simply realising that you were there, sitting somewhere, talking somewhere. Breathing. I was almost beginning to believe in the sincerity of the scenario with Ellen and Andrew because it felt ordinary, and natural. As if I could trust in the truth of it. And then you telephoned, and I remembered the falsity of it all. I remembered you.

15

The French Alps, December 2016

We ate that evening in a mountain restaurant high above Chamonix, only accessible on a snowmobile. The engine sounded monstrous, choking its way round the track, and the fir trees shook white as we flew past them. The pathway became narrow and steep. Nearer the restaurant, torches lit the way and the engine quieted to a growl as we followed lights strung between frosted branches. When we arrived, you helped me from the snowmobile in the sudden silence with an ironic, knightly flourish and the silver reflector pads on your ski jacket glinted like steel in the moonlight. We had to walk the last bit through a twisty, tree-lined path. The dark had a texture to it, as if the sky had collapsed under its own velvety weight and plummeted to earth in a silent crumpling. The headlights of the snowmobile had parted the way like they might a heavy curtain and now without them, and with the moon and stars invisible above the trees, where the mountain become the sky and the sky fell into the mountain, it was impossible to tell.

Inside La Marlenaz we stripped ourselves of our ski gear, and for a moment I felt oddly vulnerable, as exposed to you as if I had just undressed. Our coats and trousers hung stiffly from the antlers of a Chamois, side by side like empty suits of armour and you slid into a booth, patting the seat beside you. 'Don't sit opposite me,' you insisted, 'sit beside me.' And very quickly water from our de-frosting jackets began to collect in dark pools on the stone floor and I watched the icicles slipping from the waterproofs and felt the heat staining my cheeks red, while you ordered for us in your faltering, stubbornly applied French. We ate cured meats and pickles without cutlery from a shared wooden board and drank the local red wine, enveloped in the fug and steam from the nearby kitchen. It had been a long time since company felt so right, you said, between mouthfuls. I asked, cautiously, if there was anyone you ought to tell about me, and you laughed. 'My cleaning lady?' You said that you were impelled to know more about me, everything about me and then never specified what. You did ask about Mum and Dad but when I told you, you did not dwell on it with any platitudes or display any ghoulish interest. I thought it to your credit at the time. You dismissed my tragedy and I was grateful. You did not want to get that close. You preferred to weave the story of us from some sort of fragile make-believe fantasy of your own, one spun from romantic fairy-tales and in them, it was enough for you, Prince Charming, I was orphaned and alone. The details surrounding my circumstances were an unnecessary surplus to your requirements and would have been rather too alarming, too messy for you to cope with.

We did not talk about me any more. We talked about you and what had gone before me. The odd birthday party, trip or occasion. I never knew it was possible to feel jealous of moments; of all the moments before me, the ones that had passed without me being there. And then you talked about the ones yet to come as if they would include me. A fierce sort of joy, mixing with the heat in the cavernous room. I remember you mentioned your friend Anna in casual passing and it never occurred to me she might become an adversary.

The chunks of bread arrived and the fondue bubbled like a cauldron between us. You asked for another demi-carafe. 'I'm going to look after you now,' you promised. 'I'm going to feed you up, I'm going to spoon-feed you breakfast, and then lunch and then I'm going to feed you cake and buns, like Lussekatter – it's Swedish – and then wine and dine you and then start all over again the next day. You need meatballs and potatoes.' And then there were the plans. 'When we've ticked off these restaurants, I'll take you to these hotels. These cities. These countries.' You speared bits of bread onto your fork and into the bubbling cheese. You blew on them and offered them up to my mouth. I did as I was told, and listened to you making lists.

You made so many. It felt like you had planned out the rest of my life and that from that evening until one of us died, you had a plan for each day. Perhaps you didn't realise what you were saying, after all that wine and then the colourless digestif that tasted like poison but was an apparently crucial finale to the feast. Perhaps you didn't look properly at the figure curling through the heat towards you, souping up everything you said with wide eyes. Not even the bitter night air and the freezing ride home dampened your spirits. We sped through the crevasse and emerged back out onto the open mountain. Close above us, stars poured down their own clear and blackened track. When we had been dropped at the bottom, we stumbled across the snow together to the hotel. 'I'm so in love with you,' I said, and you squeezed my hand very tightly. We stood for a while listening to the church bells chiming in the valley.

16

The two of them have their heads bent together, talking softly. It's hard to hear, standing between carriages in the train, but I do catch Andrew saying, 'She seems older,' and then Ellen adds, 'And rather intriguing,' before she looks up and sees me.

When the train slows down and approaches Edinburgh Waverley, your father says that they should take my email address, and Ellen adds that it has been lovely to meet me. Then she remembers something administrative about the surgery and then the train judders to a halt. One by one we step awkwardly down the step and then we are at the end of the platform and we all shake hands. They're disappearing.

'I hope your son is OK.' It is a desperate parting shot and Ellen says that they will find out at dinner tonight. With Anna, she adds, presumably to inform Andrew but it feels like she wants me to know. 'Johnny asked if Anna could come.'

They never do ask for my email address. They just bid me an airy goodbye and leave me on the platform in the grip of a newly remembered fury towards Anna; and now the Strachans are evaporating, dissolving into the smoggy air with automated train announcements in Edinburgh station. The backs of Ellen and Andrew are being swallowed up by a group of tourists and then they disappear behind Caffè

Nero. I stand still, thinking, so this is going to be the end of it all, and what did I expect anyway. It was like I threw a pebble into the water and naturally, it is just sinking without trace. I am thinking that I will simply go back to tracking Ellen and Anna on Instagram; back to the misery of electronic snooping. Soon Abbotsford will seem like a woodland dream, of the type in a Shakespearian enchantment when everything gets muddled up and goes topsy-turvy for a moment. I start walking down the platform, gingerly testing my ankle. The Strachans re-emerge the other side of Caffé Nero. And then they stop. And Ellen is turning around, clapping her hand to her mouth. She begins to stride briskly back to me.

'So silly,' she calls. And then when she is nearer: 'So rude. Andrew says that we don't even know your name. It's not Alice, or is it? I am an idiot, I was confused for a minute.'

How is that? I wonder. How is it that they had only just thought to check my name? Perhaps, caught between the two of them at the conference, I hadn't needed one. Perhaps between defining episodes of my life, it is only right that I should have been nameless for a while. Either way, it seems as though they haven't thought me deserving of one and this makes me screw my courage to the sticking place.

'And we can't just part ways having met like this. I want to know that you get your ankle seen to.'

I'd like to say that I name myself on the spur of the moment, but it wouldn't be the case. It wouldn't be true. I remember the name from the library, the one that I have had up my sleeve. There is time for one final examination of it – 'I just said to Andrew, how peculiar to meet someone and immediately get on so well, and he realised . . .' – and she looks at me, questioningly but also reproachfully, as if it is my fault that the three of us have shared a meal and a train journey without me supplying a name.

'Molly. It's Molly,' and then all I really feel is a rush of relief and gratitude that she isn't going to abandon me after all.

'Molly,' she echoes. 'What a sweet name.' Molleee, leaning on the ee sound. 'We live in Stockbridge,' she says. 'St Bernard's Row. Will you send me your details?'

'I'd love to,' replies Molly. 'I really would.'

'Tell you what. Here's my card,' and Ellen pulls the card from the pocket of her navy jacket. 'Here you are.' A slip of white cardboard, covered in every sort of contact detail anyone could possibly need for Ellen. 'I'd like to know that your ankle fully recovers.'

'I'll be in touch,' I promise and we return slowly together to Andrew who is waiting munificently outside Caffé Nero, a smile playing about his lips.

I say my second goodbye to Ellen and Andrew at the taxi rank. But I don't want to go back to Dalkeith Road just yet so I take the bus to the beach at Portobello and I sit on a rock and watch the sea rolling in and the darkness rushing in from the west. I'm trying to make sense of what has happened, and of what I might do next. I've met Ellen in my mind so often and I feel I know her quite well. It seems almost harmless that the imaginings have become reality. The deceit is very minimal. At least, this is what the person I am tonight persuades herself. I suppose you could say I was putting myself back together, just not entirely correctly – like forcing a piece of a jigsaw where it doesn't belong; it doesn't feel quite right, but it has to do. Molly will do.

I wonder what Ellen had seen when she looked at me. Had she seen someone that her son might have dated? Wasn't there anything about me betraying the intensity of my feeling for you? There was so much left that might have given me away, is it not like water seeping from an overflowing container? I look at my nail-bitten fingers and pull my parka around me. Nothing at all? I'd wanted to tell her that it had been me that turned your bedside light off when you had fallen asleep, who picked your T-shirt off the floor, the T-shirt that smells of you so painfully. Once, I could have told her, it might have been me having dinner with you all tonight, hugging her hello, having my hand squeezed. Would she and Andrew have exchanged satisfied glances? All of us united in mutual approval and contentment? But tonight, the quartet is to be completed by Anna. Shortly you will be having dinner together. The four of you, with no evidence of me, all remembrance of me vanished. You have let go of me, Johnny, I know you have. You assume that I have done the same to you. You haven't yet realised that you left your shadow behind: along with all the other less original tenets of heartbreak, you left your shadow attached to me and I cannot shake it off.

The oystercatchers that are always here in December and January are pecking in a loud, sociable group on the shoreline. I sift through the gravelly sand and listen through their peep-peeping to the voices gathering in my head. I hear the sounds of the restaurant you were all in, the clink of your glasses, the cutlery against the china and the muted asides – *what are you having for first course* – and the scrape of a chair as Ellen asks to be excused and another scrape as Andrew half rises for her. Of course, this is all in my imagination but what is interesting about it is that for the first time, your parents are as illuminated as you. Tonight, you even seem slightly more shadowy than them. You are slumped in your chair. Are you sullen for some reason? Perhaps you are hung-over, as you often are on a Saturday. Perhaps you are dwelling on the ignominy of your bruised arm. I don't like that I can't conjure you clearly, or guess the reason for your lacklustre. It is as if you've faded, ever so faintly, and the convivial images of your parents have dulled yours. But it doesn't matter. I know it won't last. You will take over again tomorrow.

I clasp the reassuring shape of Molly's name to me and later that night, back in my own bed that Saturday, I fall asleep around the soft 'm'; curled around the 'o' and held by the twin peaks of the 'l's. Molly. She knows where you live.

17

The French Alps, December 2016

I remember when we went sledging and I was so cold – you unzipped your coat and I felt my way into it, cautiously at first and then my arms crept around your waist. *It's all worked out perfectly*, you told me. *Doesn't it all make sense?* And I let you wrap your cushiony jacket around me and I laid my cheek against yours and felt breathless with the sculptural clarity of contact with you. There were icicles in your hair. When I told you that I should go back to Edinburgh, you gripped my face and said, *You won't. Not without me*. I can still feel the numbing rub of your thumb across my mouth and hear your voice telling me, *I think I've been waiting all my life for you*.

We had two more weeks together. There were other things to do, but they were the gaps; merely holes between the pattern, and the point. We did our own thing, inter-mittently, during the day and were reunited in the late afternoon; usually on our balcony, often in bed, sometimes sleeping, wrapped together in sheets sticky with sweat. The bind seemed so durable.

On my last morning, we made our plans to meet again at home and we kissed goodbye upstairs (regretful, neces-sary – temporary) but I saw you again amongst the noisy exodus leaving the hotel. Your group was milling around their minibus, and people were trying to pack skis and boots and find their seat. You were wearing your jacket and carrying a rucksack, joking around with your friends, smacking your hands together; gearing up and ready to go. I remember the perplexed feeling that your evident merriness gave me. I pulled my old coat around me and I headed across the road. But not before you had seen me. And you threw me a wistful glance, one that seemed to carry some admiration and regret. The look cleared a path through the noise and laughter and reduced it all to frivolous chaos. Then you mouthed something but I couldn't make out what and I turned for the bus station. You were going to let me go here.

The sky was dark even though it was mid-morning and there was an ominous steadiness to the snowfall. I slipped slightly and I sensed your eyes still resting on me and I wondered if you would come to steady me but there was only freezing air behind me, and the thick snowflakes swirling aggressively. The stillness, and the clear air that had characterised so much of my time here up until now, had vanished.

But I never left. As soon as the bus arrived at the airport I knew something was wrong. I was buffeted about in a confused swell of angry travellers and I couldn't hear what the tannoy system was trying to tell me. Everyone was yelling in a variety of languages. I tried to get back on the bus and was prevented. I fought back panic and pushed my way out into the road where it seemed you were waiting for me. There you were.

'I've come to get you,' you said simply. 'No one is leaving today.' You were standing by a taxi and you told me that the weather was set to worsen and that all the planes were grounded. You held on to me when the ice caught me unawares again and you said things like, 'This sort of thing happens all the time out here,' and then you said, 'What about a coffee, you're very pale,' and I think this was when you gathered my scarf into your hands and carefully coiled it around my neck, when you assured me, 'It's meant to be.'

It's strange but the parts that are real are the parts that read like a fairy-tale. You picked up my suitcase, and decided. You said, 'Let's go.'

The room was called La Marmot. I sat on a sofa with white fur from some pitiful animal over it, and stared at the pictures on the wall of mountaineers in old-fashioned kit. The largest of all the photographs was a sepia-coloured summit of the Matterhorn. There were two isolated climbers dangling from ropes beneath it, their legs kicking in the sunlight. I think now that they were doomed and had died there. They looked unreachable.

I emailed Gillian at work in Edinburgh and she told me to enjoy the enforced extra holiday. I noticed how the sun caught the glass of the photographs, and how the dappled light seemed to bring the climbers in and out of life. When you were done with my bags, when you had found me in La Marmot, you announced that the airport was closed now (rather as if you had given the order) and that you had asked for hot chocolate. I remember that I really began to believe the weather was part of a heaven-sent conspiracy. And you, in turn, became more practical, wondering if there was anyone that I should call. I thought of Nora who wouldn't know or care if I was late back but I was suddenly glad to have someone to telephone.

'Where are you?' my aunt asked more than once.

'I'm away, in France, Aunt Nora, but my flight's been cancelled. I just didn't want you to worry if you went looking for me. If you called. And I didn't answer.'

She was silent, and confused maybe. I don't know. Maybe I was the one who had sunk away into another world.

'I'm not alone.' I looked at you, looking at me. 'Don't worry.'

I wonder, if she had been well, as sharp as she had been in the past, would she have questioned me, told me to be careful? She might have said, 'But you've only just met him. You don't know this man at all.' Perhaps my call to her was really a plea to hear this sort of reason. But the truth was that she wasn't well enough. And another truth; she could have made many salient, cautionary points and more for all the good it would have done. I was disappearing fast, the drop was too delicious, the sinister shade of the lure to happiness obscured by how unavoidable it all seemed. It was too well masked for me to recognise it as anything but an exquisite dissolution of resistance. 'I hope you're sleeping,' I said. 'Call Marion if you need anything. Don't forget to turn the fire off each night. Nora?' But she had already hung up. 'Bye,' I said. 'See you at Christmas.'

And at some point over the next five days I called Tam and she was just relieved to hear from me, and I checked in with Gillian again and she was unconcerned. I could barely remember the city I had left. Now there was only you.

Back at Geneva airport a few days later, you carried my snowshoes for me, the rucksack bouncing off your shoulder; you had peeled a part of me away and harnessed it to yourself. We discussed Christmas and presents. You told me that every year without fail you get a cashmere jumper. You asked me for help in choosing a Christmas present for your mother in duty free. You said your mum was easy because she was indiscriminately overjoyed with anything (from you, I suspected) but your father was impossible. 'Quite often,' you said, in between sniffing the scented candles, 'Mum wraps me something to give to him. Our secret, he's no idea.' I finally settled on Ellen's candles, green eucalyptus-scented ones, with silver lids and black ribbon wrapped around the glass. 'Like the ones in your hair,' you commented approvingly, pulling gently at my plaits. 'I'm going to miss you,' you mused. But I thought, I'll be taking you with me, to the Highlands. I've got you in my heart and distance can't break that sort of possession.

We had one last *vin chaud* in the bar. I wanted to buy sachets of it but you told me unequivocally that the stuff didn't travel. You had grown quieter and you don't like silences. You pretended not to hear silence, you filled it with doing stuff; opening your bag, playing on your phone. You checked your pocket and then said something about being short-changed at the bar.

I frowned, and whispered, 'Johnny, the barman can hear you.'

You shrugged. 'I had a teacher like you when I was at school. Not nearly as sexy . . .'

I tried and failed to look disapproving.

'. . .and not nearly as influential. She used to say things like that. She tried to better me too.'

'That's your parents' job.'

'I think mine did all right.'

'I think you might have benefited from a smack or two.'

'Now you're talking. I like it when you use that tone of voice.'

'Were you ever disciplined at all?'

'My mother's idea of discipline was one kiss goodnight instead of two.' Yawning. 'Now, are we going to our gate or not?'

Without waiting for an answer, you stood up but before moving past me, you put your finger under my chin and leaned down. I'd learned that this was the sort of affection that you scattered, idly and whilst on the move. Your lips grazed mine, and then you became businesslike. 'Time to go home. Back to the real world.'

'Did you really come to get me? When we were last here and the storm grounded the planes?' Something made me ask. Something made me want to hold on.

You cleared your throat. 'As good as. Let's just say it all worked out, someone leaving, someone staying.'

I let it go. It didn't matter now anyway. We were coming back to Edinburgh together.

It was beautiful outside. Behind the plane, the mountains were disappearing in clean sleety snow, falling like pink butterflies against the setting sun. Taking off, you began to gaze again at the spectacular view through the frosted glass of the window. Your hand slipped, distracted, from mine. I didn't look, but I felt the ground falling away beneath me and just took your word for it about everything – about the beauty and the challenge and the fear and all the other words you groped for and couldn't find – and buried it in the snowdrifts of my mind.

We landed in Edinburgh in the late afternoon on Christmas Eve. Time with you was running out, only I had no idea. Was there anything different to say? Would it have altered the course of events if I'd done this, laughed at that? You had become impatient waiting for the luggage, that was obvious. You'd been on your phone, concentrating on a flurry of texts, I didn't know who to. I was totally oblivious to the avalanche that was rumbling just over the hill. I smiled and laughed, flushed no doubt, thrilled with the newly found fluency of our togetherness and said point-less things like, 'It can't be long now,' and you scowled rather. And when the carousel had finally delivered our bags, you marched towards the exit. You were getting flimsier all the time. I suppose there was a bit of desperation in the way I gave you your Christmas present. I pushed the wallet I'd wrapped so carefully that morning into your hand and the way you looked at it; it was as if I'd given you something rather nasty. You looked almost offended.

'By the way,' you added, after your bland thank you, 'Anna, my friend, has come to pick me up. I promised I'd go to a drinks party with her so we'll go straight on.'

And you pointed at her, she was there, coming towards us, with gleaming black hair, a camouflage jacket, glowing with her welcome – and then she realised I was with you.

'Hi, Johnny.'

'Hey. You OK? This is Skye,' and you nudged me with your passport and Anna nodded, her dark eyes unfriendly. 'We were on the same flight back. Skye, you're staying here, right?'

Anna jingled car keys.

'Yes, my connection to Inverness is in an hour. But I'll be back on Boxing Day, remember.'

'Will you be all right?'

'Of course. Only . . . Johnny . . .' Anna did not back away. Anna yawned and looked at her watch. I changed my mind and said it to myself. *I love you*. 'Happy Christmas. See you after.'

'Enjoy mad Aunt Nora.'

'I'm double-parked. Come on, Johnny.'

'Happy Christmas. I'll call you. And see you when I see you.' And you turned and walked away.

18

I imagined you at your parents' house on Christmas Day, wrapped in the privileged caresses of the cashmere jumper and your mother's happiness. I thought of you all together – Ellen (relaxed and pretty), Andrew (magnanimous then drowsy), the aunt and two young cousins – in amongst fairy lights and flutes of champagne. I was relaxed at first.

I was waiting for you in Dalkeith Road by lunchtime the next day. I pictured you attempting in your laid-back manner to extricate yourself from your family at around teatime. I began to think it odd when you obviously failed to do so and my messages were not answered. I went to the Boxing Day sales and then tired to keep busy arranging the flat. Shots of anxiety were peppering my thoughts but that was all, at least until around midnight when I sat up in bed and realised I couldn't reasonably excuse your silence any more. It feels as though I haven't really slept since.

It began to dawn on me how little I actually knew about you. That whilst giving the illusion of openness and vulnerability, you had actually been concealing anything that was worth knowing, everything that was based in concrete fact. Where you worked, who for, where you hung out, who with; all these crucial aspects of day-to-day living had been held back. There was a huge blank hole around you, you had existed for me only in your own entirety.

There was not immediately a specific moment that I knew what was happening. There was a void at first, a confused and griefless void; no sadness, because I expected to hear from you. Expectation dominated each second and every slow, drawn-out heartbeat – if not in this minute, then in the next, then the next. There was a vague, mounting sense of some sort of horror, not absolute shock ever, because it wasn't the result of something but the lack. I didn't have anything to hold on to. Rather, the shock built itself up behind me, and I couldn't look it in the eye. At various points during the day it would rear up, threatening attachment, but I could not confront it. Instead, I texted again – What is going on? Where are you? It would have only taken one reply. I would have moved on eventually with just one message, just a brief acknowledgment from you of my existence, but you refused me even this courtesy. You didn't just leave, you see, you *blanked me out*. You ground me to dust and then, with your back-turned sigh, I was expelled from your life. I was silenced, absolutely cancelled; negated even.

The incredulity was constant but the waves of bitterness and anger fluctuated and there was growing humiliation as well, one too immense to articulate. I did not want to confide in Tam. And anyway, I reasoned, you may call soon and explain it. So I waited, and looked at your Instagram and then I found Anna Stewart's. But the minutes and hours carried on falling away without you arresting their march. Time ticked on, red-faced, and the year strained horribly towards its end but I stayed somewhere else, trapped between the remembering and the reality, becoming a stranger to myself as I fell apart.

Delete delete delete. Is that how it went for you?

By 29 December, five days after we landed, I convinced myself that you had died, and if it hadn't been for Anna, I might have believed for ever that you had, actually died, and that nobody knew to tell me. It became a comforting but ultimately unconvincing lie which I didn't bother telling myself for too long, and anyway, on 30 December, I saw you had been active on Facebook. No, you didn't die. It was not as clear as that.

I went back to Anna's Instagram. @anna_banana_xo has a few pictures of the two of you together, like this one. You are on a beach – I think it is Portobello – and you have your arms wrapped around each other. Your faces are partially obscured by matching waterproof hoods, which are pulled tight around your chins, one red and one blue. It had been pouring with rain that day, and whoever took the photo zoomed right up close because I could see the droplets of water on your face. Your smiling, inscrutable face. The badly spelt caption read: **Gorgeous day at the beach #notthecaribean #scottishriviera #loveditanyway #takemeback**

I had to rummage through crap to reach you. I had to steel myself, and like a semi-reluctant groper, delve through this sort of soiled version of you in order to find out if you were dead or alive. And on New Year's Eve, seven days after I last saw you, I decided I couldn't face 2017 without making an attempt to get something from someone. Darcy, my neighbour's rabbit, was chewing thoughtfully by the sofa as I typed a message to Anna on Instagram direct.

Hi. Sorry to trouble you. We met at the airport with Johnny. I can't get hold of him. Do you know if he's OK?

Anna messaged straight back. I mean, straight back, immediately. There and then.

Yeah, fine. He's with me.

She didn't bother to take some polite amount of time, to consider a tactful response. There was nothing she had to think about it or wanted to sugarcoat.

The champagne bottle found itself hurtling through the air towards the wall. Darcy rushed under the sofa. Who was **fine?** Who was the agreeable, tickety-boo, Johnny Strachan? And what did **He's with me** mean? With me right now? Sleeping with me? I asked the questions over and over again. And something switched inside me. The certainty I'd had that I knew you, that you knew me – it had been so intense, so absolute, that discovering I hadn't at all was akin to a computer crashing. I lost myself as well as you and I couldn't find the woman you'd met; I only knew that if you didn't want her, neither did I. You put me out with the trash and there I was.

Meeting your parents was the restart, a regeneration of sorts, the computer rewiring: but it was a haphazard recalibration as if I hadn't any choice about what the reboot threw up. It happened to be Molly, and Molly went to Abbotsford the first weekend in January.

19

I just want to check out Brunswick Street. I've finally got something to go on and I just want to look at it, I simply want to see where Johnny lives. I don't want to see him, at least, I don't want him to see me; I haven't the strength for that yet. I want to act on something that I've been given. And maybe it was being opposite Ellen on the train when he rang her as well. Maybe it is (minor) concern about his arm and an ongoing (major) concern about the nature of his relationship with Anna. Maybe it's because I miss him.

I walk to Leith, past the shopping centre and onwards to Brunswick Street, and wait for him on the corner, half-turned away from his road and my hair under my woolly hat. If the ominous thought that it is a crazy and creepy thing to be doing slides across my mind, I chase it away. I think maybe two hours go by but I am fortified by coffee from Starbucks and the vague idea that this is a one-off and I won't resort to another underhand tactic ever again.

He comes out of his flat with Anna. I can't believe it. I turn away into the Starbucks entrance, choking on my coffee and hope, and hear her raspy voice. 'Arthur's Seat,' she is saying. 'Do we have to go there?' Her complaints fade, her dark head of hair bounces off her shoulders. One arm is supporting Johnny's, held in a sling. I stare into my empty cup, speckled with dark spots, then push into the café and throw it away. And then I run out of Starbucks again, suddenly desperate, panic overwhelming me. I haven't seen him properly, Anna got in the way. I need to see his face. I dart around the corner just in time to see him disappearing into a car. Anna swings into the driver's seat. What the fuck is she doing with him?

I follow the black Golf to Arthur's Seat in a taxi. It doesn't make sense but that doesn't seem to matter right now. Why not, why not? Tears keep filling my eyes on the journey and I know that I'm tired and what Nora would call overwrought and what Tam would call overemotional but I don't care. I ask the driver to wait while I watch them. Johnny pays for the ticket in the car park. He's wearing the black puffa, one sleeve empty, loose over the sling and he seems nonchalant, if not happy enough. His dark-blond hair is a little shorter at the back. I can't see his face properly so I just drink in the shape of him, the way he walks, in great thirsty gulps. Anna sticks the ticket in the window and he puts one hand, his good arm, in his jeans pocket. They start the walk up the soggy path, Johnny skidding and slightly behind. Anna turns around and begins to jog backwards, gesticulating and smiling. Johnny, following, seems to shake his head slightly.

The driver deliberately keeps his face away from me when I pay him. He has actually had someone in his taxi who said: 'Follow that car' or something like that but he hasn't taken any satisfaction in it. Grim-faced, he has avoided all eye contact with the mess in the back. Faced with Johnny, my sadness has risen unchecked to the surface.

It had been snowing when I came here last year, kindly snowflakes falling like wet blossom. The landscape, supremely uncaring, has evolved to a point of muddy unfamiliarity. How had the seasons kept turning, when I had just stopped? Johnny and Anna are trying to decide whether to sit down or not on the green bench on the brow of the hill. I daren't go further. Anna sits – and Johnny stays standing. If only he'd leave her there and come back down. Then, for a moment (with the ghastly hope clawing at me), I think he's going to. If only he would come and explain. I don't even want kindness any more – any kindness, or pity, would be hopeless because there's nothing I can do with that. I want him to explain, in the harshest possible terms. Then I remember that he is implacable. Never explain, never apologise.

From below, in the car park, someone sounds a car horn, and I turn around, shielding my face from them as they both look toward the noise. When I look back, they are walking away up the hill. He reaches for Anna's arm with his good one, and tugs at it and they walk like that, *like that*, towards the bleak summit. He likes climbing, he liked climbing with me. He's climbed Ben Nevis too and, in his pride, seemed to claim a sort of ownership of the mountain. I remember I told him that Ben Nevis was not there simply for him, and he had laughed (a little). But now I know that for me, it is there only for him. It doesn't have any purpose without him climbing it, what use is it at all to me, all that magnificence, without him? I'm watching him like I'm stuck to him. The two of them, hand in hand, are pulling each other over the brow of the hill and he disappears. There's nothing I can do about it. It feels as though he is pulling my insides with him, my insides are dragging behind him on the muddy grit. When he is gone, there is nothing left. Not even any pride.

Cars roar past the roadside bench that I have found and I feel suffocated. I don't know what to do with myself now.

I feel completely out of sync with my old self. I remember another little ditty he was fond of: *You can't fit a square peg in a round hole*. We were returning to our room after an Italian meal a few days before we left Geneva.

'What a silly expression,' I'd said, noticing that the gap between us was so wide and tangible it was like a third person. 'What does that even mean?' Please walk closer to me.

'It means exactly what it says on the tin,' he'd said shortly. 'It means you can't force people to be someone they're not.'

'No. But aren't you who you are?'

There was a long pause and then he laughed at the nonsensical question. 'I'm a hexagonal peg in a square hole.' Anxiety had surged through me, as it always did when he said something I thought meaningful, and I'd told him a little about Tam then, trying to remember and illustrate her unequivocal nature. He had been partly disinterested, mostly facetious. He'd said, 'Sounds a bit militant,' and then asked if I was bi. I'd been horrified at the thought there was anyone else for me. I'd said, 'No, no. I'm you.'

The thing was, I thought now, remembering the snowy street in Geneva, was that I hadn't been able to dissemble. I had been completely authentic, I had been full of pasta and love and I'd said, 'You make me who I am. You mean the world to me,' half-wishing the words back as soon as I'd uttered them. He'd done that thing when he smiled, shrugging with palms outstretched, and raised eyebrows, half-rolled his eyes in a *well, what can I do?* sort of way. If only I had learned to be inauthentic earlier, if only I had grown my second skin and learnt how to dissemble then.

Perhaps I would not be slumped on a bench by Arthur's Seat, reduced to nothing better than a stalker. Because that's the truth of the matter, that's what I am now, as sure as I know I don't want to be one, I know that I am. A stalker, and an imposter.

20

I don't think that, after you, I could go back to being me. Knowing now what colours the world had to offer but living in monochrome again? If only I could have bottled us. If only I had managed to hold onto some of it, any of it, if only I had learned or copied the secret, or whatever is was that you showed me existed but felt I wouldn't ever rediscover. Without you everything leaked away, effervescent and ephemeral. When you left, you took me with you.

I open Instagram and log out of @scottish_skyegrant, obsolete and full to bursting with the past, and sign in again, this time as @Mollyspics. It's a blank canvas, fresh and unsullied and somehow innocent in its embryonic state. Perhaps, Johnny, in my situation, you might not have seen any real harm in it either. Perhaps Ellen's smile, hopeful and charming, would have tempted you, too. Perhaps a small, stubborn part of you might have felt you were owed something of them. Perhaps you might have decided that your old life, with its padding and routine, was no longer going to suffice. That the way it used to be wasn't going to work any more, that it had been proved counterfeit and unreal. Because you were the real.

I look at Ellen's Instagram again and I hover over the inviting blue Follow button, longing to make contact, for her to see me and acknowledge me, but I stop myself. The account is public, and I need some followers of my own first.

It can wait. I think for a minute instead, legs swinging on the edge of my bed, and then I check the theatre listings. Next, I create a new hotmail account and finally, I write to Ellen, carefully copying her address from the card she had thrust into my hands.

From: Molly Hirst [mailto:Mollyhirst@hotmail.com]
Sent: Monday 9th January 7:25
To: ellen.strachan@me.com
Subject: Hello

Dear Ellen,

It was very nice to meet you both this weekend. Firstly, I wanted to thank you very much for being so kind about my ankle, which is completely better by the way, thanks to your advice. I felt very grateful that such a friendly face was there to help.

Secondly, I have two tickets to *Macbeth* on Thursday . . . I know it's short notice but your husband thought that you might enjoy it. If that's the case, please do come with me? It starts at 7:30 and it's on at the New Theatre.

I hope you had a pleasant evening with your son on Saturday. Here's my email address as promised.

Thank you again, Ellen,

Kind Regards
Molly

Using the name like this, writing it in an email, is quite a different thing to voicing it. The moment between the platforms at Waverley; caught between a sudden jolt of fear and the encouragement in Ellen's brown eyes, I'd said it and surprised myself. It was truly as if it was the first name that had come into my head, seeming a little embarrassed by itself and I suppose I sounded, or felt, unconvinced by it. But seeing it now, in print, is believing it. It doesn't surprise, it affirms. The text makes it real and almost persuades me. When I'm creating an account for myself at Abe Books, I use Molly's name, just relieved to be stepping away from who I used to be, putting distance between me and another blow to that damaged person. This was how Johnny made me feel at the start; like someone else. I liked the feeling of foreignness he bestowed upon me, those twinges of exoticism coming back to me now. A beat like a butterfly's wing.

If there is any nugget of doubt, any small misgiving, it disappears when I remind myself that Ellen will probably never reply anyway.

Ellen replies. Quite quickly, on Tuesday morning, when I'm at work at the clinic. But she declines my invitation. When I read her short but not unfriendly refusal, I feel disappointed but not too downcast. She seems to want to see me again. Despite her unavailability on Thursday she signs off, Till next time and much looking forward to it.

White sunshine winks through the branches and the grass is a bright, cold green. Someone is mowing a path around some early yellow flowers in the park near work. I walk through it, and tell you, Johnny, that at this point, I'm imagining that things are on an upward turn. I wander through Princes Street Gardens, listening to the sound of children playing and feel strangely unbothered by Ellen's choc a block diary. Till next time.

I'm thinking about Nora as I get ready to walk on Wednesday. She's not mad. I went to live with her when I was fifteen; she took me in because she didn't have a

96

choice. She didn't want me and I didn't want her, but she did what she had to. As soon as I could, I got away and I spent weekends and holidays walking somewhere, usually the Highlands, and when Tam introduced me to snow-shoeing, I could walk in the winter and venture further. I even ended up in the Alps but that won't be happening this year.

My aunt used to say, in her dismissive and critical way, *you'll walk your own legs off*. She has always had a steeliness to her, as long as I can remember. She even looks steely, with shorn and sharp grey bristles for hair, and fingers like a miniature Edward Scissorhands. Some cold (but not cruel) air from the hills hangs about her. She considers hobbies like hill walking and running something that only tourists from the south indulge in. She likes to sit, wraithlike, at her window in Torcastle with the cats purring on her knees and watch for the campers and waterproof-clad hikers to pass by. She will turn away, feigning disinterest and then succumb to silent lip-pursing at the foolish audacity of the invaders. Hers is the last cottage on the Dark Mile before the loch ends, petering out into potholed impassability. The only other shelter is the ruin of an old castle, home to wild cats and the osprey. Often her door is knocked on by victims of the hill or the weather. She still charges a satisfied fifty pence for the telephone call and the stupidity. When I joined the walkers' ranks, she couldn't help but see it as another attempt by me to annoy her. Friends at Lochaber High, with the exception of Tam, thought it peculiar as well. The hills were just there, an immovable and ancient part of our landscape, and exploring them was something only outsiders needed to do.

I loved school and stuck to the classrooms which were not only empty after school, but warm. Huddled under clanking radiators, I read whatever I could find, escaping into parallel worlds. The problem was *my* world, the wet or icy trek to the bus stop, and the long walk along the Dark Mile to the cottage. And Nora, who was more adept than the schoolchildren at acting on what annoyed her. She hated my hair, for instance, which was just too red. *A sign of your temper*. She would cut it herself once a month with the enormous kitchen scissors close against my neck, the shears that she also used to chop fabric and chicken breasts. Dad used to have a temper and I think Nora expected me to inherit it along with the colour of his hair. He used to get angry. Sometimes for no reason at all, just after a bottle of whisky. Like Johnny, he had said *See you when I see you*. I can see him now, large in the doorway with an early morning mist from the hills rising around him. It meant that his homecoming, unspecified and vague, always had the element of surprise. If Johnny meant his return to be arbitrary when he had said it at the airport, Dad's was threatening. I'm not like he was but Nora had decided otherwise. *Difficult child*, she'd say. *Stubborn miss. Off again, are we?* she'd ask, sighing fatalistically. *You should slow down*. Well, I hadn't, I had sped up and walked three miles every day for three years to another bus stop, which took me to the West Highland College in Fort William. And after that I had walked to the train station and gone south with Tam, away from the rain-smudged mountains and the midges, to Edinburgh.

Sunlight is causing fissures of silver down the metallic grey buildings and spreading warm across my back. On Princes Street itself the theatre is advertising its modern Shakespearian production. I check my phone and keep walking.

21

There is an unread email from Ellen in Molly's hotmail account. It couldn't be anyone else. The stamp in the dock is bouncing and I have the same lurch in my stomach. I think I say, 'Oh,' aloud and I lean forward. 'Oh,' I say again to the flat. 'It's Ellen.'

Ellen has been blown out on Thursday night. If your lovely invitation to the theatre still stands, I'd adore to come. She suggests meeting half an hour early in the foyer for a pre-performance tipple.

I don't know what has prompted her change of heart or if her cancelled plans are genuine. My heart is beating against my chest, and in the silence, I do wonder if I can hear a warning. But all sensible thoughts get mangled by the temptation to see her again and I don't hesitate before replying.

I've arrived early so that I can be sure to be there before Ellen. I need everything to go as smoothly as possible. I buy the drinks, and get a table that is slightly tucked away, before the crowds make it impossible to sit down at all. Bringing out a little mirror, I check my face, conscious of how desperately I want to make a good impression. I spent a long time on my outfit as well, trying to appear sophisticated and urban. I settled on black trousers and red coat, an unremarkable combination in the end, no doubt but safer to be understated.

I find myself constantly searching the throng for anyone I might know and the fuller the foyer becomes, the edgier I feel. Then, just as I am convinced that the risk isn't worth it, I spot Ellen on the street at the entrance. She pushes through the doors and stands at them uncertainly with some of the tension about her that I noticed in the hotel dining room; she investigates the crowd with a slight worry on her face. Perhaps she is concerned that she won't recognise me, that she won't recall my face from the train journey we took together only five days ago. And then she is walking over to the table.

'Molly.'

'Hi, Ellen.'

'Hello, Molly,' she says again, unnecessarily. 'I'm sorry I'm late. I hope you haven't been waiting too long.'

'Not at all,' I tell her. 'I've got you something to drink. Sauvignon.'

'Thank you,' she says. 'My favourite. How did you know?'

'A lucky guess,' I reply, smiling.

'Clever you. What a treat.' A charming thing to say but I know it isn't really a treat for her to have a small glass of Sauvignon Blanc. Not when she drinks it by the bucket, daily.

'How's the ankle?' she asks as we sit down, and she starts to take her coat off, changes her mind and keeps it on.

I wave hands dismissively. 'Good as new. I spent Saturday evening following your instructions and it was back to normal the next day.'

'Still. I hope you're not walking on it.' Her blonde hair is loosely clasped in a tortoiseshell clip and she is wearing the same lip gloss as before. She crosses her legs and one furry boot-clad ankle starts to swing up and down.

100

'It's fine now. I'm just grateful to you. And really pleased you could make it tonight. Thank you.' I've nearly finished my red wine. I must slow down, be careful.

'It's me who should be grateful. I've been keen to see this. I'll give you some money,' she goes on, 'and for the wine.' Now she wriggles out of her coat. Underneath she is wearing a soft beige cardigan with a furry collar. A gold pendant hangs over it.

'Absolutely not,' I insist and she shakes her head in response, taking a long sip of her drink and pronouncing it a godsend. Her crow's feet are etched finely around her eyes tonight and the lines around her mouth are deeper than I remember but she's still elegant, in a strangely rural and comfortable way.

'I love your cardigan,' I offer.

'This? Ha. It's very old.'

'The old ones are the best, aren't they?'

'Aren't they!' she agrees. 'Although your gorgeous coat looks new? Très chic.'

'No, really old.' The red coat had been bought in the Boxing Day sales. When I had thought her son might still come. 'I don't like shopping much.'

'Neither do I. Although it's not as though I don't have the time these days.' She places her hands behind her neck and fluffs up her hair. 'I've dialled back a bit at the surgery. Let Andrew take over.'

'Is it your business? I saw that it is called after you both.'

'Yes. We're contracted to the NHS but we own the building, and the business. It used to be called after the street, Scotland Street Practice.' She drops her eyes as if she is used to being embarrassed by the eponymous title. 'But Andrew was terribly proud.'

'I'm sure you are too.'

'Yes,' with another smile. 'It's grown quite a bit in size but we're still a very close band. A family business, small but tight.'

'I'm glad you were able to come tonight, in the end. What happened?'

'We've Andrew to thank. He thought that I would really enjoy it. You were right about never getting him here. Anyway, he let me off the hook – a work meeting.' So not really blown out. 'He sends his best,' she remembers to add, politely. And before I can say anything else, Ellen says quite firmly, 'Enough about us.' She leans back in her chair. 'You must tell me about you. Andrew was rather impressed by you.' She pulls her gold pendant backwards and forwards across her chest.

'I don't know why.' And it feels as though Andrew has encouraged the meeting tonight. It makes me uncomfortable.

'I've promised him we'll do something he'll enjoy next time.' A faint pause. 'What do you do, Molly?'

I pick my glass up and take a sip. I have rehearsed all this. It would have been stupid not to have prepared these answers. And I have had time, so much time since Johnny left, to think carefully about many things: what he knows about me, and what he may or may not have passed on – and I have come to the depressing conclusion that he never said anything about me to anyone. I don't think anyone knows I exist apart from Anna. I think in this instance, I can tell the truth.

'Something so boring it's not worth talking about. I'm a receptionist-slash-secretary.'

'Whereabouts?'

'Near Princes Street.'

'It's a nice place to work,' she says generously, and I nod.

'Yes, but it doesn't feel as though I'll do it for ever. It feels more like a stepping stone. I'd like to do something more worthwhile,' and then, nonchalant, I pull out Johnny's inhaler from the pocket of my coat.

'Oh,' exclaims Ellen. 'You're asthmatic too,' and I catch the sense of connection, the faint but tangible sympathy for an asthmatic. She is encouraged to continue, to confide a little more. 'Like my son. All of us.'

'Bad luck,' I say calmly, with thrashing heart.

'Oh, it doesn't bother me. I so rarely get an attack, I forget I have it. And it certainly doesn't bother Johnny. Nothing gets him down.'

'How was your dinner on Saturday night after the conference?'

'Lovely,' she says emphatically. 'Lovely.' She leans forward. 'I'm always secretly delighted to get him to myself.'

'It was just you? Not. . .what was her name? Anna.'

'Happily, just us. He was going to bring someone and then he wasn't and Andrew decided to leave us to it. He does sometimes.' She pushes her glass in a circle.

'And does he. . . what do you . . .' I falter slightly, and she looks at me questioningly. *Think, Skye. What might Molly ask? Remember to be clever about this.* 'Is he married?' It is what he had asked me.

'No!' she chuckles. 'Mind you, he never tells me what's going on in his life. Conversations with him – well, it's like playing tennis against a wall. He keeps himself to himself. You never get anything back.' Her expression becomes indulgent. 'But boys of his age probably don't confide in their mothers, do they. I don't think there's anyone he's too serious about.'

I try to laugh back and a croak comes out of my mouth.

'Are you? Married, I mean?'

I shake my head wordlessly and then the warning bell sounds for the play. Relieved, I put the inhaler back in my coat pocket and with a last, nervous glance over my shoulder into the dispersing crowd, walk into the darkness of the auditorium with Ellen.

It's not in space, Andrew had exaggerated, of course, but it is acted out in a futuristic world so I suppose he merely tinkered with the margins of truth. Ellen enjoys it and her own reactions are theatrical. She gasps when she is appalled and she purses her glossy lips when she is dismayed. She uses her elbow to nudge me when she wants to emphasise something in the plot and right at the end, just before Macbeth is killed, her hand swings violently up over my knee, hovering for a moment before perhaps remembering it's only me. I'm not sure Molly enjoys it so much. Her mind is elsewhere. She can pretend either way though, so it's no problem.

I stay in my seat as long as I can when the curtain has gone down, keeping Ellen chatting about the performance, giving the audience time to leave before us. Finally, she stands up and stretches and we go through the bright lights of the chattering foyer, me slightly behind and keeping my head down. Into a windy night, with Ellen pulling her coat back on and a pair of chunky suede mittens. Time is running out, and the evening doesn't seem to have achieved much. Hard as I have tried, I have not been able to think of a way of bringing up Johnny again, not without arousing suspicion anyway. We get to the corner of the street and the Balmoral Hotel is looming above us. Ellen is trying to find a way to say goodbye, I think; I am just trying to find a way to talk about Johnny some more but it's impossible to pluck his, or Anna's, name from the blustery night. I just want to stay here with Ellen till one of us can mention him. I want something more to take away with me.

It's clumsy but I come up with this. 'So Andrew hates the theatre. Does your son as well?'

Ellen doesn't seem to find anything wrong with it. 'Erm . . .' She considers. 'No, I don't think so. He's really very easy-going about most things.' And then she stops walking, and looks at me thoughtfully. 'You know, you ought to meet him. You should meet Johnny.'

A little of the shock I feel must have slipped through my face.

'Or not,' she amends. And she looks at me, and then something occurs to her. She's wondering something about me, there's something about me that she's hitherto been uneasy about, unable to pigeonhole.

'No, it's not that. It's . . .' I flounder. 'It's just . . .'

'Give it some thought,' she says easily. 'If you like. You'd get on with him, even just as a friend.'

'It sounds as though he's got plenty of those.' I take a deep breath. 'Is he just friends with Anna?'

If she thinks this forthrightness is odd, she doesn't show it. She just concentrates on finding something in her bag and considers, while applying the lip gloss she retrieved. 'Do you think,' she muses, between smacking her lips together, 'friends between men and women is even possible?' Infuriatingly, she answers her own question. 'I'm not sure.'

My hair is blowing about my face. I stare through it, into the dark.

'Everyone likes Johnny, you're right. You couldn't not.' She zips up her bag again.

'Yes.'

'Well, up to you. But let me know if you'd like an introduction.'

'I think . . . I think . . .What does he do?' Another stupid, useless question.

'Ah, I see I've piqued your interest.' Her eyes sparkle a little. 'He's a solicitor. Quite a bored one at the moment. They're not really seeing his potential.' She sighs. 'Although Andrew says he just lacks ambition.'

I remember Johnny's take on this. Any mention of the office had been accompanied by slight derision. Johnny is a visionary. Work is slightly beneath him and the business of earning money is purely a means to something, only he doesn't know what.

'I'll give it up when I've saved enough,' he'd said.

'And do what?'

'Ski,' with glinting eyes, daring me to have disagreed.

'Whatever makes you happy.' Thinking, whatever can include me.

Ellen interrupts. 'He keeps really busy. Saturday afternoon football. Every Wednesday night at a gym class, that sort of thing.' She moves away, belting her coat around her middle and then she says, not bothering to hide her regret: 'He's too busy for me, that's for sure.'

I think Ellen is lonely. I think she misses her adult son, who she still refers to as a boy. And before I know what to say next, she confirms what I am thinking. 'I hardly seem to get out of the house now and I'm probably twice your age, but if you're ever at a loose end, I'd love to do something again. I expect you're inundated with invitations and places to go, someone as lovely looking as you. I'm sure you're busy but—'

'I'm not,' I say, trying to sound stoic in the face of the truth.

106

She looks at me. 'It's hard to believe. But don't be lonely on your own.' A small, half-laugh.

'Well, I'd love to do something too. Anything. And you're hardly twice my age.'

'I will be in touch then,' she promises. 'Now – can we share a cab anywhere?'

'No, thank you. I'm going in the other direction,' pointing somewhere towards Newington.

She looks at me when she says goodbye. I stand there uselessly, with my arms hanging by my side. She may have been going to step forward, warm and almost teddy-bearish, and my fingers start to fidget in anticipation of her embrace, but just as I reach forward she suddenly hurries back, her paw-like hand flying skywards. She has spotted a cab with its light on. She climbs into the cab, the belt on her coat flapping behind her. The door slams. The cab pulls away and she is mouthing something through the window. Perhaps: 'see you soon!'

The wind gets even stronger during the walk home. By the time I have collapsed into bed, my mind whipping between Johnny and Anna and Ellen and Macbeth, the tail end of a hurricane has hit Scotland. I hate the wind.

22

Although she is in her death throes after her Atlantic crossing, the hurricane is still powerful. Rain is lashing down and the wind is so fierce I can hardly pull the door of the flat shut. The lid of a dustbin comes flying towards me just as the door slams, and misses me by inches. The rain feels like needles. I shouldn't have bothered with the umbrella, which rips itself inside out as soon as I push it open. I leave the spikes in a bin and stagger across the road.

Tam is at the bus stop. I haven't seen her since November, the night we ran to my local pub through the puddles. After that came Johnny, and when I was with him, I didn't care and afterwards I didn't care even more. She looks good in her black lycra leggings and a neon vest is bright beneath the waterproof jacket. Her hair is slick with the rain, her cheeks are fresh; she looks healthy and wholesome. The wind and the wet weather do not bother her. She checks her phone, straps it to her arm and redoes her shoelaces. She is looking around, jogging vigorously on the spot and then, from nowhere, another woman appears in her space, and fits into it, like a jigsaw piece. My eyes sting a little in the wind. I don't think we ever forget the shape of someone who has been important in our lives. Not the shape of their body I mean, but the angle of them, the way they move through a crowd and make space fit around them. Their slant against the world. I miss Johnny's shape.

Tam and her friend embrace, their arms slotting comfortably around each other and then Tam is laughing and pointing through the rain at the grey racing sky, and I start walking towards them and just as they are setting off in the direction of the Meadows, I say, 'Tam,' but she doesn't hear through the wind. I say it louder, with a sudden urgency, and then I shout at her. 'Tam!'

But they are running too fast, shoulder to shoulder, weaving in and out of people, not breaking stride or losing rhythm. She is soon lost from sight. I wanted to ask her what to do now I know that Johnny goes to the gym on a Wednesday evening.

Wednesday arrives. I'm sure there are lots of things going on in Edinburgh. I'm sure there are lots of things happening all over the bloody world but all I know is that on Wednesday, Johnny goes to the gym. Johnny goes to the gym. I can't contemplate the library when all I can think of is this.

I make a cup of tea and take it back to bed. I wonder again what the name of his law firm is. A search of his name in Google combined with 'solicitor' doesn't reveal it. He's probably too junior. He probably spends too much time skiing in the Alps for them to take him seriously.

At around eleven, I get up and get dressed. I shuffle down to the coffee shop in Newington and buy a latte and a newspaper and shuffle back. Tam practically lives at the gym. What do people do at bloody gyms? Which gym does Johnny go to? It could be in Leith. Near home or near work? Could be Leith.

Lunch is a tin of baked beans and then I try and do some work. *Purified water makes perfect pebbles for curling. It is sprayed through a wand onto the surface. This is called pebbling. Everything matters; temperature, humidity, air quality*. I pick up my snow globe and shake it in my hand, watching the snow descend, slower and slower, and then settle. I open up Anna's Instagram. Nothing new, certainly nothing about Johnny's gym. I bet the gym is in Leith. @Mollyspics has two follow requests, one from a healthy juice company that Ellen follows and another from @visitscotland. Nothing new from Ellen.

At three o'clock I make another cup of tea and this time, sitting down at my desk, I Google gyms in Leith. Of course there are loads – Pure Gym, Leith Victoria, David Lloyd. I suck in my breath, annoyed and then, simultaneously, I have a thought. I open Instagram and start typing a message to Ellen. I keep it short, and don't give myself the luxury of reflection. I simply ask her for a gym in Leith that I can recommend to a friend and she is entirely obliging. I read her quick, informative response sucking in my breath. **Hello. Yes, no problem. David Lloyd – my son goes there. It's a good one. exx** I let my breath out in a slow whistle.

I get their number from the website and ring it. 'Hi. I'm calling to see what classes you have on tonight?'

'Two to choose from if you're a member.' Only two. 'Swimming only for the general public.'

'I'm a member.'

'So, you'd be looking at Hatha yoga at five thirty or Body Attack at six.'

'Great. Thanks.'

I think it is safe to say I'm looking at Body Attack, 6 p.m.

I shower and then I spend the next half hour choosing clothes, blow-drying my hair (I leave it long, the way he'd liked it) and carefully applying subtle make-up. I am going to be just passing, after all. Not stalking, just passing.

On the bus, I sit on the top and at the front. It seems as though everything is lurching from side to side. The trees are reeling in the wind, the clouds are unsteady, the pedestrians are tiny. I watch myself — that figure in the red coat with hands gripping the bar at the front — from outside the flying bus window, such a huge window. I wonder what I am doing. I wonder at myself. But the bus is fast and it's swooping down the streets. It's not going to stop and I'm not going to get off. The temptation to see Johnny again is too strong. Really, compulsion alone could have carried me there.

I've guessed the class, which started at six o'clock, lasts an hour but to be sure, I am waiting from six forty-five outside David Lloyd gym. Strangely, I had never imagined that I would doubt who it was when I finally saw Johnny again, but I am quickly made unconfident. Several times I start forward because I am certain this figure, head bowed, black coat, is him. It isn't. None of them are him, and I slink back again, confused. Very quickly I am cold. The new red coat is not a thick one, I had not bought it to be kept warm. It is dark and there's a drizzly mist coming off the water. I can smell the sea now, coming at me through the semi-darkness. I watch people leaving the gym, and more occasionally, some going in. Seven-thirty. Johnny is nowhere to be seen. I'm getting colder. The sounds are different down here, muted and muffled as through a fog. There are thumps and bangings, the occasional shout. The sound of a boat chugging out to sea. He's not here, he's not coming.

At quarter to eight, I give up and begin to walk away from the docks. I'm freezing now. I ought to have guessed that he wouldn't stick rigidly to his gym commitment. He goes when he feels like it, not because he has to. Embarrassed tears, ones of frustration and self-pity fill my eyes.

23

The next day, for no reason other than I am thinking about the Strachan family, I walk to Stockbridge in my lunch hour. And the next day, and the next. I look out for Ellen and Johnny all the time: I never really expect to see either of them but I imagine I will. Around this corner. Around that one. It's her . . . it's him. My neck prickles sometimes, believing one of them to be behind me. Coming up to me at the bus stop in the centre of town. By the Water of Leith, on the bridge. Too often, I start, mistaking a swing of someone's blonde head for her, or a long stride in the crowd for him. At the end of the day, alone with myself, I make up the story of what would have happened had I actually seen one of them. I listen to our conversations in my head and correct my responses until I have absolutely the perfect ones. Sometimes, meeting Ellen, I decide to tell her the truth, and always, in these imagined exchanges, Ellen is . . . unsurprised. She is never angry. And Johnny: he is always sorry. He regrets leaving, the way he left, more than anything. He wishes it could have all gone differently and he is sorry. He never manages to explain though.

And then, leaving work early on Monday afternoon, tired of the usual routes, and suddenly exasperated with the stagnant state of affairs, I decide to go to the Strachan medical practice. It's north of the centre, on Scotland Street. I suppose it is a strange thing to do because this time, I don't want to be seen. I just want to watch them. I just want to see how they go about their life; as if I can't remember for myself how this is done. At least, not without Johnny or Ellen clogging up my head, saturating my imagination, my thoughts and my actions. I'm nervous of going quite so close and I know full well that I could never explain any of this if I were asked to. But I'm still going, and I remind myself that I'm not doing anything wrong.

Up Dublin Street and around leafy Drummond Place. And drawing close, thinking about the doctors in their surgery, I know which of the Strachans I would rather see for an appointment. I expect that for Andrew, meeting his patients is a task as perfunctory as breathing, and less memorable. I imagine him tilting back in his chair, fingertips pressed thoughtfully together whilst he thinks about something else entirely, counting down the ten minute consultation and dispensing traditional, careless advice. Try walking every day. Lose some weight. He'd better ask Ellen about that book he wants. Warm milk before bedtime. She can get it after surgery hours. Next, please.

Yes, I think, crossing London Street, I wouldn't want to see Dr Andrew. But then I am here, arrived at Scotland Street, and a little way along it is a building with the over-sized, immodest words STRACHAN MEDICAL PRACTICE nailed across the front. I wait for a minute opposite and then, too exposed, move behind a low wall. I crouch uncomfortably behind it, horribly aware of both my prurience and my determination despite it. I seem to have become unstoppable.

Ellen leaves first. When I actually see her, and she is on her own, the reality of the situation becomes clearer for just a moment. I must be insane; spying on Ellen from behind a wall. Her face is as kind as I recall, open and inviting, but her brow is furrowed. I so nearly approach her but that won't improve things; can anything now? She is wearing the same coat she put on in the train, a blue woollen one. I remain staring at her from my place of hiding, rooted to the spot and fixated by just watching her go about her life at that moment. She is looking for something in her bag, she can't find whatever it is. She seems to sigh, rubs her forehead with a weary hand, and turns back to the surgery door and then, digging around again, she must feel the elusive item before she reaches the door. She shakes her head, bringing her phone out of her bag. She presses a button and puts it to her ear. She walks away down the road and leaves me gazing after her.

When she's out of sight, I get stiffly to my feet and walk over to where she had been, and stand in her space. I imagine I catch the fresh, elegant breeze of her. Strangely, I think there is something of Johnny in it. Perhaps families share a scent.

I ought to go. But I'm still standing there when someone behind me says: 'Molly?'

I can feel the blood drain from my face.

'It is Molly, isn't it? What are you doing here?' Andrew.

'I . . .' I hold my hand up to my forehead as though the sun is out, to shield myself from him.

'Is there something I can help you with?'

I force a smile. 'I came on the off-chance that Ellen would be here. I said I would . . . at some point. It doesn't matter.'

'Well, shame you missed her. Only just, mind.' He looks at me more closely. I lick my lips, suddenly dry. 'Look who you got instead.' I suddenly have the awful feeling that he does not think my appearance here is anything to do with Ellen.

'It was silly of me to just turn up. I'm sorry.'

I turn to go, to run, but Andrew bars my escape. 'She's no grafter, my wife. She leaves on the dot of. You're better off looking for her in a wine bar. Not the work place.'

Behind him, the doors to the surgery are swinging open again and this time, a woman in high heels with short brown hair comes out.

'But her loss is my gain.' He pulls a pair of glasses out from somewhere within his jacket. 'Did you bring a car?'

The woman walks past us and Andrew says, 'Bye, Amy.'

'Bye.' She looks at me as she goes.

'Bring a car?'

'No. I walked.'

'Walked? From where?'

'I walk everywhere.'

'Yes. It looks like you do. Very trim, aren't you. Well – I'll give you a lift. Where do you need taking?'

'We'll be going in different directions. I don't want to trouble you.'

'No trouble at all. A pleasure even. I'll tell you my direction if you tell me yours.' He shoots an arm out towards a car in the corner and something beeps. Lights flash on a silver Volvo. 'In you get. I won't take no for an answer.'

I think he won't. His habitual expression of benign condescension has settled again, the look that won't brook any argument. I get into the passenger seat and fasten my seat belt. 'It would be great if you could drop me in the centre.'

It's as if I haven't said anything at all. 'It's good to have run into you.' He pauses before he starts the engine. 'I have to admit I felt rather jealous of Ellen's little soirée with you.'

Andrew's conversation leaves me blank, utterly blank. Unlike Ellen, he doesn't invite replies, or at least none that I can think of. He just makes statements that I'm unable to respond to. And he's too large for the car, everything feels as though the airbags have burst and there's hardly room for us to breathe. I shrink into the seat, a small, pale splinter.

'But it worked out for us all, didn't it? Ellen gets to take someone under her wing and I get to make sure we see each other again.'

'Excuse me?'

'Ellen likes scooping people up.'

That wasn't the part of his sentence that I wanted answering.

'Where are we headed then?' He sounds jovial.

'I'm meeting a friend at the cinema,' I say. It sounds plausible. 'But please just drop me anywhere.'

'Which one? Vue multiplex is on my way. What's on? I hardly ever go to the pictures now. I remember it from the good old days. Back row and all that.'

I turn to look out of the window, my cheeks flushing, searching – unsuccessfully again – for a reply.

He indicates and pulls smoothly out onto the main street. 'I'll drive you there then.' He takes one hand off the steering wheel and runs it through that thick white head of hair.

His unsubtlety is frightening. It has no filter and also, no sense of him actually really minding one way or another. His solicitude is ground up with his indifference. He can take it or leave it. He turns the radio on and taps his leg with his fingertips then points to a bottle of water in the coffee holder between us.

'You couldn't undo that lid for me, could you?'

I do as he asks. His fingers touch mine when I hand him the bottle. He tilts his head back and pours the liquid in; he doesn't drink from the edge of the bottle, he chucks it into his throat.

He says, 'You're thoughtful. Penny for them.' He turns his head slightly sideways to look at me and doesn't wait for or want an answer. 'Who are you meeting then? Is it a date?'

'No.'

'What's it like for you, being single in Edinburgh? They must be beating the door down.' He tilts his head and chucks the remainder of the water down his throat.

I turn to look at Andrew. 'How do you know I'm single?'

He doesn't take his eyes off the road. 'Are you?'

'Yes.'

He doesn't say anything for a while and then carries on. 'You've got to get out there. It's no good waiting for exciting things to happen to you. You have to go out and get them. Can't just sit at home – waiting for the phone to ring.' He looks at his, held between his legs. 'You're a very attractive woman. Easy on the eye.'

I have no sense of any control with Andrew. I don't know if it is my fault or his that we are in the car together. Andrew slows towards the lights and runs his thumb around the rim of the water bottle.

'It's been nice chatting. We should do it again.'

We most definitely should not. 'Thanks again, Andrew.'

'Thing is, I think we may have more in common than you realise.'

The lights stay stubbornly red.

'Ellen. We both like her. Well, of course I do, I'm married to her.' He chuckles, without sounding amused. 'But she's only got time for the surgery and her son. We haven't really got anything going for us at all any more.'

'Apart from the surgery. And your son.'

'Well.' He is dismissive. 'I run the surgery, pretty much on my own. And Johnny is an adult now. Supposedly.'

I don't respond.

'And I'm just a disappointment.' When I don't argue with this or offer my sympathy, he flings the bottle into the back and shrugs. The lights go green.

At the multiplex, Andrew gets out of the car as well and comes round to my side. In the open air, now I can get away, it feels even more wrong to prolong our time together.

'I'll see you soon,' he promises. 'I'll make sure of it.'

I set off towards the cinema complex feeling his eyes on me. I risk a glance behind. He is walking in circles, swaggering around the car. He's on his phone, and scuffing the ground with a forceful, kicking motion. He stops, leans against the car, smiling. One leg is bent back against the car and another hand is in his pocket. It's a familiar pose of seduction.

24

'Boo!'

I'm standing on the steps outside the cinema, watching Andrew and lost in my thoughts when Tam comes up behind me.

'Tam,' I say, my hand on my heart. 'You made me jump.'

'Hello, you,' and we hug each other.

I'm suddenly deeply glad to see her. 'What are you doing here?'

'If you'd bothered to stay in touch recently, you'd know that on Monday afternoons I take classes at this gym. But don't worry,' she adds. 'I've missed you. Where have you been?' She looks at me closer. 'Skye?'

'Tam,' I start to say and stop.

'Oh, Skye. I knew something was wrong,' and I don't actually cry but I can feel tears inside me, trying to flood something dried out. She takes my arm and leads me to the side of the steps. 'Here, sit down,' and she pulls some tissues from her bag.

An age seems to pass, an age in which, pulling the tissues to shreds in my hands, I realise, truly realise, I have just come from spying on a kind and unsuspecting doctor in Scotland Street. It is a blinding moment of awfulness exacerbated by the poisonous car journey alone with Andrew.

'Come on now,' she says, after a while. 'What is going on with you?'

'Haven't you got a class to go to?'

'No,' she says, 'I'm on a break.'

Down in the car park, Andrew has finished his call and is getting back into the Volvo. I watch it circle the bus stop and head away into the traffic.

'Tell me,' she says, with her arm around me and takes my silence for acquiescence. 'Go on then. Start from the beginning.'

So I do. I can't not. I start in Chamonix, under the glittering slopes of Mont Blanc with your eyes and your attention and your charm. I tell her about the days of unrivalled perfection and how I had fallen under your spell. I tell her about Anna waiting for us at the airport. Tam listens gravely. I tell her more about you, about our weeks together and then how the attention and the charm vanished for good between Christmas and New Year. She interrupts once to say that she wishes I had confided in her. She says, towards the end, that she does not like the sound of you and it is my turn to shake my head. When I have told her the story of you, I drop my head against her and shut my eyes.

'I'm so sorry,' she says finally. 'I'm so sorry.'

'Yes,' and I sniff into her arm.

'You've had a bad time. I'm afraid you've been led a merry dance.'

I lift my head up. 'What do you mean?'

'I think,' she says carefully, seeing my expression, 'I think – and you must see this, even though your heart has been broken – you must see that this man has tricked you.'

'No. Not tricked. Why would he bother? You make it sound as though he didn't mean any of it. I know he did. He felt it too.'

'I've no doubt he liked you,' she says, in the same cautious tone, 'who wouldn't be glad to have a romance

120

with you? But the likelihood is that he has either done this before, or he's got a wife or something, anything like that.'

'Married? Of course not. In fact, I know he's not. You make it sound as though he's some sort of a conman. That's ridiculous. I'm not stupid.'

'No,' she agrees quickly. 'You're not. I think he's been clever.'

'He's not clever. He's . . . he tries. He means to be honest.'

Tam looks at me oddly. 'I don't get it,' she says finally. 'Well, I do, but what I mean is, why don't you? Why are you defending him?'

'You don't know him, Tam. You weren't there, to see us together.'

'OK, OK. Tell me. What is it about him that's so special?'

I shake my head. 'I can't explain. You wouldn't understand.'

'Try me.'

'Fine. I will. He's not special – not in the sense you mean. Yes, he's good-looking and funny and all the rest of it, but he's not Prince Charming. I know that. But he's important to me. Something happened out there between us, and I know that I'm not making it up.'

'Do you still love him?'

'Yes.'

'And how do you explain his behaviour once you got back here?'

'I can't explain it. That is what has been so dreadful. None of it makes sense. None of it adds up.'

'The likelihood,' she says caustically, 'the probability is that he's evil.'

'Evil?' I stand up. 'That's just unhelpful.'

'OK, not evil. An arsehole.'

It's too late. I don't want to hear any more. 'As you say, you don't get it, Tam. It's not a simple thing. He's . . . he's . . . I'm not suggesting he's perfect. I'm just saying that he's the one. There was something between us and I can't let go of it. Not till I know for sure. And it's not just me, he saw it too at the beginning. He just talked himself down.'

'Or he was happy for someone else to talk him down.'

Anna. I bite at my thumb miserably and then try another angle. 'I remember you saying the same about Gemma last year. You do know what I mean.'

Tam makes a face. 'Gemma? Who I'm still with and who feels the same way? Come on. The situations aren't comparable.'

'Why shouldn't they be though? Why is it OK for you to say someone is the one for you, but not for me? And he did feel the same way.'

Tam lets a judicial silence lengthen before trying again. 'There will be someone else for you. You will meet someone else.'

She really doesn't get it. I do not want to meet anyone else. I want him. I push my hair away from my face.

'He really pulled the wool over your eyes,' she says eventually, and then stands up too. 'But you need to get it together now.' This is more like the Tam I know. I must leave, quickly now. 'You've been had, by someone verging on criminal.'

I cannot try and explain it to someone who has it so wrong. I do not want to talk to her any more about Johnny. She has made me want to defend what every now and then, in moments of clarity, I could see was indefensible. I run away from her, jumping down the steps, and she lets me go.

*

The same evening, I hear from Ellen. Molly's inbox is jumping up and down in the dock of my computer and I immediately feel worried that Andrew has told her about the lift and the conversation in the car and that she is angry with me somehow. But no: Ellen had forgotten to give me the money for the theatre ticket and the wine, and it's simply awful. She says she couldn't be sorrier and that Andrew is furious with her. Did you even get home alright? To make it up to you, can I persuade you to supper here? 22 St Bernard's Row. This Friday 27th. She hopes that I can come. In the meantime, could she have my bank details?

I don't say yes straight away, and obviously I have to ignore the request for personal information. I feel tainted by my encounter and car journey with Andrew, who seems to have engineered the dinner. Above all, it's far too risky to spend the evening at their house. It would be a crazy thing to do. I chew my nails and stare at the message, at Ellen's floral, genial sentences and reread the encouraging words.

I know that getting away with it today – being discovered outside the surgery but Andrew assuming he knew why I was there – is no excuse for allowing the deceit to continue, and maybe this is where I run out of excuses because in the end, around midnight . . . I just do it. I pour myself another glass of Rioja and then, braver, increasingly defiant, another one. Tam has only succeeded in pushing me closer to Ellen. Ellen makes everything all right. I say yes to dinner at the Strachans'.

25

It takes me over an hour to get through town to St Bernard's Row on Friday night because there is some sort of security alert in the city centre. When my bus has been stationary for twenty-five minutes because of road closures, I jump off it and start to half-walk, half-run in my black velvet dress, towards Stockbridge. I can hear sirens as I hurry beneath the castle esplanade, sirens that are punctuated by short, eerie silences. I try a shortcut down a cobbled street but lose my way a little. I'd left plenty of time but I am still late. It is eight o'clock, half an hour after I have been asked to arrive when I cross the bridge and eventually reach St Bernard's Row.

I stand in the street with the sense of foreboding larger than ever; the sirens fade, the dread grows. I ought not to have agreed to come. Despite my frequent checks and Ellen's steadfast assurances that it is just us, I feel worried now I am actually here. It is too much of a risk, surely. But there it is, number 22. Their front door is navy blue, the letter box and matching doorknob gleaming silver. I shiver slightly, feeling goose-pimples springing up on my arms and legs. It feels as though someone is behind me and even though there is nothing but a slight breeze to be felt, I can't help turning around. When I look back at the house, the navy-blue door has opened.

Andrew is filling the frame.

'We were beginning to think you were a no-show. Saw you from the study window. Better come in,' he says. 'What held you up?' He barely masks his impatience. It will simmer under the generous folds of his skin, this unflattering pique, until it is dissolved by alcohol.

'I'm so sorry.' I don't move from the street.

'Please don't worry.' Ellen appears behind him. 'We heard about the bomb scare. It's lovely to see you.'

I don't have any choice. I walk through the door and slowly through the long straight hall behind Ellen. My footsteps echo on the white marble floor. The wallpaper is pale green with gold beetles or bugs dotted unevenly across it. Everything feels sophisticated and untidy; it is becoming a tunnel of evidence, testimony to their busy and stylish life. I do not belong here. Two or three umbrellas, huge and multicoloured; a line of leather boots, furry things and coats and walking sticks and a contemptuous smattering of parcel delivery attempts pushed to one side. 'Thank you so much for inviting me,' I say, hovering near a gold-leafed antique mirror and she doesn't reply, she is disappearing. 'Is anyone else coming?' I call. I'd got the dress code wrong for a kitchen supper (Ellen is wearing jeans) and I may have got other messages mixed up too. Perhaps just us meant just the whole family.

'Come through,' she calls back and then Andrew is behind me so I am half-pulled and half-pushed into the kitchen. The open-plan space is vast. The kitchen is clearly the hub of the house. Like a beating heart. Everything that might be separate has been flung together: Moroccan rugs and Nespresso coffee machines, laptops and loaves of artisan bread, newspapers and trendy pottery and unrecognisable plants in Egyptian-looking vases. There are four places laid at the table.

I start to back away.

'Ellen,' I say desperately, but she doesn't seem to notice my distress. 'Who else is coming?'

'I mentioned my son to you, didn't I? I feel so sure you'd get on. Just as a friend, mind,' and she almost winks. 'But he never commits to anything with us. Such a shame because you look so pretty. What a beautiful dress. Will you have a drink?'

Andrew is slicing lemons lethargically on a central island and he offers me whatever drink he is preparing by raising a tumbler and his eyebrows.

'Is your son coming, or not coming?' I can't see any other way out of this room other than through the garden and over the willow trellis.

'Like she says,' Andrew says, cutting in before Ellen can reply. 'I wouldn't like to bet either way. A law unto himself.'

I take the drink with trembling fingers. I do have to bet one way. The black dress feels tight over my constricted ribcage. At the far end, Ellen is sinking serenely into an armchair by garden doors, beckoning me over. She kicks her shoes off. I just see the red flash of her painted toes before she tucks her feet beneath her. I wipe my palms down the sides of my dress and try to breathe deeply.

'Cheers,' says Andrew. 'Thank God today's done with,' and he takes a long sip of his drink. 'It's been a long one. Let's eat asap, darling.'

'Please don't mind him,' Ellen says steadily. 'We'll eat when it's ready. I'm sorry if he comes across as abrupt, he doesn't mean to.'

I think he absolutely means to. I can imagine Andrew saying to Ellen: 'Drink, grub and out the door. Bed by ten. No messing around.' This is to be a snappy affair: some brief, bearable charity and repayment for the theatre. I stare at him and he considers me in return.

Ellen gestures at the sofa where a large grey cat – Witchy – is shedding hairs. 'There's absolutely no rush.'

Andrew glares.

'Do sit down, Molly. I hope she won't irritate your asthma?'

I must have looked blank for a second. Then I remember but I still can't think what to say. Say something. Nothing comes. The room, and the fear has silenced me. Whilst I am standing it occurs to me that I could still run, but an old instinct to keep quiet and obey means I do what she suggests.

'It's fine. Thank you,' I manage, joining Witchy on the sofa. Witchy scrambles away.

'Yes, strange, she doesn't irritate my asthma either.'

Short silence. 'It's very nice to be here.'

But it's not at all. It's one thing imagining them and quite another experiencing them, as they dole out their reluctant hospitality in the large and colourful kitchen. On the edge of my seat. Andrew goes to sit on the arm of Ellen's chair. They look at me expectantly.

After a few seconds, she asks politely, 'Have you had a good week?' There is a side table along the wall next to her with two scented candles on it. Black velvet ribbon is tied around the glass. Christmas, courtesy of Geneva airport's duty free.

'Yes,' I say, 'thank you, yes. It's been fine. You know how it is.' I can smell the eucalyptus now, and it is suddenly overpowering. It wafts around me like the fear prickling on my palms.

Her fingers creep towards the gold pendant around her neck and she does that see-sawing motion across her neck to free it from the clasp, nodding in agreement. Andrew smacks his hands onto his knees once or twice. He seems to have forgotten our meeting. Or at least not shared it with his wife.

'I've had the week from hell,' he announces. 'Busy, and pointless. Never get yourself a medical practice. The bureaucracy is a nightmare. And I saw nobody, not one person who was seriously ill today. My patients today consisted of a list of gibbering hypochondriacs. The most interesting thing about my day was hay fever.'

Ellen says, 'It doesn't matter what the complaints are though. It's what we do.'

'Yes, well. I should have been a neurosurgeon.'

Ellen smiles but she lowers her eyes as well. She's heard it before and I assume she also hears the belief in the statement. Carved into the groove of the humour is the belief that a brain surgeon is exactly what he should have been. I nod blankly at Andrew and he surveys me over his glass. It occurs to me that although he is attractive in his determined and confident way, I only consider him so because he is part of this family. Without Johnny, without Ellen, he would be entirely ordinary. I'm staring and then I realise we haven't broken eye contact. Andrew looks away, satisfied. The eucalyptus swirls over me again. I look at the door and look back at the French windows.

'I hope you like stew,' says Ellen. 'I'll put some rice on. We won't wait.'

Andrew is tetchy again. 'I didn't know we were. Honestly, Ellen. He's not coming.' He says this last bit looking at me, in a patronising tone meant for Ellen. Can I relax slightly?

'Ten minutes,' she says lightly. 'And then we're ready. Any wine with dinner?'

Andrew ignores her. 'Ellen is late for everything. She is unable to ever get dinner on the table before nine o'clock.'

'Don't you cook?'

Ellen shakes her head, as if to say, don't bother, and indeed, Andrew is pleased. 'Often,' he says, gleaming. 'Not often enough.'

'He's a good cook,' admits Ellen. 'We take turns.'

'It's my fault tonight. I've made everyone late,' I tell them but Andrew glides on.

'She'll be late for her own funeral.'

She is used to him but her cheeks colour slightly. 'It's true,' she says. 'He's right.'

He pulls a scornful face. Being right doesn't mollify him and plucking a bottle of wine from a rack in the central island, he turns back to Ellen. 'Corkscrew?'

'It's my fault,' I say again, weakly. 'I went straight into this bomb scare. I'm really sorry.'

'In the usual drawer.'

'Yes, the measures they take – it's all a pain in the proverbial, isn't it,' he says, yanking out drawers.

'They're just doing their job,' Ellen insists. 'Keeping people safe. This drawer, darling.'

'What's it doing there?' he says, turning around with his glasses on. They have steamed up. 'Is there any veg?'

Ellen shakes her head. 'Sorry. It lives there, that's what. Andrew, take your glasses off, you don't need them.' She adds: 'He thinks he looks like that actor with them on. What's that actor called?'

It's my turn to speak, I think, but in this freewheeling three-way conversation it's not always clear to me. I have no idea what this actor is called so I stay mute and though Andrew obviously does, he doesn't humour her, he foils the attempt at camaraderie. He just runs his hands through his thick white hair. 'I do though, don't I. You said so yourself.'

She says, 'Oh, honestly,' and I look between them while they continue their jousting, Ellen organising cutlery and deflecting his blows. Is this a show for my benefit or is this actually how they are together, in private as well as public? I had thought at Abbotsford that it was mutually enjoyable banter but now I think it is the verbal way by which Andrew tries to accumulate power. He says things like, 'I've told you a million times, don't exaggerate,' and 'Andrew to the rescue.' Ellen never snaps. She is calm; but not always passive, I realise. She has her own weapons. When he criticises the ('monstrously ugly') Moroccan pot the stew is in, she says, in a wistful way: 'I'm so fond of that pot. I remember buying it. My family used to own a riad in Marrakech.' She tells me, but seems to be reminding Andrew: 'Long before his time. We used to go a lot. We hardly go away at all these days.'

'Something wrong with your memory? I took you to Sardinia last year.'

'You didn't take me. We went together.'

'Yes, darling,' raising his arms in bewilderment at me. 'It would help if you didn't hate flying, of course.'

'Yes,' she agrees, letting him win that round after all, and beckoning me to come and help myself to the rice.

I wonder when they are done with their sideways swiping, when Andrew tires of putting her down and Ellen has had enough of placating him, and then I think I know. I think they silence each other upstairs in their bedroom, or probably in the kitchen, in the room where they seem to do everything else. I think Andrew silences Ellen here on the granite-topped island between the salt and the fruit. Why not?

26

At last, as the protective persona that is Molly settles over me, I begin to find some courage. Andrew is generous with his red wine. Ellen's home-made lamb stew is delicious. I start to relax. His father is right. Johnny isn't going to turn up now.

I look round the room from the table in front of the French windows. There is nothing visible of him. And yet . . . this is where he has grown-up and been nurtured. They had moved into the house immediately after they were married and Johnny came along practically nine months to the day. And sewn into the furniture and atmosphere, admittedly in a way that perhaps only I could tell, is his attitude. His nonchalance and slightly cruel humour were fostered in these comfortable and chic surroundings. Even Ellen has it too, this easy, eloquent manner. Just without the spikes.

She is telling me that she finds she doesn't have much to do outside work. 'I don't know why, only that when I found I had more time, I found I didn't have anything to do with it. Perhaps we're just getting old and boring.'

'Speak for yourself,' says Andrew, neatly slicing through a chunk of lamb.

'Next time, we'll find you some more exciting company, Molly.'

'You mean, next time you'll find someone younger than me,' he says drily. 'Someone better-looking than me, hmm?'

'I'm merely pointing out that Molly is probably nearer Johnny's age than ours.'

'Let's see. How old is Johnny now? Ellen had Johnny when she was pretty young, Molly. She's forty-seven this year.' Andrew flashes four fingers at me, twice.

Ellen says, 'Thanks.'

'But he is a good-looking chap. I'll grant you that. We know that, don't we, Ellen darling. Think he takes after his father?' Andrew uses a spoon to scoop up the gravy.

'No,' she says, mildly enough, but something about the set of her mouth makes me think she is exasperated. 'He takes after me.'

'Well. He's certainly a lousy lawyer.'

Now she is visibly indignant. 'That is not fair,' and to me, 'I'm very proud of him. He's doing well.' My face must be so blank, she continues helpfully. 'At his law firm.'

'Run by an obliging friend of mine,' supplies Andrew, and then he says something that sounds like gobbledegook. Something like Nedders, Nedders. 'It won't last long. He is useless. Can't hold anything down, job, girlfriend; you name it.' It's hopeless, I didn't catch the name of the company and there isn't an opportunity to interrupt.

'It's simply not true,' Ellen is saying crossly.

I look from one to the other.

'It is true. Just wants to bum around on ski slopes. Except he suffers from vertigo.'

I must have made a small sound.

'He's a wonderful skier,' Ellen is saying, first to her husband and then she repeats it to me. 'Wonderful.'

Andrew finds a grape in the fruit bowl and begins to skin it. His face darkens and Johnny's comes into focus. I remember Johnny's careless wolfing of food. Andrew is as fussy as Johnny was indiscriminate. He would eat

132

fondues with the cheese hanging over his lips, tearing the bread apart with gusto, he was always ravenous, snatching food on the go, munching Haribos at the airport, finishing anything on my plate that I was too slow with. I have a sudden vision of him in the alpine sun: I can see him on the veranda of the hotel in Chamonix with the pine trees behind him and the skiers in the distance like matchstick men on the mountain. There is the smell of sun cream. Oh, Johnny. Leaning forward, the light in his hair, his eyes crinkling. *Why couldn't I have come here to St Bernard's Row with you*? You are so completely unlike your bitter and bullying father, now looking at Ellen with something like spite. I would have been on your side.

And Ellen is looking at me – she has stopped chattering on – so now this kaleidoscope of images must fade and I need to respond, and discuss Johnny as if, as he used to tease, I was someone more like his schoolteacher, or worse, an older and rheumy-eyed grandmother. The type who just nods weakly and wrings her hands in her lap. I can't see how I've become this person, when I used to be the girl who sat on Johnny's knees and felt tonic water fizzing at the back of my throat. He used to mix gin with tiny strawberries. We used to have strawberries bleached white by the sun in Geneva.

'Sorry, Ellen. What were you saying?'

'Men are just hopeless about commitment in general, aren't they, Molly?' and Andrew makes a pshaw sound.

'I don't know,' I say desperately. 'I wouldn't know. I expect so.'

'I think your son is, Ellie. I expect they'll all carry on coming and going. Who knows?' Andrew is dismissive, but he adds, 'I doubt anyone would put up with him for long.'

'Who knows?' repeats Ellen sadly.

Coming and going?

'I'd have liked a daughter,' says Ellen and then I am surprised by a flash of tenderness.

'I know you would, darling,' he says, more softly. Then he pushes his plate away and sits back. He looks at the large roman numerals ticking in the huge black and white clock above the stove and hardens again. 'But we've been dealt our hand. And now . . . we must make the best of it.' He is bored with talking about Johnny and presumably is letting Ellen know he is done, both with the meal and their son.

'I don't need to make the best of it. And there's nothing else to eat,' Ellen says, putting her knife and fork together, 'except some cheese if anyone wants it.'

Andrew has been mellowing as the night closes in and the wine is drunk. 'Why don't Molly and I have some whisky?'

It's not a question, it's a decision, and his opinion of the evening – which is that it hasn't proved so bad after all. Their guest, despite being disappointingly late initially, was still 'easy enough on the eye' and not bad company. But it's ten o'clock. Should I leave now? When I've helped load the dishwasher? I pick up my plate and move awkwardly between the central island and the table under Andrew's urbane gaze. After the whisky? The bottle is on the side between the Fairy Liquid and some gardening gloves, and he pours us a measure each.

'None for you, Ellen?' He knows the answer. 'She only drinks white wine,' he tells me. 'Gallons of it.' I know.

'Not tonight,' she says, yawning.

'How do you take your whisky, Mol?' He doesn't wait. 'Neat, I suppose. Straight.'

I nod, dumbly.

134

'So, it'll just be us then. Settling in.' There is a slight gleam in his eye again and I don't know how Ellen can miss it.

'I'll just get my herbal tea from the larder. Would you like one, Molly?'

'Of course she wouldn't.'

'I would love one. Thank you.'

Ellen disappears and Andrew tilts back in his chair. Like Johnny. 'I tell you what I was wondering.' Even further. 'I was wondering . . .'

There is silence until Andrew's chair leg thumps back down to the floor. He hasn't been wondering at all. This is something Johnny used to do as well. He'd say, 'So . . . tell me . . . tell me . . .' and all the while be thinking what to say. If no inspiration came, he'd say anything that came to mind. 'Tell me . . . you love me.' As if it were a game. I told him once, between the cold peal of church bells. *I'm so in love with you.* I think now his silence had been a horrified one, not the harmonious agreement I'd taken it for.

Andrew finds something. 'Do your folks come from round here?'

'I haven't got any.'

I shouldn't have said that. I'd wanted to shut him up though, it's what I would always say to prevent people asking any more questions. But now I'm in a muddle. I've also drunk too much red wine. But he acts as if he hadn't heard me and refills my glass, even as I shake my head. I wish Ellen would come back in. Andrew is drumming the table with his fingers. He gets up again and there is some noise behind me as Witchy claws at the sofa and when I turn around again, he is at the mirror above the small wood burner picking at his teeth. When he sees me watching him, he smirks, unabashed, and then moves forward. He

135

puts his hands on the kitchen table and his face near mine.

'When are you and I going to see each other alone?'

'I don't know.' I shake my head in confusion. I really hate Andrew, and I tell him so, in my head, because I can't be rude to him and blow everything.

'Tch,' says Ellen, coming back in. Andrew straightens up. 'You haven't touched the cheese I wanted finished up.' There is a slight edge to her voice. 'I feel tired now.'

'What cheese?' says Andrew lazily. He sits down again and rolls his whisky around his glass. I watch the liquid rise and fall, twist and turn.

Ellen snaps the kettle on and doesn't respond. And then their doorbell rings. 'Oh gawd,' he drawls. 'Typical. He always arrives late. Arrives in time for the Laphroaig.'

Ellen makes a face at Andrew. 'I'm so glad he made it. It's not that late.' She is smiling now. 'I'll get it.' Her fatigue is forgotten.

'The thing is, Ellie,' says Andrew, 'the thing is—'

'I have to go,' I interrupt. My face feels as though it is on fire but my legs won't move. 'I have to go,' I say again, my voice rising. My legs just won't move. And where even can I go?

'The thing is—'

'Com . . . ing,' Ellen coos. 'Andrew, talk to Molly while I get the door.'

'You see?' Andrew complains to me. 'She never listens to a bloody thing I want to say.'

'I've got to go.'

'Nonsense. The night's still young. What have you got to get home for?'

How do I go, where do I go? 'Where's your toilet, Andrew?'

He waves towards the hall. 'Far end, turn left,' and finally my chair scrapes back and I force my faithless, dream-like legs to the kitchen door. I dart left as quickly as I can, not looking down the hallway, and there is a door slightly ajar by the gold-leafed mirror. I open it just as Ellen is pulling the front door wide.

It's a storeroom, not a cloakroom. The light has been left on. It smells faintly of cardboard and it's no bigger than a cupboard. It's lined with shelves stacked with things like herbal tea. Some tins. Some toilet paper and light bulbs. I can't shut the door with me in it so I hold on to the handle with my forehead pressed against an ironing board hanging against the door. My legs start to shake.

This is it. I don't have any choice but to face them, all three of them. Oh God. I should have left ages ago. Or maybe while they are in the kitchen . . . maybe, I think wildly, I can run for the front door. I'll never see any of them again, I promise myself. If only I can just work out how to escape. My legs are knocking against the ironing board. Oh God.

I don't think much time passes but before long I begin to imagine that breathing is becoming difficult in the confined space. And once I have that thought, I find I can't breathe properly at all but still I stay where I am, my chest constricting and the longing for air becoming torturous. I don't leave the cupboard, I stay there rather than have to face Johnny, Ellen and Andrew. Eventually I think, when I am almost drifting to the floor, an old instinct for survival means I turn my head to the door. It creaks open and I fall quietly into the hall. I lift my head and straighten up, gasping noiselessly. I let go of the door handle. Strangely, my first thought is how cold it is. A draught from somewhere sweeps over me, and it helps. I'm calmer now. I'm going to run for it. I can

137

make it: I can see the front door at the far end of the pale green tunnel and the gold bugs flying towards it. I take another breath.

'Molly?' calls Ellen from the kitchen. 'Is everything OK?'

Now or never. Run.

'That was our neighbour. She's gone now. Sorry. She's a frightful bore.' And her face appears round the kitchen door. 'She's a night owl and thinks we are too.'

'We are,' says Andrew from the kitchen. 'I am.'

I want to sink to the floor.

'Is anything the matter? You look like you've seen a ghost. You're white as a sheet.'

'I . . . I wasn't feeling too well all of a sudden.' I'm starting to shake again. 'I'm better now. I'm OK.'

'Andrew was having a cigar in the garden. The smell makes me feel ill too,' she says sympathetically. 'Have your tea and come and sit on the sofa with me.'

'I'll go now. Straight away . . . but thank you.'

Andrew's face looms towards me as he comes into the hall. 'Don't want to finish the whisky?'

'No. No, thank you.'

The front door looks like a Tardis at the end of the tunnel. Andrew opens it for me with gusto. 'Come again, won't you.' Just concentrate on saying goodbye. Look at Ellen, look at Andrew.

'Molly,' Ellen has a little diary in her hands that she is flicking through. 'I'm near Princes Street doing a home visit on Monday. Shall we grab a sandwich for lunch?'

'Yes. I'm sure that's fine.' I would have agreed to anything. 'Good night.'

'Good-ee.' Ellen's chirpy words are the last I hear before I stumble into the night. I don't look back.

I shouldn't have ever gone. It was punishment for going

that first I had to endure them talking at me about their handsome and wayward son, so full of life and energy, and then find myself hiding in their musty store cupboard, suffocating like a trapped rat. Alone now in the dark street, all I am left with is the ghastly, sickening vision of him finding me in there. And of all the girls, coming and going. Presumably, I was just one of the girls who had gone.

27

It feels part of the punishment that, barely recovered, I should see Anna the very next day. I'm walking towards the Randolph Hotel, phone in pocket, hand on phone, thinking about the Strachans, and I turn the corner expecting to see the railway station and I see Anna.

I'd know it was her anywhere, even if she wasn't striding out of the gallery where she works. I would have remembered her just from the airport even if I didn't have @anna_banana_xo's photograph to remember her by. She isn't the sort of person who fades into backgrounds and memory and she is never far from my thoughts because in my mind she is always near you. She is just a blink behind you, triumphant, sassy, pushing her way through you, and when you began to fade, when I couldn't see you any more, she emerged in glaring, vivid Technicolor.

Today she is wearing bright red lipstick, and red sunglasses are perched jauntily on her head. Her tight black T-shirt says HELLO SAILOR on the front. She's talking loudly to the woman who is with her in that raspy voice of hers. They just swing out of the doors together and then she stops to get into a woolly cardigan and pull on a pair of multicoloured stripy gloves and then they turn away from me and head down Princes Street.

The sight of her makes me gasp. All roads lead to you, Johnny. It's like walking in circles, there's no escape from the inevitability of you.

'It's such a shame,' Anna's words float back to me.

'Yes, shame,' giggles the other woman. 'Anna. Shame on you, more like.'

And Anna responds with a bellicose shout of laughter.

Anna is like a blast of cold air. A shiver runs through me as I watch her sashay down the road. She took you away at the airport and when you're playing football she spends Saturday afternoons guarding you from the sidelines. She drives you to Arthur's Seat when you want. She constantly places herself beside you on social media and I expect she does the same thing physically whenever she can. I imagine the two of you have Chinese takeaways, your favourite, in front of a TV in your sitting room and she sits in the armchair that won't ever hold a trace of me, and she leaves her belongings on it as if she had bagsed the seat; and adds to the dishes that never get done, so that between her and you they become 'our' washing up. And perhaps at some point she might say, 'D'you remember that girl, the one you met skiing that time, I've forgotten her name, what was she called again?' And you would shrug and say, 'Which girl, turn the telly up.' I hate Anna, even if there is nothing going on between you. Anna's got you.

Ellen seems genuinely pleased to see me on Monday and makes me feel guilty all over again so, despite the relief, and despite feeling safe for once, with Johnny presumably in his lawyers' offices and Anna at the gallery, I still feel uneasy.

'You look fab.' She says it in a simple sort of way, managing to be just admiring, without any caveat or judgment. Even Tam can't help adding extra comments such as, 'That jumper must be new,' or 'Don't lose any more weight.'

141

I sit down opposite her, shaking my head. 'I hope you haven't been waiting long.'

'Not at all,' she says cheerfully. 'And it's good to see you. I hope you like the café.' She waves her hand around proudly, as if it's hers. 'It's only small . . . but it is sweet. Isn't it sweet? And perfect for a weekday snack.'

It is nice. It's warm and red-and-white-checked and every time the door opens, napkins fly out of their loosely packed holder which she carefully replaces. 'And these,' she says, 'are for you.'

It's a handful of reviews on *Macbeth*, carefully folded.

'Ellen, thank you. That's really thoughtful.'

'You've probably read them all. But just in case, I wanted you to know that all the critics loved it and I'm so glad we went.'

'I haven't read any.' I haven't had time, I think to myself, my head is so full of the Strachans. 'I'll look at them later.'

She nods, pleased. 'Are you OK with fizzy water? I'm not sure they do anything more fancy.'

'Just water.'

She reaches across for the bottle and fills our glasses. 'Andrew hates it here.'

The thought of his ill-disguised snobbery and loudness in the café makes me cringe. 'I can imagine.' I don't think he ever did mention the lift to the cinema. My hands are on the table between us, and Ellen and I look down at the nails, bitten down to the pink edges of soreness. I remove them from our gazes.

'My son likes it though,' she amends, as if making up for her husband's lack of taste and she looks at me earnestly. 'Johnny loves it here.'

As long as he's not coming today. As if she reads my mind. 'His office is in Old Town. Bit far for lunch.'

'How far? I mean – where is it?'

'GMT?'

The abbreviation – thank God. It had been impossible to make sense of the long-winded name. And it is in Old Town. 'Yes.' How my mind whirs beneath my smile.

Ellen says, 'They are in . . . oh, you're not interested, surely. Now – lunch is on me, remember,' and she pushes the menu over. 'Let's order.'

I look at the writing and because I'm thinking about a firm of solicitors in Old Town, I just say randomly, 'Soup?'

'Just what I was thinking. I come here on my own quite often and always have the tomato and red pepper one. I bring my sister when she visits.'

We talk for a while about Ellen's family, her sister Ivy and her nephews who live in Oban. And then she asks about mine.

'I'm sorry. Listen to me, banging on. I must sound very self-absorbed. I'm sorry, because I've got a feeling you don't have family, do you?'

'Not really,' I say in a monotone, after a moment. 'It doesn't matter.'

'Molly. Your parents. They died, didn't they?'

I feel myself go cold. 'How do you know that?'

'I'm so sorry. Andrew seemed to think you'd implied it, during dinner at ours. You've never mentioned them either.'

I've guessed that Johnny never gave his parents any information about me at all, let alone an introduction. But it's a fairly unique detail. I need to be careful.

'Don't be sorry,' I tell her. 'It was a long time ago.'

'And Molly, I've always thought you seem sad. I mean, you're lovely, but somehow I feel you need looking after. Let's just say I thought Andrew was right about your parents.'

'There's nothing to be done. Let's talk about Ivy.'

She ignores me. 'What happened?'

I stare at her. Not everyone is courageous enough to ask, especially after I have put them off. And sometimes (most of the time) I choose not to answer even if they persist. But Ellen makes me want to tell her. 'They were on their way to France. They were going on holiday, and they chose to drive.'

She nods encouragingly. 'Go on.'

'Mum refused to get in an aeroplane. She had never been on one. She had barely left the Highlands, let alone Scotland, so they had to drive to Portsmouth.'

'And what happened?'

'There was an accident.'

There are details that most people wished they had never asked for. But I want to give Ellen some sort of truth, even though the truth is ugly. I want her to know. It suddenly seems important to talk about them and give her the details that Johnny did not want, that he had not asked for in La Marlenaz.

'We think they had been stretching their legs. Or stopped for a break, something to eat maybe. And a car, out of control, mounted the pavement. Mum was hit head-on.' I pause and watch to see Ellen's pity dissolve into shock, but her solemn expression doesn't waver. 'My father was thrown clear. The driver ploughed over him in his panic, trying to veer away. He later said he thought he'd run an animal over.'

'I'm so sorry. Was the driver drunk?'

'No. Lost concentration.'

'And how old were you?' Ellen asks.

'I was fifteen. I used to wish that I had been with them just because it would have been easier.'

'Easier . . . in what way?'

'Oh, easier to have died with them. I expect Nora, who had broken her leg, wished it too. But Nora couldn't get herself up and down the bloody stairs so I stayed to help her. I didn't want to go with them. I was an angry teenager.'

'You were a teenager,' she corrects, with a small reassuring smile.

'I went with Nora to collect them though, and we flew down to Luton because Nora refused to get in a car and Mum had to fly back to Inverness after all, if only to be buried.'

'And did Nora bring you up?'

Ellen. I look at her, and sigh inwardly. In another time and another place, it would have all been so much simpler. I wish that I could have told her all this without worrying that one day, if not today, she will make the connection. For the first time, I am glad that Johnny has clearly never told his mother one little detail about me.

'Yes, I went to live with my aunt, six miles away from home. Down a long road called the Dark Mile.'

'That sounds mysterious.'

'It wasn't mysterious, it was simple and straight-up. Verging on bleak,' and I give a mock grimace in case she takes me too seriously. 'Poor Nora, really. She didn't want me, but she got me. She'd wanted someone else but the man she'd hoped to marry drowned. It's why I never learned to swim, we never went near any water after that if we could help it.'

'I hate swimming,' she says. 'It's cold and wet, and overrated.'

'Do you know,' I say, 'the driver got six years for manslaughter but he was released after two.'

'Two years? Surely not.'

'He was driving the family Range Rover. His father paid for my college education and I got my flat with Mum and Dad's life insurance.'

'But still,' she says. 'That seems too lenient.'

'He was contrite,' I say, blandly. 'Contrite and wealthy, which got him lawyers and sympathy. And he was English, and they were Scottish.'

'Oh no,' says Ellen, appalled. 'You can't think like that . . .'

'I can. You think if the trial was in a Scottish court, he would ever have seen the light of day again?'

Ellen shakes her head and says again, 'I'm so sorry, darling. Life. It's unimaginably cruel.'

Darling. No one has ever called me that. She makes Johnny's use of endearments at the start of our relationship sound wry, a pale imitation of something. There is no effort involved in her spontaneous 'Darling'. It is the sound of someone who is used to being called darling and used to saying it.

Ellen leans forward sympathetically and then I sit back. This isn't something she can fix. It's not like a wall that she can break through. It's a permanent and relentless thing, it's how day meets night. It's how blood dries. It's part of me.

But she comes closer and takes one of my hands.

'Number twelve,' calls the waitress.

Ellen looks at me with her controlled, uneffusive sympathy. I like the feel of her smooth dry hands on mine. Her motherly manner, but still so practical and unsentimental. It's so unfamiliar and yet . . . I recognise it. Without warning, my eyes fill with tears.

'Number twelve!'

'We just keep going,' she says, 'don't we. Soldier on however we can.'

146

I stare at Ellen, biting down on my lip and refusing to let the tears fall. Just looking at her, not daring to move in case I jog them out of my eyes.

By the time we have eaten our lunch, we are back to normal but when it comes to saying goodbye at the door, she takes my shoulders.

'Please take care of yourself. And let's do this again.'

'I'd like that.'

'Shall I email you?'

I nod, and she adds, 'Are you on Instagram, by the way? I'll look you up if so.'

Briefly, I am muddled. The conversation about Mum and Dad has confused me. Am I on Instagram? Which one can she know about? I quickly have to pull myself together. 'I am – although only just! @Mollyspics. I don't completely understand it and have about one and half followers.'

She giggles. 'Oh, I'm mad about it. I don't do Facebook but I do love people's photos.'

We collect our coats and there is a bell above the café door that tinkles cheerfully above us as we move into the street together. Ellen says, 'Bye for now, darling,' and I am leaning towards her hug, smiling, and I have forgotten to be on my guard when someone says, 'Well, hello, stranger.'

28

I look up slowly to face the greeting, the smile fading from my mouth. Tam is standing in front of us, looking from Ellen to me and Ellen is getting her umbrella out waiting, looking at me. I feel disorientated suddenly, dizzy. What is Tam doing on Princes Street? She ought not to be, the gym is miles from here.

'Hi,' she says again. 'Twice in a week.'

'Hello,' I manage. 'What are you doing up here?'

She shrugs. 'Why not?' And then confesses. 'Lunchtime shopping.'

Ellen chuckles politely and they both wait for me to make the introductions but I'm not thinking quick enough. I can't think.

'Hello,' says Tam in the end, holding her hand out to Ellen.

'Hello,' echoes Ellen. 'Ellen.'

'This is my friend Ellen,' I say, like a robot. 'We've just been having a bite to eat.'

'Hi. Tamsin,' and Tam looks at me questioningly. 'Did you get my last message?'

I shrug helplessly. 'Probably. Sorry. Look, I'm running a bit late now.'

'No, you don't get away that easily,' says Tam. 'I was just going to grab a quick coffee. Will you come? And you, if you've time, Ellen.'

'I must get on,' says Ellen, wrapping her silk scarf around her neck. 'I'll have to leave you and Molly to it and make a dash for it.' She looks up at the clouds and I look down at my feet.

'Molly?' says Tam her brow wrinkling. Very carefully I lift my foot and place it back down on Tam's. I press, hard. Her mouth opens and then shuts again. I press again. Tam. *Please*.

'How do you two know each other?' Ellen pushes up her umbrella and we are suddenly all underneath the large canopy, our faces reflecting a paler hue of the racing green.

'How do I know Molly? We go a long way back,' Tam answers, keeping her eyes on me. I take my foot off her trainer. 'Yes. A few years now.'

My tongue feels huge in my mouth. I lick my lips wet and try to speak but nothing comes out.

'Enjoy your coffee.' Ellen looks between the two of us. 'I should get back to the surgery for the afternoon session and see what Andrew's up to,' and she moves away down the street.

'No,' I say quickly. 'Or rather, I must go too,' and Tam says, 'Well, bye,' in a weird and doubtful kind of way and it makes me want to run, very fast. I don't reply and dart across the road, covered with shame and guilt.

Tam, unsurprisingly, rings me in the afternoon. 'Are you going to tell me what that was all about? Why did that woman call you Molly?'

'I'm at work. I can't talk.'

'Bullshit. What's going on? Who is Ellen?'

'Let's leave it, please. You don't know her, you don't need to.'

'No, Skye, seriously. I haven't seen you properly for weeks and I feel I don't know what's going on with you

149

at all. First this Johnny and now a new name and hobnob-
bing in your lunch hour with older ladies.'

'Tam, please. I'm not feeling well. This is none of your
business. Don't ask any more.'

I don't want to tell any more lies. I know Tam will be
shocked. What on earth can I say that won't make what
I've done sound as though I've gone mad? Even madder
than Tam already thinks?

'Who is Ellen?' Tam says again, more urgently. 'Where
does she fit in?'

'You won't understand. I don't really understand.'

'So there is something. Come on. Who was that woman?'

I sigh. 'She's Johnny's mother.'

'What the fuck?' Spluttering.

'Well it's certainly not funny.'

'It certainly is not. I'm not bloody laughing. I thought
Johnny had vanished. Oh God. You're not back with him,
are you?'

'No,' I say quietly. 'No, he's not been in touch.'

'I am not getting this at all.' I can almost see her scratching
her head. 'What are you up to, Skye? What does she know
about you and Johnny?'

'She doesn't know anything at all. She doesn't know that
I spent half of November and all of December with him.
That I love him.' I add this last bit warningly.

'Seriously? Who does she think you are then?' and then
Tam answers own question, flatly. 'Oh. Molly.'

'For what it's worth,' I say, 'I like her. She's married
to a vile bully and I don't think she's got many friends. I
think she likes me too.'

'I'm sure she does, but so what? That doesn't mean
anything. She doesn't know who you are.'

She does know, I think. I've just been telling her who I am.

150

'All this aside,' says Tam, warming up now, 'how come she doesn't know Johnny went out with you? Or at least with anyone who looked like you?'

'How would she know what I look like? There aren't any photos of me on the internet.'

'No,' Tam agrees slowly, 'I suppose there aren't.'

'Exactly. And no, it seems that Johnny didn't ever mention me to his parents.'

'What a surprise,' she says sarcastically.

I ignore this. 'And I don't think they're all that close. The Strachans. I mean, she adores him but they don't know that much about him. It has been horribly easy to do, really.'

'But . . . why?'

There is a long silence.

'Because,' she goes on, 'you can hardly meet Johnny now. Can you? You can't start again with him, having made a mate of his mum.'

'Sometimes I think I could tell them the truth.'

'Tell Johnny you made up a new name? To get close to his mum? He'll freak, and run a mile.' Her amazement at me, although I had expected nothing else, is hard to hear.

'I know. I know.'

'Doh. And by the way, you don't love him. This isn't love, it can't be. You're just being stubborn.'

'Shut up. Tam, I'm not arguing this with you, I mean it. It is what it is. I know exactly what it all sounds like, but it is what it is.'

'Do you, though? Know how it sounds? Because I'm afraid it sounds completely bonkers, Skye. *You* sound bonkers, but you're not. I know you. You just need to get away from this family.'

I am suddenly cold, and I catch myself swaying a little. Tam must see she has been too harsh, and she changes tack. 'Let's have a drink on Saturday night. Come on,' she coaxes. 'We'll really catch up. And we'll sort this mess out. I know you feel undone by this man, but you've just lost your footing. We can make it OK again.'

I give in because my head is starting to thump. I don't want to meet her on Saturday though, and have to keep on justifying what she refuses to see. And she doesn't seem to have anything to do with my life now that it has been derailed; she is irrelevant and unconstructive in the face of its chaos. She has just proved herself – and I know this to my shame - beside the point.

She used to be my best friend. I think now that Johnny broke far more than I'd thought. He didn't just break me, he managed to destroy the carefully arranged codes and algorithms of my whole existence. 'Lost my footing'? I'm afraid it's more than that. I'm afraid I'll never be the same again.

29

February

Without Ellen, I would feel entirely isolated. The same
evening, she requests to follow me on Instagram. And
finally cementing our friendship, I press follow in return.
And it was really nothing to do with Johnny, what began
with Ellen in this way. At least, it was easy to pretend it
wasn't because it began with Instagram and then there were
the emails, so I couldn't see her face. There was nothing
ostensibly to connect her with anyone. Distanced physically, and obscured by our computer screens, we were both
hidden from each other, crafting our considered, soundless
sentences in isolation. Perhaps we barely noticed when the
words slid from polite to meaningful and then we really
were friends.

The frequent exchange of emails is a conversation really,
with varying (significant) lengths of time left between
responses. There's a rhythm to the way this electronic,
promissory exchange is conducted. The words are well
thought-out and chosen; entire sentences pondered upon
and rearranged before they are released. What has been
left out, deleted, is known only to the author. Pauses can
be heard, intakes of breath illustrated; even a keyboard
has nuance and emotion. Usually there are little jokes in
her news, bracketed trendy sound bites. Note to self and
Seriously? are in her subject box. She begins with Molly! I can

hear Ellen in the words. It suits me, this paced and artful method of communication and I like Molly on the screen. She's amusing, and she has a clever turn of phrase that Ellen picks up on and bats back at her. I wonder where Molly is getting her digital eloquence from and how she's learned to be like this, but then again, it isn't hard to respond to Ellen, and especially not from behind a screen. Dialogue like this can flow in a way it never can face to face.

This is how I really get to know the Strachans. I start to find things out about them. Ellen tells me that Andrew is very pro-union, probably because his family is from the Borders. That he doesn't feel wholly Scottish or English, that he feels British. Were the union to dissolve, she tells me, he would be a displaced person. Johnny has no political conviction, in fact he is uninterested, disdainful even, about all politics. What else? She is nomadic by nature because as an army family, they travelled all over the world, living in countries I couldn't even spell. Andrew doesn't believe in climate change. She secretly always wants to leave the theatre in the interval (*Macbeth* excluded – no exclamation mark, so I know that she's serious). She sees a reflexologist. She collects four-leaf clovers. She keeps finding more grey hairs. She only ever writes in purple ink. Ivy, her sister, has mild scoliosis and twin boys. They still live in Oban. Her son (there is plenty of interesting stuff in amongst the ordinary details of her life) is a great worry to her. She wishes he would settle down.

Despite everything, I begin to feel as though I am one half of a meaningful relationship again. Pathetic perhaps, but she just seemed to be saying, *Look. I like you.* And all the . . ., all the :), all the ?! It's filling the hours, and taking up headspace and I am enjoying the friendship. I know she is too. Solitary herself, she fills the vacuum that her son creates for me. *Is that what we do for each other*, I wonder? *Plug moments of loneliness*? But I can't get away from the knowledge that I'm watching and waiting for mentions of Johnny, his name always the bright spot, the letters in neon on the page. He refuses to fade from my mind. Why can't I ever focus on anything else, just for a minute? My thoughts have built a prison around him; around his slow smile, and his spectacular, confusing eyes. Nothing else truly permeates this fortress of thoughts. And now I know what his company is called, the Dickensian-sounding Gilfedder, McBains and Thorley, I can't let go of the knowledge. I've looked it up, the elusive GMT, and I even know where it is (a gloomy building on Guthrie Street behind Parliament Square). It's been two weeks since I went to the David Lloyd gym and never saw Johnny. But now, thanks to Ellen, there is another option.

30

I dress casually that morning. I put on jeans, ankle boots and my old green parka, not daring to hope I would actually see Johnny later. I had begun to believe, I think, that I was chasing something imaginary, that he wasn't flesh and blood, that he was hardly real except in my mind and in the snippets that Ellen threw me. I think I was beginning to lose belief in him. I needed to see him. I needed to prove Tam wrong about him.

After an hour in Old Town, browsing in the National Library, I step back out into the shadow of the cathedral. The light is murky and one by one, as I walk slowly around them, the Gothic towers are illuminated by the steady switching on of street lamps. Like Andrew had said about Ellen, I shouldn't think Johnny stays late at the office. Guthrie Street. It is mostly empty, I have left the bustle and noise of St Giles and the Royal Mile behind me and the quiet is punctuated by the hard click-clack of male feet, (briefcase, overcoat) hurrying away down the road. Number 40, 42 . . . 44. It's there, the other side of the road, baronial and imposing. I stare across at 35 Guthrie Street where he spends his days at GMT. Is he really inside, somewhere in the jaws of this intimidating building? Two people, a man and a woman, push the heavy door wide as they leave and I catch a glimpse of the glossal hallway, a red carpet stretching thickly behind them. I lean back against the railings. After only ten minutes, the black door opens again and he is there.

I don't have to feign the absolute horror, the shock of seeing him. It is exactly as if I had unexpectedly bumped into him and my first instinct is to hide, to duck behind the railings. It's him, it's really him, and alone. He comes down the four or five steps, looks left and then he looks ahead and sees me. I suddenly clutch for the railings. *Johnny. Why did you bother? You didn't have to. You didn't have to say everything you said.* As if in a dream, I push myself off the railing and get myself across the road. He is wearing a suit. He looks ordinary, he looks like the rest of them. He looks different. How is that possible. *You are the most beautiful thing I've ever seen.*

I know what I was going to say, but I don't. I am suddenly poleaxed by the futility of vocalising these thoughts. These words don't belong on this chilly doorstep, to have their hollowness made so clear. The words, so risible, to avoid humiliation, get stuck in my throat. All my longing stays concealed, and the tears freeze before they form and the question I ask isn't *How could you have done what you did to me?* but a flat: 'Gosh. Goodness me. Is that really you? What are you doing here?'

He is shocked and then he is simply surprised. The fright I have given him quickly disappears. There is nothing but sangfroid. *See you when I see you.*

'Skye?' I had just taken him unawares. It does not take long for his expression to rearrange itself into customary benevolence.

'Yes. It's me, Skye,' and then your face gives you away. Just a hint of embarrassment. A lopsided smile of chagrin. And in that split second, as the surprise dissolves into the dusk, it is clear that you have absolutely no idea what you have done to me. You never took the act of leaving seriously. Your effortless disappearance was not deserving of any sustained contemplation, let alone admission of guilt. You, I see now, did not imagine serious wrongdoing, or much injury to speak of, and there is, therefore, no blame to apportion. You are not a cruel person, after all. You just had no idea. And in a way, this helps; of course it hurts, but it helps too. I can keep the hurt hidden for now – and during our consideration of each other (yours with increasing calm and mine with a passable pretence of indifference), I do catch that your eyes look closer in colour, as if the hazel-green is becoming more like the brown, or the other way around. It's just the light, no doubt, but right now they almost match. It reminds me that you are not that complicated and I take some courage from your run-of-the-mill eyes. 'Weren't you sure?'

'Of course I was. I'm just . . . surprised. Really surprised. Skye. Well I never.'

'Hi, Johnny. Yes, very strange.' I manage even to sound casual. 'How weird to run into you like this.' *I thought you must have died.*

'I work in there.' He gestures behind him.

'Do you? That *is* a coincidence. I'm taking the short cut down to the university from the library.' It does not sound as convincing as the preparation had.

'Ah. OK. Well, I suppose Edinburgh's a small city.'

'Indeed it is.'

'And how have you been?'

Bitterness threatens to well up and I force it back. *Happy Christmas. I miss you. Bla bla bla.* 'I've been fine. You?' *Please call me back.*

'Not too bad. You know, Skye, I didn't mean to . . . I meant to reply to your email.' My email? Is that what he is calling my rows of texts, my endless messages? 'I would have got around to it, one day. You know me.'

I look down at the ground. Scuff my boot lightly into the gravelly road. Clench my fingers into my palms, squeezing tighter and tighter. When I look up again, I have carved a slight smile across my face.

'Don't worry. These things happen. I expect you've been busy.'

'Yes.' He is relieved, encouraged. 'Good of you to understand. Work started in earnest in the new year. It's keeping me really busy.'

'Johnny, I understand. I'm busy too. This is work then? The solicitors' place?'

'Yup,' he gives that half-laugh. 'This is where the magic happens.'

'You're back in the swing of things then. After all the time off before Christmas.'

'I wouldn't go that far.'

'No.'

'And how's the world of ice?' and then before I can reply, he says, 'Icy, I suppose,' and laughs again in a way that reminds me of Andrew. 'You look well.' He looks at me closely and then says it again, this time more as if he means it. As if he is reminded of something. 'You look really well.'

'Doubt it, but thanks.' I attempt some briskness. 'Well. Don't let me keep you. I'm going . . . thataway.' And gesture vaguely into the North Sea.

'Great to have run into you, Skye. I'm glad. I didn't mean for it to work out exactly as it did.'

Nothing to say. After a moment, he carries on.

'Sorry I can't hang about, I've got to get to the gym over in Leith. I've missed the last session or two.'

That's why I hadn't seen him. He hadn't been, perhaps because of his arm.

159

'I understand, no problem. You'd better go.'

'This really was a strange coincidence. Bye for now. I'll be in touch.'

I manage a polite laugh.

Johnny walks away. The whole encounter can hardly have taken three minutes. My eyes, dry and wide, stare blankly at the door of 35 Guthrie Street. Emptiness and disappointment sit in the pit of my stomach like a dead weight.

What had I expected anyway? An apology? Johnny, on bended knee, with contrite and plausible explanation? No, not that, but something. Something more than the dead-end nothing I got. But he just can't do it. Nothing. I know nothing more than I did before.

When I get home, I turn to Ellen. It seems like the natural, the obvious thing to do; she helps, she is a never-ending supply of warmth and words. Tam's wisdom, of course, is no good to me tonight. Tam would tell me what I already know – that I seem to have lost control of myself. Ellen, oblivious and trusting, does not know this.

I don't lie to Ellen, I tell her I'm feeling glum, and she emails back me too! As always, she comes back to me with speed and sympathy. Let's cheer ourselves up next week and go out, somewhere fun. My husband is officially missing in action. There is so much to do at the surgery and with family but there doesn't seem to be anything that he'll let me do. I rearranged my sock drawer this morning!!

And that does cheer me up, I feel better about my strange, dislocated self. I'm messaging back when my phone bleeps at me. The notification comes in, it bleeps again. Another notification. I look away from my computer and down at my phone. I have two text messages and they are both from Johnny.

31

I have waited so long for communication from him that I do not know what to do. I hold the phone in my hand and stare at it, the email to Ellen unfinished. The phone is shaking. I don't want to read the messages. Everything he might have found out tumbles through my mind. He has spoken to Ellen. It wasn't a near miss, after all, at St Bernard's Row. I have been caught. I am not strong enough for Johnny, I never was. I feel the weight, the terror of connection with him.

Finally, I open the messages.

Both are made up of just a few words. As usual, my expectations were too high and my reaction excessive; he retains, obstinately, his abysmal inability to say anything worthwhile. Careful not to say too much, he ends up not saying anything at all. He has written, Hi, how was uni today? and followed up with Good to see you earlier. Give me a call sometime.

And now that this, the long-dreamed-of, long-hoped-for scenario has arisen, my imagination fails me. I cannot think which way this might go, I have no idea what Johnny wants or what I might do. And there is this curious disappointment in him again, like the emptiness that I had felt outside the solicitors' office. But ignoring it, and Ellen's confirmation of our drink next week, I spend the night returning to the bland messages, trying to read something into them.

And on Friday evening, he calls me.

'Did you get my text? I thought you were going to ring me.'

I've fixed my eyes on a tiny hole in the corner of the room, not even a hole really, I don't think. It's just a space where subsidence or something has caused sagging between the skirting board and the floor.

'There's nothing to stop you ringing me.'

'No,' he says, cheerfully. 'Although I've got an ulterior motive. Pub quiz on Saturday, and I've got a feeling I could do with some help. From someone with half a brain.'

'Tomorrow?' A sudden gust at the window catches my attention and rattles the pane.

'Yeah, seven p.m. at the King's Wark on the Shore.'

I am silent, and embarrassed by the silence. I just can't fill it. I look back at the hole in the corner. Johnny keeps talking.

'Hope you can make it. Just turn up if you can.'

'I might be busy tomorrow.'

'Don't decide now. Send me a message if you feel like it.'

'Maybe. OK.'

'Hope so. We should catch up, as they say.'

Silly expression. Catch up. I can't begin to catch up with you.

Saturday comes and if I ever thought I wouldn't text Johnny confirming the pub quiz, I was just kidding myself, although I draw it out in a tumult of spurious indecision until 5 p.m.

There's a sort of dogged determination about me when it comes to him. Of course I'm going to go. And it may be misguided but it seems like a chance to prove something, only what and to whom, I'm not sure yet.

When my phone pings at me five minutes later, it's only Tam. She suggests meeting at the tapas bar which of course I can't do now and which arrangement I hadn't put in the diary. Diary dates don't mean anything since I met Johnny. Because he's the only thing that matters, nothing else gets put in. And anything to do with him doesn't need to get entered because of course I won't forget. I message her back cancelling and promising to arrange something soon. She doesn't reply and honestly, I don't especially care. I go to the pub not caring if I'm bonkers.

I am expecting to find Johnny alone. He's tucked into a corner with someone else, female. I immediately turn for the door, I am going to leave, but Anna — because it is her — is too quick, and she sees me. She stares at me, I hesitate, and then Johnny looks up from his pint and waves me over. He gets up and this time, unlike outside his office, he kisses my cheek.

'Great you could come. I wasn't sure, so commandeered Anna this morning. Anna, this is Skye, Skye this is—'

'We've met,' says Anna acidly. That scratchy voice. The airport. That Instagram message. She stands up and I hope she is leaving.

If Johnny remembers, he doesn't show it. 'We need all the help we can get.'

'Do we?' She's staying.

'Get us another pint while you're up,' Johnny says to Anna and unsmiling, she turns away to order. Johnny says, 'What are you having, Skye?'

He sits down, relaxed and unbothered, leaning back with his arms spread along the top of the bench. I'm hovering there, undecided now, thrown by Anna's presence but it is her, in the end, that makes me stay. She's not getting rid of me that easily, not again.

'I'll have a half.' I find the change in my pocket and give it to Anna, sitting down.

'Johnny, love,' she says. 'I thought we were . . .'

'What?'

'Never mind,' and she turns away again.

The endearment, common as it is, grates. 'How's your arm?' *Love*.

'My arm?' he repeats and I could kick myself. Oh, Skye, you could not possibly know about the arm, with no sling in sight and the gym classes restarted. You idiot.

I shift a little. 'You know. Something on Facebook maybe, I can't remember now.'

'Turned out to be a sprain,' looking at it, 'which healed fast.'

Anna, who has been seemingly preoccupied at the bar, turns around. 'A sprain?' she says mockingly. 'It was a bloody bruise in the end. Didn't stop you doing anything apart from getting twenty-four-hour care from too many people. And getting out of gym class.'

Johnny looks livid and Anna looks away, saying she is going to say hello to someone. 'And then I'll get the drinks.'

There is a small silence and then Johnny says, 'You decided to come then.'

'I nearly didn't.' Liar, liar. On they go, some big, some small.

'I'm glad you did.'

'I'm not sure it was a good idea really.'

'Why not?'

I can't keep the bitterness from my voice. 'Apart from the obvious, you mean? Where do I start? And it certainly looks like I'm interrupting something.'

'You're not interrupting anything. I promise you. Anna's pleased you turned up.' Actually, I don't think she had any idea I'd been asked, same as me. 'I am, anyway and that's all that matters.' And then his smile fades. 'I've been thinking about you since Wednesday.'

I try and fix him with my stare, I try and sound normal. 'Johnny. Come on. You made it pretty clear how you feel about me.'

There is the smallest flicker of contrition. 'I'm sorry if I went a bit quiet. I really am.'

'A bit quiet? There was nothing from you. Nothing.' My voice is too shaky. I stop.

'I know,' he says. 'I know. Things got complicated around Christmas. I couldn't . . . I didn't want to . . .' He gives up. 'I just couldn't be there for you.'

'Sure,' I say, looking at the crisp packet on the floor. 'Whatever. Let's leave it, shall we? But it's best you don't say things like that.' I bend to pick it up.

'Things like what?'

'Don't pretend you've been thinking about me.'

'I'm not pretending.'

Anna returns with the drinks then, as if we have gone far enough, and bangs the tray on the table. 'So – you met skiing, didn't you?'

'I was snowshoeing, not skiing,' I say, as much to remind Johnny as inform Anna, and as I do, I remember something myself; how I had not been entirely convinced that he was as impressed by my dull-sounding sport as he insisted, and that the first flicker of disappointment in me had grazed over his interest.

'Snowshoeing,' she echoes blankly.

'Anna can ice-skate,' Johnny says, as if that means we will all understand each other.

'I'm sure she knows what snowshoeing is.'

Anna has the smallest beat to prove me right before Johnny says, 'No, she doesn't.'

She takes a long slug of her drink with narrowing eyes.

'It's just hiking in the snow, wearing a special snow-shoe,' I explain.

'It all sounds like hard work to me.' She means boring. 'Walking in the snow.' She tosses back her black hair. Her jumper is black and tight. *Why is she here?*

'It can be hard,' I say. 'But it's worth it. You can walk higher and further than anyone else. You can literally disappear above ski stations.' I stop, and look at Anna, conceding: 'But figure skating is hard work too.'

Johnny has been looking at me, smiling, but now he snorts and Anna stares at him angrily, saying to me, 'Really? What do you know about it?'

'Only that figure skating needs the softest surface. For digging-in, spins and jumps. It's tiring, apparently.'

'Do ice sports need different surfaces?' asks Johnny.

'Of course. That's what I'm doing, what I'm studying. If you remember. Ice-technicians make the best conditions they can, especially for curling rinks, where it's crucial.'

'I'm so impressed,' says Johnny. 'Didn't Highlanders invent curling in the fifteenth century? I think they used to play it on frozen lochs.'

'Well, you'd need to do something to pass the time, wouldn't you?' Anna says. 'Till lunchtime, when it got dark and then the heathens could just get drunk.'

'I'm from the Highlands,' I tell her.

Anna just laughs, without humour. 'So's my dad. Nothing personal. I don't think it's a secret the Enlightenment got to you lot last.'

'Not being very polite, Anna,' chides Johnny. 'An ice-technician is beyond you and me.'

I shake my head. 'It's not complicated – but it's

166

interesting. They work to see if they can persuade nature to do what they want it to do, instead of doing what it wants to.'

Johnny may not have been listening, but Anna is. She laughs again, this time a genuine one. That indiscriminate and throaty chuckle of hers.

'Now that's a battle you won't win. What a weird hobby. What's your day job?'

'I'm just a receptionist. Secretary to a plastic surgeon.'

'I'm "just" the receptionist at an art gallery.'

'I didn't mean . . . never mind.'

Johnny flicks her arm. 'Hardly call it work.'

'It is work. You prat,' she tells him but she flicks his arm back.

I look at Johnny, lazy against the plaid seat. Anna drums her fingers on the table and Johnny takes a gulp from his pint.

'When are they starting?' Anna breaks the silence.

Johnny looks at his watch and then over at the bar. 'Jock! When's this great quiz?'

The barman shakes his head. 'Not tonight. Not enough teams this week.'

'Shame,' I say.

'Relief,' counters Anna coolly. 'Finish up then? I quite want to go.'

'You can,' Johnny tells her. 'You might stay a bit, Skye? I'd like another.'

'Sure,' I agree. Anna downs her drink, pushes her chair back and ignoring me, addresses Johnny.

'You'd better not be late back tonight.' She puts her camouflage jacket on and the door swings behind her as she goes.

Alone with Johnny, I look at him. 'Why had you better not be late?'

He says, easily, 'I have no idea.'

'Is there something going on with you two?'

'No,' he shakes his head. 'No.'

'Hmm,' is all I say in the end. 'She's pretty possessive.'

He doesn't answer. Instead he says, 'Can we not talk about other people? It's good to see you.'

It's inexplicable, this charm that I am not immune to, and how he can turn it on, and turn it off. 'It's been weeks, Johnny. Weeks of not hearing one single tiny thing from you. I thought we wouldn't ever see each other again.' And it makes me mad that I am still not madder with him about this.

'You mean, I made my bed and I can lie in it?'

'Yes. Something like that.'

'But bumping into you outside work. Too much of a coincidence to ignore it.' His lips twitch.

I don't argue with this.

'Another one?' He jerks his hand towards my half. 'I'll get them,' and Johnny slides away leaving me to look at the picture that was above his head. He comes back from the bar with a bottle of red wine.

'You see, I remembered. Jock recommends this one. Rioja.'

'We won't finish a bottle,' I say tartly.

'You always say that, and we always finish it,' and some silvery fish jump a little in my stomach.

'Johnny. I thought we agreed.'

'We didn't agree anything,' he says, pouring the wine. 'And I can't help it. I was thinking about you,' he says. 'Only the other day.'

I can't answer because Johnny's hand swings casually from the bench to my knee. It is only momentary and it is just a light touch. Too light to be a friendly pat and I move my knee away.

'How's your friend Tam? Tamara.'

'Tamsin.'

He shrugs. 'Tam. Tom.'

'She's fine. She doesn't approve of you.'

'Not many people do,' and then he says, 'I approve of you, by the way. You're looking amazing. I forgot you were just legs and long hair.'

There is a moment of something grazing tenderness. Johnny's hand goes back to my knee. I let it stay there this time and drink the wine and Johnny moves a little closer in and starts telling me about the evening he'd had the other day . . . I let him talk on and despite everything, begin to relax. His company has always been easy. When the bottle is nearly finished, he brings the backgammon board to our table and I realise that the world, so drab since he left, has changed colour. I am lulled back into an outlook, an attitude that has always seemed so peculiarly his. I don't want to let that go.

I let him win, or he lets me lose, I'm not sure which. He pushes the board to the side and kisses me.

'God, what do you do to me? I'd forgotten.' He is laughing slightly. He leans forward again, an afterthought, to stroke my hair.

All the time I was with Johnny, it was as if none of it was happening to me. It was a fantasy that I had to work at all the time and it was so hard. But this feels real, too real.

'You shouldn't have asked me here. It was a mistake to come.' It is like standing on the cliff again. I can't go back to the precipice. 'This is just the wine talking, isn't it? For you?'

'It's not the wine talking. I wanted to see you. It wasn't a mistake.'

I nod, not because I'm sure I agree but because my head does it.

'You know me,' he says but it is apropos of nothing and really, I don't think I do know him. I don't think that I had ever been allowed to. I always had to pretend not to know him too well. He'd hated the suggestion that I was getting too close, if I'd guessed what he wanted to order or knew what he'd do or say next, he'd be unable to hide his irritation. As if predictability was the most heinous and boring of crimes; but I had staked everything on exactly that. On predictability, on certainties. 'You know me,' he insists and he spreads his arms and raises his eyebrows, shrugging helplessly. 'I never could resist you.' I don't know him.

'Johnny . . .' I begin but he is standing up and coaxing me towards him.

'You're a green-eyed witch,' he murmurs, into my hair. 'We were so good, we never had a problem in this department, did we,' and the 'we' he uses – even now, as he looks at me, those faithless fish twist a little. It is possible. We could go back to the way it was in Chamonix. And then he closes his eyes, as if he saw something impossible leaping in mine. 'Come on,' he whispers. 'Let's go.' *Let's go.* After a while, he pulls me towards the door, out of the pub and into the cold Edinburgh night.

I don't resist. I need to feel something. I'm not sure if it is you or it is me, but we are not gentle with each other. You have my arm, pinching, and I have yours. The alleyway is deserted. The shadowy expression on your face is new. You have lost the veneer of amiability and there is a violence in the way you push me against the wall. I don't think that you are thinking as my hands slip around your arms, my nails pierce the softness of your inner wrists, my mouth snatches at your skin. I will not give you time to think. I need to feel something. The sky is framed heavy and black around you and the street lights a little way away don't shine, they just blur and mist in the background. You are all there is.

For some minutes, you are mine again, but then I realise or remember something. I am yours. Your kiss is not soft, it is the savage kiss of ownership and possession, mine the feudal kiss of submission. You take hold of my hair and my head lands heavily against the wall, my throat exposed and your fingers running down it. If you pressed a little harder, you would stop my breath. And now your hand is over my face and everything goes black, and I can't see you but you are struggling to get into me, without looking at my face. You are saying my name over and over and it sounds strange to me.

It is all over quickly. The cobbled side street had been pitch black, unexplored innards with just the street lights showing the way. There had been no moon, not one that I could see. I couldn't hear anything, not even the sea which had quietened, which had been listening for us. I couldn't smell the salty tang that is blown in waves over the docks, I could hardly breathe whilst it was just us. Just us, for those brief, blind minutes.

32

I know what Tam would say. I know what most people would say. I'm not saying I disagree with them.

I had noticed a picture in the pub that reminded me of the sepia photographs in La Marmot, the photographs of the climbers on the Matterhorn. This was an oil painting, not a very good one, I suspect, but like the photographs there was no colour and it was a grim scene. It was black and white and grey and it was of a boat, an old trawler on the Firth of Forth. It was caught in a storm and the sailors were scurrying across the desks, ropes and sails were billowing and flapping in the wind and water was pouring across the decks. It was a horrible picture. There was a smaller detail and I expect it mostly went unnoticed but I had been unable to escape it because the picture was behind Johnny's head, and so the sailor who had been sent up the mast, and had fallen, seemed throughout the whole evening to be falling through the picture and towards me, his tiny mouth yawning open in terror and his arms outstretched. No one on the deck was watching this boy fall, his arms and legs almost comically spreadeagled. He was plummeting unnoticed through the air.

It was just a bad pub painting. But the boy was going to hit the deck, or the water, and that was that. I was always going to go back to him if I had the chance and that was that. If I'd had misgivings and reservations, if I'd moments

172

of rationalisation, I was going to disregard them all. Even not having the same illusions about Johnny wasn't going to be enough. Even with no expectations that he can't live up to, I was going to go back to him.

No regrets then, and even some quiet satisfaction. I have not been spat out and discarded after all. I have been made viable somehow. I know that it's not right a man – anyone – has this power over me but after what happened, after Johnny's disappearance and my subsequent disintegration – well, I just needed him to want me, to give me some worth, even if just for a few, blind minutes.

Tam, as I've said, would have a different take on it but at least I go about my day now without the exhausting tension of expectation coming with me. I can make it down one supermarket aisle without having to get my phone out of my pocket to check it. I can wash up at home uninterrupted, not needing to tear the rubber gloves off the instant I think I hear a beep, and I can take the recycling down to the bins without making sure my phone comes too. I can have a (quick) shower without the phone on the floor outside. Not because I don't want him to message but because I don't feel quite so alone.

He messages the next day.

Ten out of ten for the pub quiz.

I don't text back immediately but I can't stop the slight smile. And a strange few days follow when I am in touch with both Ellen and Johnny constantly and the combination of his reappearance and Ellen's friendship is both worrying and comforting. It's strange, I suppose, that I find it so natural to go between the two. Rather the opposite – it makes sense. Perhaps it helps that they don't look alike. Take her eyes; just one shade of brown, frankly

173

unremarkable. Her hesitant smile, the one that hides the uneven bottom row of teeth – her ordinary sensitivity about any imperfection, just as Johnny, with his habitual unconcern, laughs them off. Yes, he regards any form of vanity as a sort of weakness. He doesn't suffer from either introspection or self-doubt. He has no confusion at all about who he is. And perhaps this is where his power lies; nothing I could ever do or say would alter the facts of him according to him.

It feels right but I know it's not right. It feels as though it can last. I know it can't.

> Are you able to meet for a glass of wine? Can leave
> surgery at 5, Andrew going through accounts – please
> don't condemn me to joining him! xxe

Ellen messages on Tuesday but I have to be more careful. I'm warier now, warier than I was before I saw Johnny again. The stakes have been raised a little now that I am juggling both mother and son. I'm not sure what to say to Ellen in response.

And then at two o'clock, @anna_banana_xo posts a photograph of herself on Instagram, as a baby. She captions it **27 years on** . . . and then blathers on and on **#birthdaysupper #partytime #cantwait** followed by rows of emoticons that make my eyes hurt because they are such a jumble of milk bottles, champagne bottles, party poppers, cakes and hearts. Like her spelling mistakes, she never gets it quite right. **#moron**. I sink into the caption, drawn in as usual as if by invisible threads, my head low over the device; examining the comments, following up on the likes. I am uninvited but totally submerged in this parallel world. The interesting thing about the gluttonous post is that she has ended it: @johnny_strachan and @cocos. And, for once, he has commented: **see you later**. I feel a quick, passing admiration for Anna, an almost appreciative acknowledgment of yet another of her triumphs over me, but also relief – I won't have to worry where Johnny and Anna are later. Because of Anna's promiscuous bragagramming, I can meet Ellen knowing exactly where they will be tonight. A restaurant called Cocos.

I don't want to keep Ellen waiting long on her own so I'm rushing through various bits of paperwork for Dr Philipps when a name I think I know briefly catches my eye. Amy Desmond. Have I heard that name before? The thought carries on nagging me after I have filed everything away and forgotten the context, and then because I am on my way to meet Ellen, I don't think about it again. As soon as I can, I leave work and hurry across Charlotte Square and towards New Town, eager with anticipation and for once without nerves.

There's a table for two in the window of Café Paris. I don't know this smart street, or this affluent area but Ellen, waiting for me and reading a romantic novel, looks at home here. Her aquamarine scarf has slipped off the back of her chair. I bend to pick it up as I pass and without thinking I say, 'Beautiful. Sardinia?'

'Yes,' she says, her head on one side. 'Did I tell you that?'

'No,' I say, reminding her, 'Instagram,' and she smiles, revealing the crooked teeth. Of course. Now we are friends, it is OK to have studied the backlog of her life. I will like the picture of Ellen at the market stall buying scarves when I get home. I'm allowed to.

'Right,' she says, clapping her hands together. 'I think it's drink time. And I will get them. They know me here, rather too well,' and she makes a 'yikes' face and rummaging through her bag, brings out the wallet I gave Johnny for Christmas. I had bought it at the airport. Inexplicably, the hurt is as fresh as if I had given the present to him yesterday.

'Is that yours?'

'Yes. Why?'

I bite my lip, hard, as if to divert the hurt. Completely deflated.

'Actually, to be precise, not originally mine, but either my husband or my son left it lying around so I've been using it. Perfectly nice, isn't it?'

'Yes. I bought one just like it last year.' I stare at the small black reject, rescued from the bin. Suddenly I feel a lump in my throat.

'And no point it gathering dust in a cupboard. I'd take it to the charity shop except for the fact I quite like it.'

Ridiculously, my eyes fill with tears, month-old tears and I turn away to hide them. Why does being with Ellen make me feel so sorry for myself?

'Right,' she says. 'Wine.'

I am still trying to swallow the silly tears away when Ellen comes back with the glasses so I am not concentrating when she slides open her phone. 'You look serious. Smile,' she orders, and takes a photo of me.

'Oh, Ellen, no. Please,' I say, distraught all over again. 'Please don't.'

'Don't worry,' she teases. 'You look gorgeous, as usual,' and she pushes our two glasses next to each other and then, as an afterthought, places the single rose in its little white vase beside them. 'There we are,' and satisfied, she takes a photo of the still life. She's so quick. I remove my glass from the arrangement and drink it, trying to think.

'I really don't like my photo being taken,' and it is true but it sounds churlish.

'No, I don't either,' agrees Ellen, making it sound OK, and then she points at my glass. 'Are you happy with white wine?'

Not really, I think, but the colour of my drink is the least of my problems right now. She is not going to offer to delete it, but I don't want to carry on making a huge deal of it. Think. I drink the wine.

'You've left Andrew to the accounts then?'

'Yes, but not on his own. He's with Amy.'

'Amy Desmond?' I say the name without thinking, not even sure of where it has come from and then I realise. I hadn't heard the name before, I have seen it, on Instagram. It must have been a thread I'd been following on Ellen's account, and probably more than one. And thinking of Andrew, I remember the brunette in the heels I had seen leaving the surgery when he drove me to the cinema. Amy, who for some reason is amongst my boss's paperwork.

'Yes, that's her. Oh bother. I meant to get a bar snack. Any preference?'

She looks at me questioningly but I shake my head. She leaves the phone behind when she goes. I tap my fingers on the table and then when her back is turned I reach over for it. I don't think there's anything else to be done, I have to get rid of that photo. But just as I am about to pick it up, Ellen turns around. Casually I trace patterns on the table around the phone.

'Nuts?' she enquires. 'Nuts and olives, to soak up the alcohol? Or just crisps . . . you choose.'

'Anything. I don't mind. It's up to you.'

This time, before she disappears, she stretches across the table and picks up her phone, carrying it away with her.

The rest of our time together is taken up with me desperately trying to work out a strategy to get hold of the mobile. I ask if she needs the Ladies, she doesn't. I ask to see some pictures of her sister and nephews but she shows me without letting go of the thing. I offer to get another round, hoping she will refuse and get it herself without taking the phone, but she doesn't. I get it, but because of the wine and the worry I have forgotten I am out of cash. More appalled than ever with the situation I pay with my card. Ellen chats about feeling lonely and eats the olives.

'I walk a lot, as you know,' I say. 'That helps keep me busy. I'm going to plan a long one, as soon as the weather improves.'

'Still,' she says. 'It must be difficult living alone.' She doesn't say, 'at your age' but that's what people mean.

'It's not always easy,' I agree. 'There's no sharing. Emotionally or practically. I do everything – bills, dust-bins, housework, putting up shelves . . .' I try to laugh a little as though this prospect is alarming. I don't know why. I'm good at DIY.

'There must be someone out there for you,' she says between olives. 'I know it can't be easy though. Not in this world of digital dating.'

I stare out of the window and down the cobbled street. 'There was someone,' I say. 'I did meet someone recently.'

'It didn't work out? I'm so sorry.' She pats my arm in the way that she does. 'Oh, please take these olives away from me. What happened?'

The need to talk about him is suddenly overwhelming. I couldn't have stopped myself even if I had wanted to. 'I don't really know. He was there one minute and not the next. I suppose the truth is that I found out I didn't know him at all. I thought I did.' I shrug and Ellen puts her head on one side.

'I hope you found out quickly. Before you got too involved.'

'Probably anyone else would say I hadn't time to get too involved. It was pretty whirlwind, but it didn't really feel that way to me. I was in too deep very quickly.'

Ellen nods sympathetically, reaching for another olive and then withdraws her hand. 'Plenty more fish, lots of single men around. I'll get on the case. Oh, darling. Don't look so sad.'

The evening draws in from the west and reaches down the cobbled street. Cobbled streets, like the alleyway behind the King's Wark pub by the docks. The white wine that I don't like is making my head spin a little and half-formed questions are muddling my brain. How can I get Ellen's phone? More plenty-more-fish nonsense. What has this Amy who works with the Strachans got to do with my boss? I'd been so excited hurrying from work to meet Ellen. Now, as she comments, I just feel sad, and confused. 'It's getting on. Do you think we ought to leave now?'

I stand outside Café Paris when Ellen has gone, feeling a little sick and worrying about the photo. Johnny will find me out. Ellen will find me out. What are Johnny and Anna doing now? Why has Amy visited a plastic surgeon?

On the stairs going up to my flat I meet my neighbour who asks me to look after his rabbit again for a few days. Later that night Darcy is delivered, snuffling, into my arms so at least I am not alone when Ellen messages that the waiter from the Café is insisting he has her friend's credit card, left by mistake at the bar. Name of Skye Grant. Weird?

I upturn the contents of my bag and find my purse, empty apart from a few coins. No credit card. I reply to Ellen saying Not mine and then ring the Café saying it is. Darcy scampers over to me. I lean over to scoop her up, burying my burning face in her fur. Shit. I'm going to have to go back for my card. Worse than that, Ellen has heard of me now.

33

Johnny rings on Wednesday, just as I am leaving Café Paris with my credit card in hand. Luckily, the waiter was not the same one. Luckily, it was easy to get it back. I look left and right, almost expecting Ellen to appear, before walking quickly down the cobbles and I jump when I hear my ringtone.

He says he's been busy. I don't bother questioning the veracity of this, and once he has suggested we meet, it doesn't seem to matter one way or another.

'Are you free Thursday?'

'Yes, I think I am. OK. At your flat?'

A moment's hesitation and then he agrees. 'Fine,' he says. 'Fifteen Brunswick Street. If you're cooking.'

'I'll get some ingredients,' I offer.

He doesn't object, and says he'll think of a plan, a DVD or something and then I can hear the line being punctuated by call-waiting beeps and he hangs up quickly.

I don't know what he thought he would plan but the reality (I'm aware of it as soon as he opens the door to Brunswick Street on Thursday night, laden with my shopping) is that he hasn't got a plan.

'I haven't had a shower yet. I'm only just back. Can I leave you to it?'

He disappears again into his bedroom, and just as I am heading down the hall, presumably towards his kitchen, he opens his door again. I can see his duvet is crumpled at the bottom of his bed and his pillows have been squashed flat in the night. I can smell the clean smell of him, the one like Nivea.

'If that wine is for now, open it up. 'Fraid I haven't got anything.' *Had I never noticed this lack of effort before?* Perhaps it was because we had been in hotels. We had never really been shopping or cooked together.

'Skye? Is that OK?'

'Yes, of course. I've got mushrooms, cream and cheese.' I know he likes this. Pasta.

'Won't be long.'

I go slowly into his kitchen, unwrapping the wine. The remains of breakfast are on the side and I look over the plates to the pile of clothing on the table. Clean, but not ironed, Johnny's shirts and some blue trousers, some beige chinos and his white T-shirts, presumably left for his cleaning lady. When I take my coat off, some old shells from the beach at Portobello clink in the pocket. I think they must be from the time I had gone to the beach after the train journey with Johnny's parents. There is a list of ingredients for an unpronounceable recipe pinned to the fridge with a magnet that says: 'If you're not living life on the edge . . .' The second half of the quote is cracked. Someone with different handwriting has added more ingredients to the recipe. Does Johnny even like cooking? I open the fridge door. There are two pizzas in there, and two bottles of beer. And four yoghurts. I shut it. There is a book about food called *Plenty* on the shelf and I take it down to look at it but I drop it and it falls open at the front. There is a large scrawling *thank you* in sexy black writing from Rosie and Richard. Rosie has drawn a large heart under her name. The shower is still running.

I go through the kitchen to the sitting room. The books on the coffee table are hardbacks with rings on them from mugs and glasses. Tomas Holmberg's most recent blog has been printed out. A book by an English politician, and inscription written by Ellen, I think. *Happy Birthday, with so much love from us both*. An iPad, an old one, and I just press the home button to see if it turns on. The screen remains dark; the battery is dead. A letter from the council queries his single person status in the flat. A magazine called *Powder!* with a skier on the front is on the table.

A collection of cream-coloured candles have gathered dust and wax in the fireplace. There is a group of photographs, one of an older man in regimental uniform (a grandfather?) and another of friends. Another group skiing. There is also one of his mother. This photograph is the largest. She is clutching Witchy, her beautiful grey-haired cat. I sit on Johnny's sofa looking at the picture. Wondering what I'm doing here cooking his supper for him and yet clearly unable to leave. I plump up a cushion and there behind it is a card. It is a club membership to the gym in Leith that Johnny goes to on a Wednesday after work. It belongs to Anna Stewart.

Johnny comes in whistling and rubbing his hair with a towel. 'Got yourself a drink?'

'Waiting for you.'

'Okey-dokey. Give me a minute.' He hums, looking through papers.

'Johnny? I've got . . . I found Anna's card – stuck behind the cushion.'

'Thanks. Just leave it on the table.'

'What was it doing here?'

'What, her gym card?'

'Yes,' I say.

He stares at me. 'What was her gym card doing here? Why not? She comes to the gym with me.'

I suppose she might. It's not an unreasonable thing. It's just that I'd no idea. Despite all the knowledge I accumulate, there's so much that I don't know. I am still an outsider, denied full access to everything that goes on. I wish I could just accept that fact and leave it there – but I can't, because between what I know and what I don't know is this enormous gap which I can't help filling. In a way, it doesn't matter if I fill it with nonsense or (by accident) the truth. Either one eats away at me.

Johnny throws the towel onto the sofa and sits down, picking up his phone. He is silent for a minute, looking at whatever he is looking at and he seems to send one or two texts. Then he laughs a little, 'I don't know why I bother with my mum's Instagram. Here's a new one, just up.'

Like a rocket, I hurtle across the room.

'What the . . . what the bloody hell . . .'

I brace myself, first hot and then cold.

'What is she doing in one of my haunts?' Then he pushes the phone under my nose. 'Have you ever been here?'

The picture is of Café Paris, but she has chosen the one of the two glasses of wine by the white flower. No sign of my face, but it has my foot in it, stockinged and heeled. A light has caught the edge of the photo and given it a sparkle. She has given it some sort of ice-blue filter. The wine glasses look huge, and with the velvet sofas behind them, the whole effect is hedonistic, sexy even. Nothing but the wine, and a white flower, someone's calf and the chic Parisian background. *It hadn't been like that, had it?* But at least it's not me, not my face. Yet there I am. Ellen has put us out there, inviting reactions. The location, as ever. And I have been tagged. @Mollyspics. I stifle a gasp. **#couldbeparis #lotsofwhitewine #perfect**

'Know it?' he says again, #oblivious. 'Her friend has nice legs.'

'Let me look,' I say and take the phone from him where it shakes slightly in my hand. It was posted six minutes ago and has six likes. One of the likes is already from @anna_banana_xo. So close. Too close. 'No, I don't think I have been there before.'

'It's cool. Or at least it used to be before my mother started going there. Anyway, come on, open that wine.'

I ignore him, trying to take deep, surreptitious breaths. As if he senses some reticence, Johnny gets up. 'I'll go.'

We drink the wine in his kitchen while he makes an attempt at cooking the pasta and a much more successful attempt at seduction. Later, in his bed that night, the jumbled worries return. My leg in the picture. Ellen tagging me, and getting closer to my real identity. Two of everything in the flat. Anna saying, 'You'd better not be late back.'

I lie half underneath him, my right arm bent back first uncomfortably and then painfully but rather than nudge him away, I leave it as it is. Only when I am sure that he is asleep do I carefully pull my dead arm from his shoulder and turn on my side. This can't go on.

34

The first thing I do when I next get a chance at work is dig out that paperwork concerning Amy. It takes me a while because it wasn't filed where I thought and then I can't find it anywhere. But when Dr Philipps leaves his office for a meeting, I slip in and start rifling through the papers in his in-tray.

Aha. Here it is. Some printouts of emails about Amy Desmond. I glance through the sheaves of paper. It doesn't seem to be straightforward surgery and some of the medical jargon is confusing but I have to be quick. And I think I'm getting what I need to know about her. Amy has had several conversations with my boss, Dr Philipps. She needs to have a breast augmentation. She can't wait for the NHS to do it. She seems to be using an old friendship and the fact that she works in the business to get a discount, and to get it done quickly. And there is one exchange concerning the invoice that has taken place during which she refers to her place of work and I read the words 'Strachan med practice'.

'Skye,' says Gillian, from the doorway.

'Gillian! You startled me.'

'Sorry. But I need you on reception. What are you after?'

'Nothing, Gillian. Well, something, obviously. Some of the accounts I couldn't find earlier.'

'Well, never mind them. Can you come and give me a hand?'

I manage to return to the paperwork before lunch but I only have a minute or two before Gillian will be back. I go straight to the details about the invoice. Amy emails to ask if Dr Philipps' office received payment; Gillian replied in the negative so Amy sends proof. Gillian confirms receipt of mislaid funds. Amy replies. With a smiley face. I drop the invoice back into the tray.

The bank details are Dr Andrew Strachan's of 22 St Bernard's Row. There can only be one reason, surely, that Andrew would pay for the pharmacist at Strachan Medical Practice to have her breasts surgically enhanced. Surely. Andrew only ever does anything that is for his own benefit.

Before I made friends with Johnny's parents, when I just knew of them, it would have been unthinkable that I should discover what I do about Andrew this Friday. It would have been a coincidence of the most extraordinary sort that I should come across this information. But now, I am so part of Ellen's life, I hardly feel even surprised by it. It feels normal that I should know things about them. Or maybe I just knew Andrew was this man all along. It's such a tawdry thing. I feel a little embarrassed for Andrew. I'm amazed he had the time to flatter me. I didn't know such men, married men who were so busy chasing multiple women, even existed.

At the sandwich shop on the corner of Alva and Queensferry during my lunch hour, I sit at a table and I think about Andrew grunting and heaving on top of Amy's newly inflated chest, his red face above her smiley one. I imagine how the ease of this affair has complemented his laziness as much as anything else; working late, in the same office, perhaps the pharmacist only sits a few feet from his consulting room. Perhaps he can see through slatted blinds when the coast is clear and when he gets the urge for Amy perhaps he jiggles the blinds and pokes his eyes through them, scanning the corridor for her. And, coupled with this most obligingly – almost necessary – local temptation is the frisson of it all being under his wife's nose. Yes, and when the eyes in the blinds scouring the corridors alight upon his wife first, well, it's exciting like roulette might be. It's impressive. For someone like Andrew, convenient is not the word. It is perfection.

Never could Andrew have imagined a personal connection with the plastic surgeon's receptionist. That she should also turn out to be his son's ex-girlfriend is unthinkable. We are his nemesis, you could say, Molly and I. I am almost frantic with adrenalin by the time my post-sandwich coffee provides more. I've got something on Andrew, the proof of what he is like. He's practically a serial predator. A detective couldn't have dreamed of this. It's like a Christmas present, a brown paper package, all tied up with invoices and dates; but inside – the present – is what is at the heart of it. Who was it that said power is knowledge, or is it the other way round? I've got it, whichever way it is, and this feeling is transcending all others: the knowledge that no one else has, finally something that matters (unlike all the fripperies I find on Facebook and Instagram). And then I get to Ellen.

Ellen. I'm about to turn into Alva Street. I realise that I have thought of her last and that my first instinct is to pity her. I picture her leaving the surgery without her husband because he is working late again; I have seen her doing so from my hiding place behind the stone wall. I picture her chatting with Amy. I picture her extending the hand of friendship (I know how she does that, wary of new females that Andrew comes into contact with, eager to make new friends) and I picture her cordially issuing an invitation for

Amy to join them for dinner one evening in St Bernard's Row. No doubt Andrew suggested and encouraged it. And then Ellen disappears into shadow and I picture Amy again, being given a lift home from the surgery in Andrew's car, being offered a date at the cinema in the back row, and so on. And her legs bent and spread wide over the granite-topped, multi-functional island in the kitchen at St Bernard's Row.

And then I feel furious. Furious on Ellen's behalf, as if all my own hurt and stupidity combines with hers and I have the most overwhelming sense of the injustice of it all and of Andrew's flagrant brazenness. It's not right that he should get away with it. That Ellen should be made a fool of every day. Week after week facing the full-bosomed Amy, leaving by four because she feels inadequate alongside the white-coated pharmacist, slightly out of breath, a little slow. A touch self-conscious about her figure. Does Amy wear tight tops like Anna? Is she contemptuous of blinkered, hospitable Ellen? How can anyone be on Andrew's rather than Ellen's side? No, none of this is right. Women, friends like Ellen and me, ought to stick together. We ought to be more sympathetic towards each other. She ought to know the truth about Andrew – but on the other hand, I don't have any actual proof, not yet. I alternate between telling Ellen (how?) and keeping quiet and I'm still undecided the next day when she messages.

Are you busy? How about I pop by?

Sure, I message back. Everything OK?
Heading off to my sister's for the weekend and driving through Newington ☺ Good opportunity for coffee xxe

I give her my address and wait.

35

She is wearing a dove-grey coat, unbuttoned, over corduroy trousers. A plain sweater, no sign of the pendant, of any jewellery and she doesn't have a handbag, just her car keys which she plays with in the pocket of her coat.

'Hi,' I say.

She looks older in the grey coat, washed-out even. She smiles faintly and then trails through the doorway into my flat. 'Horrid Saturday. Glad to be going.'

'Are you OK, Ellen? What's wrong?'

She sighs, looking around. 'Oh, nothing. Everything. The usual.'

'Sit down.' I gesture towards my sofa. 'I'll put the kettle on. Tea?'

'Coffee if you've got it, please. I like your flat.'

'It's not much. But it's home.'

'Hmm,' she says. 'Home.'

'What's happened?'

'It's Andrew.'

My hand stops mid coffee-scoop. 'What?'

'Much as I love him, I can't bear him when he's like this. I've left him shouting his head off to anyone who'll listen.'

'Oh. He's angry.'

'Often,' she says. 'And it's over something so silly. Between him and Johnny. They are like red rags to each other.'

'An argument?'

'Yes, but as usual, began over nothing. It started because Johnny's taken the heater Andrew uses in his study. He should have asked, I know . . .' she shrugs helplessly, 'but sometimes he doesn't ask about using things. He just doesn't think.'

'Maybe he needed it?' I offer. I keep on getting flashes of what Johnny can be like – foolish, weak and spoilt. I push the thoughts away.

'He says of course he did. Sorry, Molly. This is boring. It's just that Johnny isn't always easy.'

'I don't think, Ellen, that Andrew is very easy.'

'No,' she concedes. 'He's not. He's got to work for the rest of the weekend so that hasn't put him in a good mood.'

I take a breath. I'm being led to this quite naturally as it turns out. I'm not sure I can avoid it. 'Does he always work so hard?'

'Yes. He's actually quite determined, underneath all the joking and flirting.'

'He is a flirt, you know,' I say bravely but she just nods.

'I don't expect you're the only one to think that. But you shouldn't take him seriously. He doesn't mean any harm, the truth is he's harmless. Once you get to know him.'

'But, Ellen, it is serious. I'm not sure that he's . . . that he is trustworthy.'

She looks at me steadily enough. 'What do you mean?' The kettle, whistling noisily, clicks off and hisses quietly in the corner. 'In what sense?'

'I think there's something I ought to tell you.'

'About Andrew?'

'Yes.'

'And you?'

My mouth falls open. 'And me?'

Before I can say anything else, she says, 'Yes. I think I know what you're going to say. It's hardly important.'

I stare at her, the coffee forgotten. 'What's not important?'

'Andrew told me that he'd seen you outside the surgery. Before we had dinner.' She presses the palms of her hands together. 'Don't worry about it.'

I'm completely derailed. I don't know what I'm supposed to say. 'He just gave me a lift,' I say weakly.

'I know,' she says. 'To the cinema.'

'I didn't think he'd mentioned it.' I thought neither of us were going to say anything about that.

'He did, actually. I'm not being accusatory, by the way. I just wondered if you'd felt awkward for not saying anything.'

'I would never . . . with . . .' I trail off, embarrassed.

'Molly! Let's leave it. We're both grown-ups and it's one hundred per cent not serious. Whatever Andrew is, and I know he can be a flirt – I'm sure he's honest. As you can see, we don't lie to each other.'

I'm still flummoxed by the turn the conversation has taken, and then the mention of honesty. Andrew had obviously used me. When I had looked down at him by his car, he had been on the phone, gleeful. Arranging something, it sounds like. An alibi – me – had fallen quite neatly into his hands.

'Did Andrew say that we went to the cinema?' He had taken a bit of a risk committing me to an entire film with him.

She looks slightly uncertain. 'I don't . . . it wasn't clear if you actually saw a film, come to think of it. I assumed you had. It doesn't matter if you did, does it?'

'But it wasn't me. At least, it wasn't me who saw a film with him.'

'I must have misunderstood then.' There is a slight warning in her tone.

'No, that's what I'm saying, you haven't. I mean, I think you've misunderstood who—'

'It wasn't you who came to the surgery then? Who bumped into Andrew, and ended up going to the multiplex with him?'

I stare at her. 'Yes, that was me.'

'And let's leave it at that.'

'I didn't want to see him. I came to see you.'

'OK, darling,' and she spreads her arms. Like Johnny. 'Like I say, let's leave it now. You can tell me all about this long walk you said you've got planned. Where's the coffee?'

I turn back to the kettle and she asks me to show her on the map where I'm going. We don't mention Andrew again.

Later, I walk Ellen to her car and watching her go, headed for her sister's house, I wonder if the one to talk to isn't Andrew himself. I could give him the opportunity to confess, to come clean himself. That would be a better idea; I wouldn't be directly involved and he wouldn't get away with it.

I end up at the library later, but on Instagram. I still worry about the photograph Ellen took of me in the French wine bar. I wonder if she had ever toyed with posting it alongside the wine. Was there a decision to be made? I have to assume that @Mollyspics, with panicked hand outstretched and mouth falling open in unattractive horror, did not make the grade and was not, at the end of the day, worthy of Ellen's Instagram. I just have to hope that she will continue to ignore, or has perhaps even deleted, the unflattering evidence of Molly. I look at it again, this near perfect, false account of Ellen's life.

Ellen's post in Café Paris has thirty-two likes now, a good average for her. I look under the likes. There is a list of names, Anna's and . . . @johnny_strachan – when had he decided he likes it too? I am just there, Johnny, only just out of sight. I stare at his name. Oh, Johnny. I put the phone back in my pocket and then almost immediately I get it out again. I look at all our names, at different points in the picture; Ellen's at the top. Mine, or rather Molly's, tagged in the centre. And Johnny's and Anna's at the bottom, appreciating and underpinning the whole thing. We are all held together in the frame. Andrew, of course, is not a part of this, he is excluded, he is not faithful as I am. I am here. I am a part of it this time, and I like it too. I press the little heart and it turns red and then I go and stand outside in the drizzle to ring Johnny. Nothing else is as important as him and suddenly now, I want to be as direct as I can with him. I don't want to be like Ellen any more with my head in the sand. I want to see him.

He answers straight away. 'What are you up to?' he asks.

What am I up to? I could be doing any number of things, couldn't I? Once, I think, I would have told a lie if I thought it would have helped; I would have said, *I'm running late to meet someone. I won the lottery. I'm going to the Bahamas.* Anything to make myself seem more attractive to him. What was it he had once found so intriguing (his mother's word) about me? Weary now, I tell him the truth.

'Not a lot. Just finishing up at the library.'

'You been OK?'

'Sort of.'

'I should have rung sooner but I've been a bit all over the place.'

'I realised that. But I'd like to meet.'

'Great. Tonight? Although I'm staying at Mum and Dad's.'

Ellen hadn't mentioned that. Why?

'You could come over.'

'To your parents' house?'

'Yes, anytime. You're more than welcome, and it's more convenient for you than Leith.'

'But why aren't you at yours?'

'Boiler's on the blink. Freezing. Come on, Mum definitely won't be there. If that's what you're thinking, and Dad's at work today and then out.'

I hesitate for the last time and then naturally, am unable to resist. 'Fine. What time?'

'What about sixish?'

'All right. See you then.'

'Hang on. You'll be needing something.'

'I'm not shopping for you again, Johnny.'

'I don't mean ingredients, I mean an address.'

'Oh.' I say. 'Of course,' and repeat it after him. 'Twenty-two St Bernard's Row.'

I'm going to go to Scotland Street first. I've checked by text with Ellen that she is with her sister and I need to check that Andrew is busy. I'd also like to see what he is doing at the surgery on a Saturday afternoon.

When I get to Strachan Medical Practice, I think it is closed. It doesn't look as though anyone is there at all. The doors don't open and there aren't any lights on that I can see. I walk round to the back and peer through one or two windows. It's dark inside. I assume that he and Amy are actually away, and there is no work being done at all.

I walk back round to the front of the building and am standing by the sign pointing to the parking bays when I sense, rather than see, some movement from inside. It's him, I know it is, and strangely, instead of feeling nervy, as I had when Andrew had last caught me outside the surgery, I feel calm. I feel as though he is the one being exposed; he ought to feel guilt and shame. Not me. I look towards the window and there is nothing. Perhaps he is going to hide from me after all.

I start to walk away when Andrew decides what to do, and it is to bang on, and then open the window.

'Molly! Are you looking for me?'

'Yes.' I nod and smile, as if in gladness. 'Hi, Andrew. I'd heard you might be here. Ellen told me you were doing some work. Doing some pharmaceutical accounting. Or something.'

He inclines his head slightly. 'As you can see. What can I do for you?'

'Are you on your own?'

'Sadly not, sadly not. Next time you really must give me some warning.' I suppose we are both acknowledging in our different ways that there is no point pretending I am here by accident. The design is clear, he's just wrong about the reasons. Another movement, a brunette shadow behind him.

'I know how busy you are. But I'd like to see you, another time maybe. You say when. You're not at home tonight?'

'No, I'm away.'

Johnny is definitely on his own at St Bernard's Row then.

'But I'm back tomorrow and I'll get your number,' he promises. 'I'll be in touch next week?'

'Yes, please. I'd like to discuss something private.' I look pointedly into the gloom of the room behind him.

He just flashes me a quick, satisfied grin. 'Bye, Mol, hope you've got a brolly – storm coming,' and he pulls the window shut. He doesn't know that finding him here with Amy, seeing the invoices, plus knowing from personal experience what he is like — well, the dots are all joining up and they're very incriminating.

36

Rain is running down the navy-blue door and collecting in the silver number 22. There is a low rumble of thunder in the distance. Witchy is sitting in the bay window of the study and when she sees a bedraggled figure ring the bell, she dashes away. Johnny pulls the door open. 'You're soaking,' and in the hall he gingerly takes my coat to hang and leads me down the passageway with the bugs of burnished gold on their green wallpaper.

Everything is as I remember in the kitchen. I still haven't said anything and perhaps Johnny mistakes my silence for wonderment.

'It's a nice kitchen, isn't it? Mum keeps redecorating. Come and sit by the windows.'

'There's going to be a storm,' I say, staring through the glass.

'Do you want a drink? Gin?'

'Whatever. Whatever you're having.'

'The gin,' he says to himself. 'Where's that these days?'

He busies himself around the island and the fridge. Witchy comes in to stare at me and Johnny, slicing a lemon as Andrew had, shoos her away.

'So where is your mum? Thanks.'

'A break at my aunt's.'

We touch each other's tumblers. *Happy days.*

'What's new? What have you been doing?'

'I've been keeping busy. Trying to anyway.'

Johnny assumes his expression of pacifist innocence in case I'd meant anything accusatory by that.

'I've been walking a lot. Hiking further afield. I saw Anna actually when I was setting out a couple of weeks ago, outside her art gallery.'

'Did you say hello?'

'No. Can we talk about her?'

He stands up – 'Do we have to?' and gulps his drink. 'It'll be quite a short and boring conversation. Music?'

'If you want.'

He comes to stand by me with his phone in his hand and types his password in. A simple 4-numbered one, straight up the middle. Into iTunes and a song comes on.

He's forgotten I only really like red wine. I take another large sip of the gin so I don't have to think about the fact he's forgotten – or doesn't care – about the Rioja we drank in France and in the pub only a week ago. I tuck my arms across my chest with my glass in one hand.

'Shall we do something for lunch tomorrow?'

'Do you like smoked salmon? Mum left me some to finish up.'

'Yes. Lunch?'

'What about it?'

'Do you want to have it with me tomorrow?'

'Um. I don't think I can. I'll check the diary but I doubt it's possible,' he says. 'Tomorrow could be quite difficult because of some extra work.'

'Tomorrow is Sunday.'

He doesn't miss a beat. 'Tell me about it. It's non-stop round there.' The lazy days of December are clearly just a distant memory for him. 'What do you have in mind anyway?'

I don't have anything in mind. That used to be his role, we both know that I never came up with anything to add to his lists. 'Anything,' I say and he says, 'Well you're here now, aren't you?' then he gets some smoked salmon on slices of bread out of the fridge. 'What about a glass of wine? This tonic water is flat.'

I look at my barely touched gin. 'I'm OK, I think. Thank you,' and at the same time there is a flash of lightning. Automatically, I begin counting. '. . .four, five, six, seven.' Thunder crashes.

'What *are* you doing? I'll go ahead with wine, I think.'

'Look at this weather.' I go and stand at the French windows again. 'We get storms like this in Torcastle all the time. Here not so much.' It's as if the clouds have been unzipped. I have to raise my voice to be heard above the rain.

Johnny is opening a bottle of wine. Another streak of white light zig-zags like a spell cast at the clouds and then he comes up behind me.

'I remember that story you told me about the Cat Pool.'

I turn around. 'Do you?'

And then, as if he regrets admitting that, he starts to tell me about something else, something completely irrelevant and I have to admit, boring. 'Johnny,' I say and I put my hand on his arm to try and halt his chatter. His face is in profile and he doesn't look at me. I say, 'Do you remember the snowstorm the day I was supposed to leave Geneva?' and he says, he does, it must have been a big storm to have grounded the plane, like the one in Belfast when he was there for an arbitration . . . and again I stop him. I try to rewind again, to take him back, and remind him that he does remember some things. I remind him of future plans, ones like our trip to Skye, the trip we'd planned on the day we went snowshoeing. Not because I hope for them to happen so much any more, but because I hope for him to remember, and by doing so, acknowledge their existence. I try and talk about things he used to talk about. The storm rages on the other side of the French windows.

But it seems these things were only possibilities or of any interest at all when he had brought them up. Mostly, tonight, he pretends he doesn't remember saying them, or agreeing to whatever it was. Other times he raises his eyebrows as though we had both been a little crazy back then. He doesn't want these memories proffered to him, in carefully arranged displays, labelled 'Remember Why You Liked Me'. Sometimes he nods and carefully agrees but really everything that we had once bought into gets put on a pile, like old clothes that he doesn't want to wear any longer. He is deft at changing the subject; he has the lawyer's knack of making himself sound reasonable. He stands up after a while and moves around the kitchen, pretending to prepare things. Nothing seems to emerge out of cupboards and drawers. When he sits down again, it is opposite the sofa, on the armchair Ellen liked to tuck herself into. I suddenly think: *he can't do this*.

I take another gulp of wine and look at Johnny, easy and relaxed and chatting about light-hearted nonsense, making me smile now and again, and after a while, when the wine is finished, this time it's me who walks over to him. He opens his arms to me – they have been laced behind his head, his legs stretched out, his grin lazy – and he pulls me down into his lap.

We kiss and kiss in his mother's kitchen with the thunder overhead until dizzy with wine and each other, he takes me upstairs. This – he can do.

*

Later, after dinner and more wine, and then whisky (the Laphroaig came out again), Johnny who has been languorous and flushed, becomes soporific. He begins to mumble, then to slur his words and then he passes out in bed. I lay my head on his chest and listen to him breathing. The wind rattles and hisses at the window.

It's an attic room, made for small people. Johnny, I think, stayed here even after he had outgrown it, longer perhaps than he should. It's an immaculate, son-left-house-but-we-keep-it-as-his room. Old school memorabilia are the defining aspect. The bedspread is blue-and-white striped, the bedside table draped with a flag, probably a football one. Johnny is snoring carelessly. I quietly slide open the drawer. There is an old book of Shakespearian sonnets inside and when I open it, a tattered letter falls out. Going to stand by the window, I can see that the letter is written from somebody called Lara. Lara announces to Johnny, to me, and the empty room that he occupies her every waking moment, and that she's never met anyone like him, let alone shared her favourite sonnet. Lara's mother wants to meet him and hopes he can come south to Henley next month. She can't wait to see him in the college bar later. The date is 2011; it's a love letter from university, as pointless as my own more recent outpourings of love and grief.

There is some pathos around the old-fashioned love letter that makes me gentle with it. I carefully fold it again and return it to the folds of the book. I tiptoe down the attic stairs, past Ellen and Andrew's unoccupied room, and then I stop and go back. Their door swings open soundlessly and my bare feet sink into the carpeting. The bed is a four-poster and swathed in reams of Grecian pale gold and leafy green material. It is a pastoral scene with a courtly flautist and a deer and a woman playing a harp and also a small, gnomish fool who seems to be watching them all, hiding behind bushes. I can't see the bed. The curtains are drawn. I stand there in the silence and then for no other reason than I can, I pad softly over and part the hangings. The bed has been stripped and the mattress is old and slightly stained. The pillows, a little yellow, have been left in disarray. I stare at all four and then arrange them, two and two at the top of the bed. I let go of the hangings and go and sit at the large kidney-shaped dressing table with the material to match the four-poster. I look at the white hair in the ivory brushes with AS engraved on the front, and the large black and white portrait photographs of them all. There is a pot of Jo Malone body cream which has a rich, flowery scent that I instantly identify as Ellen's. A little on my hands goes a long way. The mirror, a curved, three-panelled tortoise-shell one, reflects my face three ways from each angle and in each one, the hulking bed is in the background. I stand up and before I go, once more insert myself through the hangings, this time to mess the pillows up.

I steal through the warm innards of the house. Shadows come too, slipping down the carpeted stairs, crossing the ghostly marble floor and then loom up at me from behind the large mirror glittering on the wall. I go into Andrew's study first, the bay-windowed room, the room with the oak chest, the wingback armchair and Andrew's desk. I pull open a drawer and rummage through the debris. I am looking for evidence of his guilt or some proof of his shame. Any receipts or correspondence. There are no clues.

Another drawer, this one with a delicate key to lock it, as if this might be the one that holds the treasure of the Strachans' personal life but apart from their passports — nothing. I am still none the wiser about anything. I can't find proof of Andrew and Amy and I can't find anything else, whatever else it is I think I'm searching for. Are the Strachans just . . . nothing? Headlights from the occasional car passing in the street outside swirl round the ceiling. With the Strachans, all of them, and in the beating heart of their house, I had expected to find things of worth, meaty things that mean something. I find sellotape and leaking batteries.

Across the hall and into the kitchen. The electrics of the cooker are whirring softly and the digital clock bleeps at me occasionally. 02:10. 02:11. I pick my jumper up from the floor, my tights. Witchy jumps up onto the island. She has already licked the oily plates clean of salmon.

Something at the French windows makes me look up. Security lights click on but don't reveal anything other than what I know to be already there; the wooden furniture and the hurricane lamp. A fox, perhaps, sheltering in the shrubbery. It feels like someone is in the room with me. Still nothing, but now I feel afraid, afraid because it's true that I have been here before and I shouldn't have been. I sat on the sofa there and pretended that I didn't know Johnny.

It is too dark to see anything much but I can see Johnny's phone is still on the side. I pick it up and press it at the bottom. It immediately lights up. The back of my neck tingles. I hesitate for a second, but no longer than that, and with my heart thumping against my breastbone, my breath suddenly quick and shallow, I press the numbers of his password: 0852.

There are hundreds of unopened emails. I go into them first. A lot of spam and a lot that is meaningless to me but it is immediately clear that Anna is everywhere. Everywhere. She forwards him things from Facebook, funny jokes, careless questions, many dates to keep free. Her name, ANNA STEWART is the defining fingerprint. Her address is at the bottom of all her emails; I know exactly which her street is. I scroll down through them all, catching through my bitter thudding heart their easy way of communicating with each other, something that I never had. She has him; she has wrapped him up in every aspect of her life and twaddle. Still warm from Johnny's arms, I feel as if I could kill her. Can't she leave him alone for one day, ever? And in amongst the deluge from Anna, there are others, a few with GMT email addresses, someone with a foreign-sounding surname . . . I don't bother with them. One or two from Ellen.

There is less from Anna in messages and it's all practical, organisational stuff. There is nothing at all from me. I do not exist in Johnny's messages. I stare out into the shrubbery, thinking, and then look in WhatsApp. Nothing from her visible but then I type in Anna's name at the top of the inbox and it is all archived but it is there: everything she has ever sent him comes tumbling out and lines up. Cartoons, possessive kisses, random photos of this or that . . . it's proper girlfriend stuff, affectionate and constant. Flirtatious and insistent: don't you like my new miniskirt? That sort of thing. I trawl through more of the same, looking now only for the incriminating evidence of Anna. And then I get to it.

Nobody else makes me come like you do. Every time. Love it xxx

It's like a punch in the stomach. Then there's a creak from upstairs and my shaking hands let go of the phone. I hold my breath, terrified Johnny will materialise behind me, listening hard for sound other than the blood crashing through my head. Then I go back into the phone to log out of WhatsApp. I take my clothes and creep back into the hall. I wait for too long, numb with cold and with the horror of what I have read.

I go back to the stairs and further up towards the roof. Into the attic and back into Johnny's room where he lies, on his stomach, with his arms curled over his head and his fists loosely bunched like a child's. When Anna told me she was with him – **Yeah, fine. He's with me** – she had meant it. Everyone else had either been lying or got it wrong about them.

There is a row of snow globes on the bookcase next to my side of the bed. I don't really sleep and I stare at them for much of the night thinking about the WhatsApp message. And slowly realising that if anyone understands Johnny, it is Anna. It is Anna who holds the key to him. Johnny doesn't give any answers to anything. It isn't Johnny and I who have unfinished business, but Anna and I.

Anna has always been there. I think she always will be, as ineradicable as I was transitory. Every time.

By early morning the storm has passed and when it is light, I open gritty eyes and make myself get dressed.

'Are you going?' Johnny mumbles. He doesn't turn over. 'I'm hung-over. You've poisoned me.' Last night's affection has been replaced with a nasty – guilty – petulance.

I walk to his side of the bed and look at the back of his head. 'Johnny?'

He moves slightly. He looks sickly and his face has a sweaty sheen to it.

'Bye, Johnny.'

He buries back into the duvet. Wincing over this latest version of farewell, I leave St Bernard's Row.

37

Everything feels subdued this morning, even the light. The sun is pallid, white rays criss-crossing weakly through broken cloud, as if the storm had sucked all the strength and energy from the sky. I look towards the grey horizon, down the hill – and in the distance, lying low in the mist, I can see the sea.

I'm going to tell Anna what I know and ask about what I don't. She knows Johnny better than anyone, if the messages made anything crystal clear, it is that. I'm going to get some answers from someone who may understand him.

The quiet of the Sunday morning is eerie. The wide avenue of Leith Walk is near-deserted. Evidence of the wind in the night is everywhere, in branches and bits of rubbish strewn across the road, and in sodden, dazed seagulls floating above it. It is now very still. After ten minutes, I pass Brunswick Street. I do not look down it. Then I am walking the presumably well-trodden path from Johnny's to hers. Reaching Dalmeny Street, I stop outside number 60, looking for her flat number, but then a man leaves, holding the door for me so I can go straight in. I start the climb up the stairs. There are eighty-nine steps to the top, to her door.

I rub my thumb thoughtfully over the doorbell and then push it. She's in, I can hear her coming long before she arrives, a heavy tread and then silence before she says, 'Who is it?'

Her low, scratchy voice makes my arms tingle. I clasp them to me, over my chest. I don't answer for a minute, gathering myself together, and so it is a shock when, presumably irritated with her caution, Anna suddenly flings open the door.

She is flabbergasted. 'What on earth are you doing here?' She is still in a dressing gown and she pulls the cord around her waist, tying a knot. 'Seriously. What the fuck are you doing here?'

'Hello, Anna. I suppose I should have messaged. Can I come in?'

'How do you even know where I live?'

'Johnny,' I say vaguely, and she looks taken aback but before she can say anything else I add, 'although he doesn't know I'm here.'

She is suspicious and then curious. 'Why?' She searches the stairs behind me.

'I just want to talk.'

She doesn't say anything, so I have to go on.

'I need to ask about Johnny.'

There must have been some insistence in my voice because she only hesitates for a moment more and then she lets me in. I walk through her hallway.

'I won't pretend we're friends,' I tell her.

'Fine,' she shrugs. 'We're not. And I haven't got long.'

It smells of cigarette smoke. In the middle of her messy sitting room is a table, an old pine one, covered in magazines, biros and coffee cups. And an ashtray, and a packet of Silk Cut. Anna walks over and pulls a cigarette from the packet. 'Want one?'

'No.'

'Well, get on with it then. What's he done now?'

'You say that as if you're not surprised I'm here.'

She blows a smoke ring. 'He's like a kid. Always in trouble.'

'With women, do you mean? Why do you put up with that? I don't understand how you could be like that.'

'In general,' she says, her eyes narrowing.

I try to find some courage, courage that has been fading fast. 'I won't beat around the bush. I know you don't like me. But ever since you messaged me on New Year's Eve I've been confused about what's going on between you and Johnny.' I raise my chin defiantly. 'And between Johnny and me.'

She considers the cigarette. Calmer than I imagined.

'How long have you been with him?' I ask thickly.

'How long have I been with him? For ever.'

'I mean sleeping with him. I know you're best bloody friends since for ever.'

'Yes. We are.'

'But I've been in the dark about him since I met him and I want some answers now. Now I know about you.'

'Know what about me?'

'That you have sex with him.' I give her a bitter smile, the memory of the WhatsApp congealing inside me. The unpleasantness is a taste in my mouth. 'You know I was?'

Anna looks straight at me. 'Yes. I heard about his activities skiing. It sounds as though he turned on all the charm. He tells me everything, you know. He can't resist if it involves appreciation from females.'

Reduced to an activity and my feelings to an appreciation. But mainly I'm flabbergasted. 'And that's OK with you?'

'Not especially. But nothing I can do about it. And we weren't really in touch in December. He checked out, basically. He sometimes does. I know that he did fuck all in the run-up to Christmas, pretending to be some sort of downhill ski champion. Yes,' she laughs mirthlessly. 'It all went down a treat with work and Father. But it's none of my business at the end of the day.'

'Not his girlfriend's business? Seriously?'

Anna shrugs. 'I wouldn't know.'

'What do you mean, "you wouldn't know"?'

'I'm not his girlfriend, obviously.'

We stare at each other before I go on, even less sure of myself.

'But you sleep with him. You're always with him. You're always together.'

She looks at me speculatively and after a second says, 'I do know what he did, by the way. At Christmas. He thought it was best. I almost felt sorry for you, at least I did until you turned up again in the pub.'

'You mean how he disappeared,' I say flatly.

She nods. 'I expect he couldn't face you to end it, but don't take it personally. It's just something he does.'

I look away then. 'Something he does.'

'It's easier that way for him. To pretend things aren't happening, didn't happen.' She looks at me straight on. 'There isn't anything serious between us.'

'But I know that's not true.'

'It is. I wish there was more, at least I used to. I suppose it's what you call friends with benefits.'

Friends with benefits. The worst sort of thing, a slippery, organic thing. And why I hadn't ever been able to get a handle on what it was between them. The worst sort of enemy.

She looks at me as if she can read my mind. 'It sounds more than it is. It doesn't mean much to him which is why it's been so difficult. My fault. I know it's not really anything.'

But it could go on for ever. This could be why Anna will last. I can't bear the thought of the . . . spontaneity. 'But better than nothing. It's there. It's something.' And yet, there is resentment on her face, and she is shaking her head. Perhaps she thinks it is worse. There is hurt there too. I think of the WhatsApp messages. They were all archived. Half out with the trash. And it's true that they weren't loving messages, and that all the attempt at intimacy had come from her.

'Actually – you want the truth? It's nothing. In fact, I don't mind telling you, I've almost come to the end of my tether with him. I don't think he's ever going to grow up.' She leans forward and stubs her cigarette out. 'I'll tell you about him, if you really want to know. Johnny has paraded women in front of me for years. Ever since I've known him. There's always been someone. He can't be on his own, you see, but he ruins it when he sleeps with them. So he runs away from them and he comes back to me. His mate, the one who's invisible when the girls are on. But when they're off, he reappears.' She stares at me, her eyes suddenly bright. 'I have to say, you weren't supposed to come back, I thought he'd dealt with you. I was surprised when you showed up at the pub.'

I wouldn't have, if I hadn't put myself in his way outside the solicitors' office. And before that, in his mother's way at Abbotsford. Yes, he should have dealt with me.

'I don't know why I'm telling you this.'

'Go on,' I say quietly.

'I say *friends* with benefits, but the truth is he treats me like dirt most of the time. He forgets about me as if I were a, were a . . .' She can't find the word to describe her inadequacy. 'Ignores me when he wants, never there for me when I need him. He's no friend, not really.'

'Have you told him how you feel about this?'

'Have you told him how you feel? Which by the way, is always written all over your face, so I don't expect you need to.'

I don't answer.

'I've always kept the truth of the matter from him,' she goes on. 'It's easier this way, easier to pretend we're mates. He doesn't want to know how I feel.'

'No.'

She hasn't asked me to sit down and she is on the arm of the sofa. She gets up now and I turn as if to leave. Then she says:

'I don't know why you came here. You shouldn't have come barging in to my flat. I've never been important to Johnny. You should be at Issy's.'

'Issy's?'

'You have been barking up the wrong tree, haven't you.' She looks at me pityingly. 'Come on, catch up. His Swedish girlfriend, Isa Karlsson. Works a treat for him because she's so often in Sweden – holidays, weekends, this weekend actually . . .'

That name. I had seen it as an email address, the name had been attached to Johnny's company's email. I had assumed they were messages of a professional nature and blindly passed over them.

'. . .before Christmas. You were the perfect pre-stocking filler, I gather.'

'He was with her in . . . in . . . December? When he was with me?'

Anna nods, and then quantifies her nod with a, 'Well, they've been off and on for quite a long time. More on than off in recent days.'

'You're saying that on the twenty-fourth he went back to her.' It's hardly even a question, not any more. Johnny loves all things Swedish. He's impressed by the Swedes. Tomas Holmberg is a god to Johnny. It all comes tumbling back. I had thought it was because of Holmberg.

She is not triumphant but neither is she sympathetic. She just nods. Thank God. I don't want her pity. 'It was her drinks party we went to on Christmas Eve.'

Issy Karlsson. 'I've got it completely wrong, haven't I? It wasn't you.'

'No.'

'He is. Monstrous,' I say finally.

Anna grins then. 'Yes. He is. I'm afraid fidelity is not Johnny's strong point.' She stands up. Walking to the kitchen, she turns at the door. 'Sorry.'

And it's not on his behalf, and she probably doesn't even mean her apology. It's probably just something to say, no doubt. But somehow, just the fact that someone said it, someone filled the space with *sorry*. I'm almost ashamed to admit how much it meant to me. 'Why do you hate me then? I'm not a threat.'

'You might have been,' she says. 'But I don't hate you particularly. It's more that I hate all of it. I'm fed up with all of us. It's pathetic.' She pours some juice into a glass and picks another cigarette from the packet. 'We're pathetic. We both are.'

'Yes,' I say. 'At least, I am. Only . . . in my defence' – and I laugh shakily, without humour – 'I thought he loved me.'

'You know, love doesn't mean much to him really. He had too much from his mother and too little from his father. He doesn't know what to do with it – longs to believe in it, mind you, he enjoys himself getting carried away, but . . .' She shrugs. 'I expect you know that.'

I rub my tired eyes.

'He's clever with women,' she acknowledges. 'I see it all the time. In bars and clubs. He says the right thing – to pretty much always the same type of girl. Quieter, older . . . younger. The ones who'll fall for it.'

This time it is me who picks up the glass. 'OK. Thanks. You don't need to go on.'

Her eyes flash. 'You're the one who came here asking for it.'

'And now I've got it. I'll go now.'

'I'm amazed you didn't guess,' she says coolly.

'Well, I did. I just guessed wrong, didn't I?'

'Needless to say, I don't like Issy,' she carries on as though she wants to keep talking. 'But she's independent, doesn't ask questions. Maybe they're a good couple.'

She must see the look on my face because she seems to relent slightly. 'Who knows. And as I said, she's not very nice.'

'I think that makes it worse.'

'You could say they're welcome to each other.'

I turn away from her then. 'I've been an idiot from the word go.'

Anna hesitates. 'Don't be too hard on yourself. I know he can be persuasive. Makes you think you're the only one in the world. And don't forget I'm only just starting to see through him and I've known him for years.'

'This Issy. Does she know about you?'

Again, that flicker of hurt across Anna's face.

'No, no way. She wouldn't put up with it. Johnny's not been interested in me like that for a few months now.'

I had never expected to leave feeling sorry for Anna. 'I'm sorry I just turned up out of the blue. I'll go.'

I suddenly need to be alone. Strange – but I'd spent so long convinced that if it was anyone, it was Anna, that this news about Issy feels like a new blow, fresh and bloody. I'd got so used to Anna being the third in our triangle. *Issy? How had this stranger slipped in without me noticing?*

'I'll admit I was amazed to see you,' says Anna. 'Funny, you looked as though you were ready for a fight. Bye. Call me if you want.'

I stop at the door. 'Call you?'

'Why not? I've got a feeling that we may have more in common than we thought. He's not treated either of us well. Neither of us get him, in the end.'

She's right, I think, as I go back down the stairs and on to the quiet misty street. She's right – and I had been wrong. I never had him. Issy Karlsson has him, Issy had him all along.

38

I did a good job of pretending to be OK. But as soon as I get back from Anna's, I shower and change and then I check Johnny's Instagram. And there is a follower with a private account called @busyIssy. Busy Issy, I see from Johnny's account, is followed in return by @johnny_strachan which is fucking pointless because Busy Issy hasn't had the time to post anything at all: 0 posts. How have I never noticed this slim but crucial part of Johnny's life? How had I been so stupid, to miss the thing that mattered? Nothing that I had pored through and no one else that I had obsessed over meant anything to him. Issy had got away from me.

Even though there's no point any more and I've got all the answers now, I log onto his Facebook page. Not that it will do any good, because it's never done any good. And he doesn't use it for anything except gathering friends, he never puts anything about himself out there and I know from experience that it's like trying to penetrate a maze; it's not possible to discover the truth of his life but it's easy to be misled. And there she is, Isa Karlsson – faint, inactive, cool – but there. No picture, just a Nordic scene. Snow, skis, a tiny wooden hut.

Who is she, Johnny? Issy. Did you tell her what you told me? Is she meant to be? Have you discovered again, with hope anew, the all-consuming passions that defined you at the start of our relationship? Are you making lists together? Are you badgering her, every hour of every day, demanding to know – *What did you have for breakfast? Did you miss me? Dinner tonight?* Do you say to her, *Oi, where d'you think you're off to?* Do you stroke her face and say, *I've got to tell you, you're amazing.* And there she is, tagged in someone else's photo. She has white-blonde hair and . . . dances. As well as being a solicitor, she's a part-time dancer and she wears sky-blue leg warmers over spindly legs. She looks delicate, and disinterested. She looks perfect, on Facebook . . . here's another one – pouting a little in a pale-pink dress, nipped in at the waist with a thin gold belt. No wonder Anna, stocky and enthusiastic, can't stand her.

Another time, no doubt, Issy and Johnny will return to Chamonix and the Aiguille du Midi. Her child-like calves encased in chunky ski boots will bring out all of Johnny's chivalrous instincts. Flattering and firm, she will persuade him that there is nothing to be frightened of. She will help him be the man he wants to be, he will finally be a square peg in a square hole. She will succeed where I failed. She is tantalisingly, crucially, busy – but I had nothing to preoccupy myself with apart from him. She will finish the list he started with me.

Unless Anna can see Busy Issy off. *Lucky Anna*, I suddenly think. Friends isn't bad, and I suddenly have to squash a quick stab of envy. Anna and Johnny *are* just friends, or at least he thinks they are, and actually they work much better united against an unlucky third, they are closer than they would be if they were actually together. All she has to do, endure, is see the women through. She knows Johnny will be back so she texts her jokes, makes herself available and pretends to agree that there is intimacy in the distance between them, in the looseness of their banter and the relaxed nature of their relationship. After all, texting is what he really enjoys, the small shots of flirtation and the trace of a connection, but a remote one. He is quick and good at that, he had loved messaging me from even the next-door hotel room in Chamonix. And Anna is cunning enough not to try and pin him down. She will ping back her sassy replies and leave it like that; but we girlfriends, we couldn't ever leave it. We had no clue we were walking tightropes but Anna would always have known. She's the one who'll last. It's like watching the Saturday morning football matches, Johnny probably thinks they're crumbs to throw out to her but they're not crumbs: the diary dates don't change when the girlfriend does. The football matches and the rugby club dinner and all those sorts of things are really important. They're the permanent fixtures, not the leftovers. She's snuck them in and got away with it because now she's permanent as well, however unsatisfactory it is for her. In a way, I was right to be jealous of Anna. I wonder if she will see Busy Issy off too.

On Monday evening, my mobile rings and it is a private number.

'Hello?'

'Andrew Strachan here.'

I'd almost forgotten about Andrew. I had been so preoccupied with Johnny again.

'Oh. Hello, Andrew.'

'Molly. It was a charming surprise to see you on Saturday. I'm sorry I was busy and that I've only just got around to calling you.'

'Don't worry,' I say, 'and it's rather late to call.'

'Sorry for keeping you waiting,' he purrs.

'That's not what I meant. It might have been a medical query.'

'Was it?'

217

'No.'

'I'm glad. And I think we ought to make a date to meet.' He doesn't give me a chance to object. 'And, as luck would have it, my wife is out tomorrow evening and I'm all home alone.'

Tomorrow is Tuesday 14 February. Neither of us remark on the date but I have been made angry by Andrew's assumption that my request to see him was because I wanted a date. How dare he? And in a flash of anger I agree to go there at six o'clock with the idea that I will tell him to be straight with Ellen or I will.

At lunchtime on Tuesday, I buy a paper at the shop and whilst I am flicking through I read a small paragraph about the death of Tomas Holmberg. He was the extreme skier that Johnny admired and has been killed in a massive avalanche. I am shocked at the violent manner of his death but I am not surprised. Nobody could live and ski the way he had and keep defying the odds. Nature, inevitably, has destroyed him. The avalanche had a destructive force of Four which suggests that everything in its path, forests included, would have been gouged out of the landscape. No chance.

Johnny will be devastated in the way a child who considers his hero invincible will be devastated. Once I think I would have used this headline as an excuse to get in touch with him, there used to be so much that I remembered considering vital that we should share. I remember him in the Alps, protesting, uselessly – *feel the fear and do it anyway* – and think that his attempt at courage in the Alps was only ever just that. An attempt. He only ever feels the fear, and talks about it. Poor, vertiginous Johnny, doomed to mediocrity. With or without Isa, I don't think he will ever ski the Mallory route in Chamonix.

Anxiety about meeting Andrew increases throughout Valentine's Day. I have seen enough of him to know that he can be unpredictable at best, at worst angry. If he is expecting one thing, but gets another, I don't doubt his propensity for fury. But I resist running away because I don't want to tell Ellen myself. The messenger too often gets shot. At least, this is what I tell myself and my heart beats against my chest all afternoon till Andrew texts.

Now I know you're a whisky drinker. Champagne as well?

It reminds me of Johnny. I delete the message and my nerve fades further. I don't want to see Andrew.

And then at around four o'clock I get a message on Instagram from Anna. @anna_banana_xo has sent a message to Skye's Instagram direct. **Yeah, fine, He's with me** is what she wrote on New Year's Eve to @scottish_skyegrant, and this is what I see first, above this afternoon's one. It makes me feel a bit sick.

You around later on?

I have no idea what Anna wants from me, or why she would choose tonight of all nights to ask if I'm around, but I'm too curious to refuse. I'd so much rather see her, and find out what she wants. This is the excuse I have been looking for; Andrew, and his mistaken, frightening lust can definitely wait. I suggest to Anna that she comes to my local, where I go with Tam. At least there's no chance of the Strachans being there and everyone can know me as Skye tonight. As me. I message Andrew with relief saying something has come up.

39

Anna arrives just before seven, clearly angry. She chucks her bag on the table. 'I've had it,' she announces. 'I've fucking had it.'

'What? Who with?'

'Johnny and fucking Isa Karlsson.'

'What about them?'

She leans over and takes a slug of my wine. 'I need one of these. Or something stronger. He's really done it this time. Even by his standards.'

'Tell me,' I say, beginning to feel exasperated. 'If they're together, it's because it's Valentine's evening. No surprises there.'

'So you'd think. And probably originally yes, but then she had to stay late in court. So Johnny suggests I have the dinner she'd booked with him instead.' *He hadn't rung me*, I think. 'Like an idiot, I said yes. The booking was at my favourite place. The Witchery, you know?' I nod. It had been on our list. 'He made it sound funny. Fun.' She takes another gulp. 'There's not nearly enough wine in this tiny glass, you know. And then by four o'clock, it's clear court will be over in time for dinner. I'd have been happy to back out. Well, not happy, but I would have. Of my own accord. But then she rang me.'

'Issy rang you? What did she say?'

'She said that she and Johnny's relationship had "moved

up a notch".' She makes inverted quotation marks with her fingers. 'God she's got an annoying accent. And that she'd appreciate me "backing off" in the future. In other words, she just told me to get fucked.'

Issy has drawn a line, it seems. She isn't having Anna spending Valentine's Day dinner with Johnny. She is going to be more vigilant from now on. Perhaps it will be the other way around, perhaps Busy Issy will be seeing us off.

'I hate her. She's so superior, with her big promotion and all her money. She earns loads, did I mention that? Apparently she's also known as the cleverest person in the office. Not that bloody clever, if you ask me. How does Johnny get away with it?' She leans over again and finishes my drink.

'He's a good liar.'

'Yes. But I also think work has always been her priority. And maybe now she's re-evaluating. Biological clock or something?'

I ignore this hint at their future. 'I'm envious of her work,' I say quietly. 'The focus on something worthwhile or ambitious.' Having headspace so full of intelligent and busy thoughts that Johnny doesn't get a look-in.

'She's tough,' agrees Anna as though that settles that. 'But she and Johnny have definitely been getting closer recently.'

'But how does that work? With you around so much?'

She doesn't know what I mean.

'Things like watching football. You do so much with Johnny.'

'Why do you think that?' She's genuinely confused. 'Yeah, some stuff, but not loads of stuff. I hate the bloody football.'

Vaguely, I say, 'What a mess. I'm sorry,' but really I'm

wondering how I'd concluded she was so absolute and so dominant in his life. Didn't she adore the football? I'd thought the train journey from Abbotsford with Ellen and Andrew confirmed everything I suspected. Or had I just assumed it was Anna they were talking about?

'Johnny thought that I wouldn't make a fuss about dinner tonight.' Anna pauses. 'I bloody did.'

I can't help a smile. I can see her 'making a fuss'. Part of me is glad too, I'm ashamed to admit, simply to have Anna on my side. 'The thing is though,' I say, 'is that it isn't her fault, not really.' Anna makes a face. 'It's Johnny, it's all Johnny's fault. Isn't it Johnny who deserves a comeuppance?'

She looks at me, picks up my empty glass and looks at it.

'He can't expect you to fill in for her,' I conclude. 'And you shouldn't have to.'

'Christ,' she says. 'What is the world coming to? Taking advice from you. Spending Valentine's evening agreeing with you. We never thought this would be an option, did we?'

And a good one; I never thought this would be a good option. 'Let's have some more wine,' I tell her. 'Come on. You never know, we might even enjoy it. And I can tell you for sure who wouldn't enjoy the thought of it, and isn't that quite tempting all on its own?'

'It bloody is,' she agrees. 'Wanker. Shall we eat as well? I'm starving. I saw an Indian opposite.'

I beam at her suddenly. 'Yes, please.'

And that's how Anna and I end up getting drunk, and having a really good time together on Valentine's Day evening while Johnny and Isa Karlsson celebrate their relationship at the Witchery. And we do have a good time. Anna is fun. She's irreverent and truculent and she has none of Ellen's non-partisan subtlety or maturity. And thinking about Ellen, I realise that she had not been so much of a surprise. Safe and nurturing, she had been who she was supposed to be. But Anna is a revelation because she is nothing like she appears on social media. I'd always assumed Anna didn't care. That because she had Johnny, and because she was direct and sassy, she didn't have any problems. I remember obsessing about them doing things together, dinners, takeaways. Films. I'd imagined whole swathes of their lives entwined, and Anna just not caring about much else. But she does mind, especially about Johnny, and she isn't OK, not totally. She just has a different disguise to me.

She has a sort of sadness that I recognise. She covers it up with being ballsy but she cheerfully acknowledges that life at home growing up was difficult. She's still got a mum, who lives in Leith, 'and not the trendy hipster part of it either.' Her father buggered off when she was six and she helped raise her four younger siblings. Oddly, her father comes from Fort William, near Torcastle. There doesn't seem to be any point or any opportunity not to be straight with her and I tell her before the poppadoms are gone about Mum and Dad dying and Aunt Nora.

But it gets awkward when we move on to the Strachans, all of whom Anna has known since she and Johnny were at school together in Edinburgh. Johnny went on to boarding school in England, Anna stayed in Edinburgh but they kept in touch. It's hard pretending that I don't know Ellen and Andrew. And lying to her, when we are having supper under the guise of honesty, is dreadful, almost worse than lying to Ellen. This is supposed to be a clean slate. But I keep quiet, because half of me still daren't completely trust Anna, and the other half doesn't want her to know what I've done. Sitting here with Anna, talking about the Strachans and Issy, it gives me more of a sense than anything else has of how badly I lost my way in those early days. This should be a vaguely normal, honest meal between us but as Tam had pointed out, no one would understand what has been compelling me. I have to keep this hidden.

And I've learnt caution over the last few weeks. I've learnt to keep parts of myself back. I keep my face bland when she mentions one of them and I try and steer the conversation away from them but she seems to enjoy talking about Ellen and Andrew, and I can understand that. They're those sort of people. Interestingly, she's got a different take to me on Andrew and thinks he is sidelined by his wife and son. She doesn't blame him for how he comes across.

'How does he come across?' I ask.

'A bit bullish, I suppose. But I've always reckoned he's just trying to get attention from old Ellen. Who's a bit bloody stuck-up, if you ask me.'

'It all sounds very . . . erm. Complicated.'

'Nah. Not really. Johnny's not interested anyway, he just stays out of their way.'

'Stays out of their way?'

'You know. Just not bothered about seeing them too often.'

But happy to use their heater, their house. Finish their smoked salmon. I think that Johnny suffers from the apathy for affection that loving parents can instil in an ungrateful child.

'Lots of arguments are about money.' Anna scoops up more rice and takes a long sip of her red wine.

'Oh?'

'Yep. You know it's Ellen's?'

'No. Is there a lot?'

She shrugs. 'Not masses, but definitely enough. Johnny would like more, of course. Ellen's rich father gave them the house, and the money to buy the practice which they couldn't resist calling after themselves. The father basically gives them their monthly allowance too.'

'Presumably Andrew finds that difficult.' Presumably it was also Ellen's money that had paid for the pharmacist's plastic surgery.

'Also,' says Anna, with her mouth full, 'Andrew's not the talented medic and they don't let him forget it, as far as I can see. Ellen was the brilliant medical student. He only did the minimum training requirement and Ellen gave up her "promising career" to marry him.' She does her finger quotation marks in the air.

'I bet the medical practice was his idea. All very convenient for him.'

'That's what Johnny would say.' Anna looks at me suspiciously. 'I don't know why you'd agree with him. I'm not convinced.'

I can't look convinced either because she adds:

'One thing is for sure. He's a right flirt. Sort of man who puts his hand on your knee whenever he can, bit of a bottom pincher.'

I shudder. 'Awful. Do you think he takes things any further?'

'No, not for a second. He wouldn't dare, he'd lose everything.'

I dislike Andrew more and more. I don't think he's bullied by Ellen and Johnny, I think he is the bully. I certainly know that he's an unfaithful husband, and Anna's just told me he's a money-grabbing one to boot. I swallow the chicken and fill up our glasses. 'People like that always get what's coming to them. In the end.'

'People like Ellen? She's such a snob.'

'She's not. I meant people like Andrew.'

Anna looks at me curiously. 'What makes you say she's not a snob?'

'I've seen pictures of her. She looks kind.' It's not good enough. I try again, twirling my wine glass. 'Johnny used to talk about her a lot.'

Anna snorts. 'The, whatsitcalled, Oedipal theory is working overtime there.'

I laugh suddenly. 'I expect it is.'

'Anyway. Nuff about those two. What on earth went on with Johnny at the weekend?'

For an awful minute, I think she knows about Johnny being with me at St Bernard's Row on Saturday night. 'Nothing,' I stammer. 'What do you mean?'

'Filthy mood, heating on the blink and Issy in Sweden. Loads of complaints and then nothing. I messaged him to see if he was OK, but never heard anything back.'

I turn to look for the waiter so she can't see my face. In the silence, it occurs to me that she is testing me. I keep quiet, pretending to be distracted by wanting something.

'Oh well,' she says blithely. 'Never mind. By the way, did you know he lost his licence at the beginning of September last year?'

'Driving?' I say stupidly.

'Yep. He often asks me to drive him around on a Saturday because he can't be bothered to take the bus to football. I wouldn't go otherwise. He didn't ask this weekend, so I'm wondering what he's been up to.' She adds, 'It wouldn't be interesting about the licence except that he doesn't want anyone to know, so he kind of needs me. He never came clean about it to anyone.'

'But why not? He's a grown man.'

Anna puts a doubtful expression on her face and we both laugh. 'He was speeding, well over the limit and it would have been really bad if work had found out. Not a good look for a solicitor, even a lazy second-rate one.'

'Yes. Aren't you supposed to tell someone? Lawyers have to be regulated, don't they? Professional misconduct or that sort of thing? At least a fine.'

'Johnny reckoned he could get away with it and decided not to tell them.'

'But he told you.' I didn't imagine I would sound sour. I sound sour.

'He had to tell me because he needs driving around sometimes. I'm just the chauffeur.'

'And Andrew,' I realise suddenly. 'He wouldn't want to tell his father. Andrew would be all over it.'

I've spoken out loud.

'Yes,' agrees Anna, 'you guess right. That's just the sort of thing about Johnny that drives Andrew completely mad.' She puts her head on one side. 'Right, any more for any more?'

'Completely full,' I say regretfully and a bit later we split the bill, swap phone numbers and then Anna takes the bus back to Leith.

I'd forgotten that evenings like that could be fun. I'd forgotten a lot of things – and been wrong about a lot of things. Anna mainly: I had imagined someone who didn't actually exist. Poring over Anna's Facebook and Instagram profile I had created a whole new persona; I had created a villain where I ought to have just left a blank. The apps hadn't told me the truth about her, they had merely allowed me to assume something.

Feeling more cheerful than I have done in weeks, I stroll back to Dalkeith Road. The evening is then destroyed by a text from Andrew which pings through just as I am getting into bed.

Playing hard to get?

40

When my phone rings the next day, I feel terrified that it is Andrew, following up on the message that I have been ignoring. But it's Marion, the old postie in Torcastle. She tells me that Nora was found wandering on the road yesterday afternoon, with no idea of where she was.

'Perhaps she was just walking.'

Marion's silence confirms what a silly thing this was to say. Nora doesn't just walk for the fun of it.

'Who found her?'

'The farmer. By chance. You need to come. She was a bit confused.'

'I'll come at the weekend,' I promise. Poor Nora. I'm looking at the trains from Glasgow when Anna messages to say thanks for the curry evening. I text back, telling her about my aunt and that I'll be going to Fort William on Friday. Anna replies: Want company? I could see Dad. I think about it for a while. It's almost as if I've become so used to being on my own, the thought of company is a little unnerving. I haven't known Anna – liked her – for long enough, surely. But it's also true that being with Anna is good. It could make it bearable, even fun, the train journey would go quickly. It makes sense to go together. I ought to say yes, and be grateful. I message back. Yes, why not.

In the end, Anna says she will drive because it's cheaper and because she likes the idea of a road trip. We then text constantly about things like who has a thermos and where we might stop for a break and if we should bring wellies and thermals. And then it's funny when we realise how we sound, she sends all those emojis that used to annoy me, saying that anyone would think we were journeying to the North Pole for six months. We're both trying hard to put the best of ourselves across to the other. It occurs to me, when I'm waiting for her to come and pick me up on Friday afternoon, that there is a sense of empowerment here too. Johnny – whose silence I have miraculously not been noticing so much (when did that start?) – is the one being left out. Anna has reported that she is not speaking to him since the Valentine's Day humiliation, so he has no idea that, quite bizarrely, we are in constant communication. He would not like it, we know that. He had never encouraged a friendship at the pub, he was probably simply flattered by our mutual antipathy. He would feel threatened, I think.

And there is nothing like a four-hour car journey to make or break it. I had guessed this and even made contingency plans to return by train on Monday if it turned out to be necessary. If the outward journey ended in bloodshed. But, for the first half of the drive, we are in something like carnival mode. We disagree over music, stop for Coke and crisps, and chat – really talk – for most of it. (Well, I talk and Anna shouts quite a lot.) Not about the Strachans this time. About us, and school and friends, and Edinburgh. Unlike me, Anna has always surrounded herself with people. Even though we had similar teenage years with either entirely absent parents or, like hers, partially absent, we had chosen, or been given, different ways of coping. Anna, gregarious and scintillating, never found being social difficult.

'I was just shy,' I tell her. 'A bit awkward.'

'I knew people at school like you,' she says sagely. 'The ones who hid behind books. They never put themselves out there, and never tried anything out.'

'I did,' I protest.

'Bet you weren't in any sports teams.'

'I bet you were,' I tell her. 'I bet you were captain of the girls' rugby.'

She looks at me sideways. 'Nah, should have been though. Too busy smoking and snogging behind the shed. So when you weren't off hiking somewhere, what did you do for fun?'

'For fun?' I echo. I had never consciously or unconsciously searched for fun. By the time I was sixteen, 'fun' had seemed a trivial and juvenile pastime. I had always assumed that one day something more meaningful than fun would find me. 'I'm not sure I had fun.'

'We will remedy that, back in Edinburgh,' she promises, gurgling her husky laughter and leans forward, concentrating as dusk begins to fall around us on the A9. We have agreed that we will stay Friday night in a B&B together and go our separate ways till Sunday. Then Anna, who doesn't want to spend too long with her father, is going to come and stay with us in Torcastle before we leave on Monday morning.

By the time we approach Fort William it is dark. We leave the city lights behind us at Neptune's Staircase on the Caledonian Canal, following the road to Muirshearlich and soon enough the blackness becomes a different sort of dark. Our phones glow and then Anna's battery goes. Soon we will be out of signal as well, and mobile-free for the weekend. A good thing for me, given Anna's manic Instagramming habit. But she has grown quiet as we've got closer.

The road becomes single track for a while. 'God, am I going back or is this moron? Did we just pass one of those passing places?' She reverses, cursing softly and the oncoming car glides past. 'Remind me why I'm here? My dad hasn't asked to see me for months.'

'You think he might give you a tenner for your birthday,' I remind her, and I can see her half-smile in the dark.

'Yeah, that's it. If I'm lucky, he'll cover the cost of the petrol.'

We go straight to sleep that night, tired. And I suppose both of us are anxious, for different reasons, about the morning. It dawns with customary low cloud and drizzle and we have coffee together in the B&B and arrange where and when to meet on Sunday.

Unexpectedly, Nora is waiting for me with Marion, a hopeless figure in the rain. The sight of her, frail and hunched, pinches at my chest. Her lined face, the colour of a pale bruise, is vacant and unwelcoming but she lets me take her arm and we walk to Marion's car together. The hills are slumped over each other like a once-vibrant cloth, the purple hue of summer long wrung out. I see one stag, and then another, dotted like prophecies on the bracken, watching us. Along the Caledonian Canal, the almost perfectly straight canal between the east and west coast of Scotland. There is a distinct bend at Moy, near Torcastle, the one I had told Johnny about. The bend that curves around Gormshuil's burial ground. The pine trees nod and swish in the wind, the broomsticks to put out forest fires still tied to their ancient trunks, as they have been for decades. Nora, chin against chest, nods off.

We turn down the Dark Mile. The loch, like grey silk, is flat; the road is undulating and bumpy. Past the old post office and then to Nora's cottage, the grey-stoned house of my teenage years. Marion helps Nora in, muttering under the canopy of rain. She says goodbye in the kitchen. I put the kettle on and leave Nora sitting at the table while I take my case upstairs. One of the steps is higher than the rest and I stumble over it, as I always do. It's cold in my small room and there are mice droppings next to a teddy bear in the corner. I still have the pink eiderdown on my bed and the faded remains of my teenage years but it's all the cheery, fake-looking stuff. It's like I was five when I left; there is nothing of the angry girl in this room, a shabby dolls' house of a room. A chunk of my life is missing. I pick up my hairbrush and the small mirror, tattooed with fairy stickers. There is a red hair stuck in its bristles, shorter but brighter. Nora used to worry my red hair was a sign of temper. But I never used to have a temper. I pull the hair loose and wind it round my finger until the tip of it is white.

There is a grainy photograph on the chest, of my parents, taken by Nora one Christmas lunch here twenty years ago. I didn't put it there. Dad is standing behind Mum with his hands heavy on her shoulders. They are both wearing party hats. I turn it face down and stand at the window. Ben Nevis, with its white-capped summit fills the frames.

When I come down again, Nora is still sitting in her kitchen. It is more squalid than ever. The room looks out on to the farmer's field and some Highland cows have broken their fence and are in Nora's mossy garden, nudging around muddy washing on the line and the old wooden swing. Nora doesn't seem to have noticed. The other visible neighbouring building is the old post office we passed, which was finally closed a few years ago. Marion lives in Banavie by Neptune's Staircase now. So it's hardly a neighbour, just an empty building that reminds us things used to be different.

'Hows you, then?'

'I'm fine, Nora. It's you who got everyone worried.'

'It's a fuss about nothing.'

'We need to decide what you want to do. Where you want to go. Marion says you can't live here on your own any more.'

She turns her face to the wall.

Nora's life has not been a happy one and she has the expression of someone who would like now to shake it off. Perhaps she is thinking about Alan. His waders had filled with water when he was fishing in the River Lochy one day, and the current had been too strong. Then her sister went to live with her new husband, leaving her alone; and then they died and I came along to live with her and remind her of them every day. She didn't choose anything that happened to her and neither could she do anything about it. She couldn't hand her cards back. The bench that the community clubbed together to buy in Alan's memory is covered in graffiti and seagull shit now. Everyone seems to have forgotten about Alan. I don't think she has: despite most of her memory unravelling like small kites in the wind, I think she has held onto this strand.

She's only seventy-five but she seems ninety years old today. She asks me where her sister Jean is. I tell her she's gone to the shops but when Nora realises that she hasn't, that her sister went to France and was killed on the way, she shuts her eyes. She doesn't ask about Johnny, the man I stayed in Geneva with. She won't remember hearing about him; to her it's like he never even existed. I wonder what that feels like, not knowing that Johnny exists.

'Tea, Nora?'

'Fine. And then maybe some gardening.'

'If you like.' I put the tea bags in her pot. 'Are you doing any sewing? Have you any work on?'

'No. Some curtains there need taking up.'

'That's something.'

'I don't know whose they are.'

'The sewing machine looks like it's gathering dust.'

'Well, what if it is,' says Nora.

Well, exactly.

Later, Nora calls me from the kitchen. I am in the sitting room, searching the hollows of the room for evidence of the others, for anyone at all, and for some affection, some laughter. There is not a speck of either. Perhaps the house can't take any more and has drawn a veil over itself and its melancholy ghosts. Nora is saying something from next door and her voice is indecipherable. 'What, Nora?' I say to the wounded room. 'What is it?'

In the kitchen, she is shredding a bit of paper.

'Are you OK? What is it?'

Tears start to fall out of her eyes.

'Oh, Nora, please don't cry,' and I try to take her in my arms but she is as stiff and unyielding as the mountains.

After a second or two, she shoves me away. 'Spilt milk. No point.'

'Do you mean Mum and Dad?'

'I don't know. I don't know what I mean.'

'I miss them too.'

'They ought not to have gone. It was only because they needed a holiday, they needed to get away.'

I leave her alone then and take myself outside into a black and clear night. She might as well have added, 'from you.' An army of stars has blown across the sky and chased the evening cloud to the sea in the west. I can hear the owls calling and one swoops past, pale above the shadow of the pine tree. The waterfall crashes through the hills in the distance and closer is the seductive sound of the shallows lapping over the Cat Pool. My parents' grave is not far. They were buried together on a lonely hill outside Fort William.

Another long day passes. There's no signal here so I don't ever turn my phone on, which is strange after the long attachment to it but also a respite of sorts. Nora never does do any gardening. She wants me to light her coal fire and put baked beans on the stove for lunch, but that's all. I try and talk to her about a nursing home, about possibilities, but it's hard to do when she can't see to the end of her meal, let alone the end of her days. She can't follow conversations or threads, she can't get anywhere. There is no connection to be made between her existence and the next minute. Life in a nursing home is too hard to imagine.

The only other person I see is the farmer, who herds his cows back through the hole in the fence on Sunday afternoon. He comes towards Nora's door scowling, but when he sees my face in the window he hesitates, and then returns to fixing the fence.

Later, he decides to stop me on the road. 'Nora's not well, is she?'

'No.'

'Who's going to be responsible for her then, if you're going back down south? It was me who found her wandering.'

'I'm not asking you to look after her. Don't worry.'

'That's not what I meant.'

He may have wanted to say more. I move away.

235

I start walking to meet Anna. An ancient blue Independent Scotland sign from three years ago is still at the end of the road. *YES*. The sign looks incongruous up here in its isolation, with the knowledge of defeat hanging about its frame. It doesn't look as though it could ever have believed in itself. I sit down to wait for Anna next to it.

41

I'm so pleased to see her. She immediately makes me laugh by brandishing 'not one, but TWO' twenty quid notes. 'Happy birthday to me.' She's bought us a bottle of wine and cigarettes for Nora and is more cheerful again. 'Dad was OK,' she says happily in the car. 'I'm glad I came. Thanks.'

Anna is brilliant with Nora. She manages to be kind without being patronising. When I have thought about bringing Johnny here, it was always cringing slightly, imagining him assiduously polite, judgemental and condescending all at the same time. Anna is just the same as she always is and something thaws in the cottage. She even makes Nora smile once when she announces, 'Thank God, a bloody smoker. I think we're the last two left on the planet,' and she lights them both a Silk Cut and grins through the smoke at her. Johnny, wheezing, would have declared himself asphyxiated by them both. Fastidious, he probably wouldn't have wanted to touch anything whereas Anna fills the sink and washes out the cat bowls that she keeps tripping over. Afterwards, she announces she is on a roll and wipes all the surfaces down and sweeps the floor, so I clean the fridge and then mop. Nora and her cats watch us.

'You'll keep those out tonight, won't you,' I remind Nora. 'All ten of them.'

Her mouth thins. 'The temperature's going to drop right down. There are only six now anyway.'

'They'll be fine in here, won't they?' asks Anna, rinsing her cloth at the sink. 'Don't be mean.'

'They'll be on, sorry – in – your bed before you know it,' I warn. Anna is on the camp bed in the sitting room.

'Oh, I don't mind,' she says gaily. 'What about that wine I bought?'

'I'm not much of a drinker,' says Nora.

'Neither am I,' Anna tells her, unscrewing the cap and pouring three enormous glasses. 'Here, happy days.'

I turn to the fridge for a second and hide in its depths before turning back.

Nora stares at her glass for a second and then carefully, slowly, raises it to Anna's. 'Cheers.'

I put the chicken in the oven to roast and Anna peels the potatoes. Nora gives us instruction from her seat at the table but she nods off before long and Anna and I take our wine into the sitting room and I put some more coal onto the fire. It glows and steams and we are quiet for a while, listening to the sound of the fire and of the waterfall in the distance.

'Do you miss him?'

I sink to my knees and hold out my hands to the orange-tinged coals to warm them. 'Yes.'

'Even though you know what he's like now?'

I sigh to myself. 'I don't know.' The heart wants what the heart wants and I'd got used to it just being what it was. 'Maybe what I mean is that I miss the person I thought he was. I thought he was someone else, you see.'

'Hard to let go of that.'

'Yes.'

Anna pours herself another glass and, changing the subject, I say that my friend Tam thinks I'll find someone else.

She snorts. 'It's not so bloody easy, I should know. It's a full-time job looking for a man. We need to get out there. Go on some dates.'

Without thinking, I say, 'That sounds like the sort of thing Andrew would say.'

'Andrew who?'

'Oh, no one you know. It's what they all say, isn't it?'

'Is he single?' and she laughs. I get up from my knees and Nora, woken from her nap comes in.

'Hear the waterfall?' she asks. 'There's been so much rain this year.'

'That noise is incredible,' Anna says.

'It's Caig Falls,' says Nora, 'the waterfall. I'll tell you a story about that waterfall.'

I know what's coming. 'Nora,' I warn, 'please don't bore Anna with any stories. Especially not creepy ones about vengeful witches.'

'Sounds brilliant.' Anna waves my dismay away. 'Which story?'

'I don't like it,' I insist. 'It used to give me nightmares.'

'Ssh,' says Anna. 'Tell the story, Nora.'

Encouraged by Anna's enthusiasm, Nora clears her throat. 'Many years ago, the chief of the clan, Lochiel, was leaving for battle. He was hugely blessed. He had a beautiful wife and an heir. He owned the land from Fort Augustus to Spean Bridge and many glens besides. He wanted for nothing but he could not control the neighbouring clan who refused to live in peace as he wanted. One fine winter morning, when the snow was glistening white and the sky was blue, the chief set out with his men to try and defeat the Clan McIntosh once and for all. As they marched over the hill towards Inverlochy, they passed Gormshuil's cottage. Overcome by superstition,

239

the chief stopped and asked the witch what he should do in order to ensure victory. The witch thought for a while about whether she would help him but she was captivated by his longing for victory and she did not think for long.

'"I will promise slaughter," she told him. "I will grant you McIntoshes dead and dying in their hundreds. I predict that their blood will run red from the hills and stain Loch Linnhe red. I swear that they will trouble the Clan Cameron no more."'

'The chief roared with pleasure at such a promise and it did not occur to him to be concerned about her blood lust. Gormshuil too was glad and shared the last of her wine with him but as he turned to leave having feasted on her cockerels and filled his flask from the waterfall near the Cat Pool, she began to wonder if she should not be rewarded for her generosity. It was not the first time after all that she had given Lochiel her protection and she had never yet asked to be repaid.

'"What will you give me in return?" she asked the chief.

The chief, well-fed and warm with the wine and sun, spread his arms wide and told the witch, "Anything."'

'Again, Gormshuil considered him, and she considered her options. It was a lonely life in the Highlands, and this was a handsome chief. She thought that perhaps she deserved him. She was not conventionally pretty but she had a certain beauty and not many men passed this way. She did not consider her request to be so fantastical.

'"When you have won your battle and the McIntoshes are strewn over the hills, you must come back this way. In two weeks from now, when the sun has slunk away to the west, I will be waiting for you and you will be mine for the night."'

'Now Lochiel loved his wife, and he loved his family but he did not for a minute hesitate. He wanted to win in battle and he imagined that a night with her was not a hardship and he looked into her eyes and granted her wish without a further thought. And so their deal was sealed.'

'Oh my,' says Anna, wide-eyed. 'Trouble ahead.'

Nora goes on. 'One week passed and Gormshuil took the form of one of her cats and raced to the battlefield where she witnessed the defeat of the Cameron enemy, just as she had foretold. Lochiel took the head of his rival and speared it to the boundary post and McIntoshes all over shook with fear and promised never to cross into Cameron country again. Back home, Gormshuil prepared for the return of her victorious chief.

'Heights,' Nora says. 'It was from the top of a very great height that Gormshuil watched the winding road. The Dark Mile – the same road that had first brought him to her. She waited and watched, waited for him to come again, as he had promised. And she waited, not for two weeks, not for two months, not even for six. For two years she waited, remembering the charm of his smile and the emphatic nature of his oath, and so refusing to believe that he had forgotten her. She didn't leave her vantage point from the top of the mighty waterfall for even one hour and she grew thin from starvation, even though one by one she ate her beloved cats who offered themselves to her in pity and shame. Gnawing on their meagre bones, she lived cowering on the rocks, listening to the rush of the water and her life cascading away with it. The man she could always have done without, the emptiness of his promise she could not bear.

'She was very weak but one morning she was roused from the rocks by the sound of a child playing. She managed to crawl down to the bottom where she found a small boy laughing in the shallow water. She watched him from the caves, instantly recognising the boy as the chieftain's son. So not him, but another had come in his place, and by now, of course, Gormshuil's all-consuming love had become something else. So she was immune to the child's blond curls and innocent eyes, and entirely immune to his shrieks of horror as she limped towards him with a rock in her hand. She bludgeoned the child to death. His mother came running on hearing his screams, and Gormshuil summoned the last of her power to strike the woman dead as well as she knelt there, cradling the bloody remains of her son. She left the bodies where they had fallen for Lochiel to find, but before she disappeared, she carved her name into the dead so that the chief would know she had taken her revenge and never forget her again. Scarred for remembrance.'

'Crikey,' says Anna, swallowing. 'Nasty.'

'But effective,' Nora tells her. 'For years afterwards chieftains on their way to battle, or even just passing, wouldn't go through Torcastle without leaving Gormshuil's ancestors gifts to ensure safe passage for them and their families.'

'Enough,' I say firmly. 'Supper time.'

Nora takes no notice. 'When the witch had killed Lochiel's child and wife she threw herself from the top of the waterfall and died. You know, the workers refused to build through her burial ground at Moy and risk more fury so they went around it.'

'It's true,' I say, despite myself. 'As late as 1805, in a sixty-mile long waterway, the construction faltered because of superstition.'

We are all silent then, staring at the fire, the coals now blazing, a crateful of orange eyes. The waterfall crashes down the hill behind the cottage.

Our supper is simple and delicious. Nora's head nods off and on her chest throughout. Anna, growing more mellow with the wine, reveals some tenderness. She is more patient and gentle with Nora than I am. When I do the washing up she helps Nora up the stairs to her bed.

'Where's all her stuff?' asks Anna when she comes back. 'It looks as though her bedroom has been packed up.'

I pass her a mug of tea and she picks up the tea towel. 'No. Not packed up. She just doesn't have much stuff. She doesn't want or need much, I wouldn't have thought.'

Anna stares at me open-mouthed. 'But there's nothing there. A photo, a book and a chest.'

'She doesn't believe in buying or keeping. She only has what she needs. She always says she'll travel onwards light.'

Anna can't believe it. 'But she must have been here years. It's impossible not to accumulate junk. Isn't it?' She looks uncertain. 'My gran couldn't throw away a cardboard box. She kept our old hamster wheel, for crying out loud.'

'She wants to make it easy for me when she dies.'

'Cheerful conversations you two must have. A riot.'

'The cottage is only leased from the estate for her lifetime and she doesn't want a fuss. I should be grateful.' I look at Anna sternly and she laughs.

'OK, OK. Each to their own. Here, help me finish this bottle. Is there really no Wi-Fi or signal here?'

'Not even a smidgen.'

Anna puts her phone down. 'It's a relief, kind of, isn't it.'

'Definitely.'

The conversation makes me think about Nora's death when I am in my faded pink and white bedroom later that night. There was a lot to do after my parents died – as deaths go it was quite public, and the papers called it a tragedy. There was administration and lawyers to deal with and so much detail. I don't think there will be any detail to Nora's death because she has made sure that she will die how she has lived; with minimal fuss. She hasn't any money or savings and as Anna had noticed, her physical possessions are few and far between. She is not a hoarder. The outer trappings and garments of her life – what she kept around her and what most gather in order to sustain immortality and stave off death – she hadn't bothered with. It chills me to think how nothing will remain of her when she's gone. Nothing – Nora's legacy is absolutely nothing. No widower, no children, no house, no savings and then she is gone. There will be no sense of her, no comforting smells, no warm or affectionate last letter, no wishes. Nothing at all, except perhaps the cats. The six who are left.

Ah, I think, turning over and closing my eyes. The cats have reminded me of something. Nora will leave her stories. It is I who hasn't even stories to leave.

The morning reveals the night's half-hearted attempt at snow. It barely covers anything but has changed the colour of the brown landscape so that for just an hour or two, until it melts, the light outside the cottage is luminescent. High on the distant mountains, white hoods have been pulled soft over the summits. Anna washes in my cracked basin staring out of the window. Between her and Ben Nevis, there is nothing but albino bracken, a sliver of road, the wide grey loch and the plump hills. 'Beautiful,' she breathes.

We go for a walk after coffee because Anna wants to see the waterfall that makes all the noise and that Gormshuil drowned in. We meander through delicate bracken that splinters beneath our feet, cobwebs frozen across our path and between branches. The sky is ashen above us. We follow the noise – it is like thunder – but the actual falls, when we arrive, although loud, are strangely elegant; the way the water sprays and mists into the air, droplets suspended mid-arc, thrown out against the pinkish sky like watery cobwebs. Everything reaching, stretching across the chasm like a corps de ballet. We watch the water and its violent, delicate dance, the silvery spray like the bracken underfoot.

We turn around after a while, and when we get back Nora is awake. Anna's car is thick with ice and she turns the engine on and then Nora boils the kettle. Anna pours half of it over the windscreen and Nora fills her thermos with coffee. I promise to come again soon and Anna and Nora exchange fond farewells. We are on the road to Edinburgh by eight o'clock.

'Thank you for being kind to my aunt.'

'Oh shush,' Anna tuts. 'Please. It's hardly difficult.'

'It sort of is. She's not the easiest.'

There's a small pause, and then Anna says, 'My gran was like her. Worse, towards the end. There's no point treating them any different, you just got to get on with it.'

Anna just gets on with it. 'I want to say thanks, anyway.'

She quickly takes her eyes off the road to dart a grin at me. 'OK. I loved her story, by the way. She hadn't forgotten that, had she.'

'No,' I agree wryly.

'It's brilliant. Bloody love that witch of Moy.'

'It's a gruesome tale,' and then I turn my head away and watch the mountains pass us by, realising whose words I have repeated. 'The wrong people get hurt.'

She shakes her head. 'Collateral damage. So what? She didn't just do nothing, that's the main thing.'

But what if doing something is worse than nothing? Sometimes nothing is better. I'm only just starting to see — too late — that inactivity doesn't always mean passivity. It might mean acceptance. But I couldn't do that. Instead, I fell into the trap of storytelling. The wrong people get hurt.

42

I had pushed Andrew to the back of my mind during the few days I had been away with Anna. I'd hoped that he would give up. I daren't see him alone and now I just want to back off from the Strachans.

His next message is on Tuesday afternoon, and he gets straight to the point. Ellen planning on inviting you over this Friday. Say you're busy, and I'll come to you.

I don't know what to do. I think about this message for the rest of the day and finally decide on what I imagine will be the best option for everyone.

I reply, just saying Sure and sure enough, the invitation from Ellen comes the next day. Molly's inbox has one message and the notification, once a source of such gleeful anticipation, fills me with dread now. I tell her that sounds fine. And then I arrange a separate meeting with Andrew. Where and when? is his charming way of sorting it out. I give him the address of a pub in Newington and tell him to go there at seven.

This way, by the time Friday comes, I can go to St Bernard's Row and be quite sure of only seeing Ellen. And she opens the door smiling, breathily saying immediately, 'It's only you and me, Molly. Andrew's had to work late.'

'He seems to do that rather a lot.'

'I'm glad. I encouraged it, to be honest.' She turns into the kitchen and I slowly follow. 'He's in a filthy mood because Johnny's done his usual and simply turned up, and put his car in our garage. Last night or first thing, I've no idea but Andrew is livid.'

'Why doesn't he just ask?' The endless liberties he takes. *Why hadn't they ever taught him right from wrong?*

'Beats me,' she says, elbows on island, chin in hands. 'Beats me. Probably because he knew Andrew would say no. Serves me right for not getting the garage door fixed when it broke last month, you can open it just by pulling. He wouldn't have needed the buzzer.'

'Hang on,' I say, momentarily sidetracked, thinking about this. 'Johnny drove his car to your garage?'

'Yes,' she says. 'Who else? Without asking, I repeat.'

'Oh. Um – where's your car?' Just for something to say.

'On the road. With a permit. We use it too often to bother going in and out of the garage. Which is rather a tight space.' I suppose she must mistake my poker face for boredom. 'Sorry! I am dull. What can I get you? It's too late for tea, isn't it?'

Effortless. That's the word for Ellen. She always gives the impression that her beautiful house, her ease and her own appearance is effortless. She has spread the Friday papers around her book and the two lamps with the pineapple-style bases are lit. And the Christmas candles from Geneva duty free. It's a conventional, urban scene, imitated by hundreds of other middle-class, bicker-filled marriages up and down Stockbridge. But Ellen is the centrepiece here, with her seemingly effortless elegance and her brown eyes mischievous, only it's not without effort. It's not real. I know that now.

Ellen pulls a glass towards her; the oily residue around the inside revealing that this drink is not her first.

'Do you know what, Ellen, I won't have anything. I won't stay long. There's something I've got to tell you. I tried before, but you wouldn't listen.'

As if on cue, my mobile pings. It must be just after seven. I clear my throat.

'Is something the matter? What is it?'

Another ping. So stupid of me not to give him something to do. 'Sorry. I'm just going to turn this off.'

'I think I'll have a drink even if you won't,' she says warily. 'If you don't mind.'

She refills the glass with the open bottle of Sauvignon Blanc on the island and I send a quick message before putting the phone away. Got held up. On my way.

Deep breath. 'I've been wrestling with something, Ellen. Something I haven't been sure whether to tell you or not. But we're friends, right? And friends ought to tell each other things.'

'What sort of things? What is it, Molly?' She has become concerned. It almost makes me change my mind. 'About you?'

'Not about me. I'm fine. I'm really sorry. I found something out about Andrew that I think you should know.'

She doesn't blink, rather she puts the glass down and says, without taking her eyes from me: 'Haven't we been through this?'

'No.'

She sighs. 'OK. What have you found out about Andrew?'

'That he's been having an affair.' There. I've done it. I've said it.

Ellen's polite expression struggles to hold itself.

'With Amy Desmond.'

'Don't be ridiculous.' She actually laughs. 'That's absurd.' She is relieved.

249

'Yes, the pharmacist.' She hadn't said, *Andrew would never betray me.*

'Well, it's just nonsense,' she says again. 'Are you mad?'

'It's not nonsense. I'm sure it's true.'

She sounds colder now. 'It's blatantly untrue. It's actually impossible.'

'It is possible.'

She stares at me very steadily, cradling the wine glass and then downs it. 'You've no idea how ridiculous you're being.' She fills the glass again.

'I'm sorry. But it's true. She had some surgery. A breast augmentation—'

'That's enough.' She slams the glass down. 'Don't you dare say her name, don't you dare.'

'I thought you would want to know.'

But she holds up an imperious hand. 'Who do you think you are, Molly? Why should you decide what you *think* I want to know? You don't know anything about me, or my family who I love dearly. You hardly know me, for God's sake.'

The look on her face is terrifying. She is pale but absolutely in control. I had thought she would fall apart. I had thought there would be tears.

'Andrew's and my marriage is our business. You know nothing about it. You know nothing about anyone and what they've been through. You have no clue. It's laughable that you should meet us one minute and the next minute decide you have some right to nose through our private life. To break up our marriage. How dare you?'

'I wasn't nosing through . . .' Then I stop. 'I just thought you should know.'

'You have added two and two and made ten. You silly child. And silly me. I don't know you at all, not really.'

I think that it's only then that the full magnitude of my deception hits me. I had honestly believed that it was something to do with me, that I was involved in their life, in their family, and that I had an obligation to tell Ellen what I had discovered. I had succeeded in deceiving even myself on this front and she's right, its risible that I had envisaged her gratitude. Now I see myself through her eyes. I'm just a younger, lonely woman they met, randomly. I don't really mean anything to her.

I turn for the door, done. I'm done. But she isn't.

'And, by the way, Molly, get a life of your own. It was very sad the way you attached yourself to us. And don't flatter yourself by imagining Andrew was ever interested in you, just because he gave you a lift once. We weren't entirely convinced you weren't gay. I wondered at the theatre.' Her gaze is absolutely withering. This is the Eleanor of Aquitaine that I had glimpsed before. This is the hard, regal Ellen that Anna knows. It brings me up short and I stop before I get to the door.

'I didn't just imagine he was interested in me,' I say quietly. 'Even whilst he was busy with Amy Desmond, he found time to harass me. And probably a few others.'

'It's not true,' she says simply. 'He is just a friendly, charming and very married man.'

'It is true,' I tell her flatly, 'and you know it, deep down. You know that Andrew's a menace and that's probably why you kept such a careful eye on me from the start. Even why you befriended me, perhaps.'

'I didn't have to keep an eye on you,' she says, shaking her head.

I take my phone out and with horribly trembling fingers, open Andrew's messages. 'Here,' I say, walking towards her, holding it out to her. 'Here, look. Here's your proof.

This pub, it's where he is at this very moment. He's waiting for me. He is not working late. I doubt he ever is.'

She refuses to look. She turns away towards the sink. I put my phone to her face and she smacks it away. She says, 'Go,' sucking in her breath. 'Can you please get out of my house.'

I go. Standing, shaking, in the street, I have to ask myself if I would ever have gone if I had known it would end like this. It's nearly half past seven, and it's dark. Andrew will have been waiting for me for over half an hour. The messages on my phone are all from him, asking where I am, is this the right pub and so on. He has been stood up and dobbed in. He will be so angry.

I double lock all my doors. I turn my phone off and sleep badly.

Nothing from Andrew or Ellen in the morning. More for something to do than anything else, I call Anna.

'I've been thinking about Johnny's driving ban.'

'Why?' she says. It sounds as if she is crunching toast.

'No reason really. Do you think he takes any notice of it?'

She swallows. 'Well, I'd say not but for the fact that I drive him around so often. He doesn't need to ignore it seeing as he has such a willing chauffeur.'

'Have you driven him recently?'

'No,' she says, 'I haven't driven him anywhere for a while, but I did actually see him on Thursday. If that's what you're asking. First time in a while.'

'Did you?' All thoughts of the car disappear. The night before last? She sounds off-hand. Casual. 'I thought you weren't speaking to him.'

'Nothing to report. He just popped in after a late night. Stayed a bit.' Too casual, cool even. 'Didn't want to go home just yet, that sort of thing.'

'Oh,' I say, flatly, and she doesn't respond or rise.

'So – what's the plan? Let's not talk about him. Let's make a fun plan . . .'

The fun has gone out of the chat. The point about knowing Johnny had driven his car to his mum's seems irrelevant. We talk vaguely for a while and never end up making a plan. When the call ends, I open the window and lie on my bed with a breeze stirring the pages of my book, and a WhatsApp message in front of my eyes.

43

I'm still wondering on Sunday, and I'm still wondering on Monday. I haven't heard anything more from Anna. I haven't heard from anyone. And then this morning, a beguiling and beautiful Tuesday at the end of February, I log onto Molly's hotmail account when I'm at work and Ellen's name flashes up. I'm so relieved, I forget to brace myself, so there's no warning. For an exquisite instant, I'm just happy she got in touch.

I remember that it was immediately obvious that it was a round robin. Given Ellen's and mine last meeting, no doubt I was only included in it by mistake. I remember that sunlight was streaming through the window in reception and made the computer screen misty.

I remember there were details too, surrounding the main message. That the family have spent the weekend planning. That it will take place this summer. That it was the most wonderful, joyous surprise. In Sweden. They are going to celebrate on Wednesday evening with them.

> Romance is in the air. My secretive, darling son has announced that he and Isa are getting married! Isa is a beautiful and talented solicitor from Sweden and Johnny says that she is the one.

The email wasn't even meant for me.

I leave the reception desk, sleepwalking through the sunbeams. I sit for a while in the ladies' toilets in a trance. And then it's as if a guillotine begins to rush towards me, something I can no longer get away from, and I have to get up off the floor. The truth is as unavoidable, and as lethal as the axe on a guillotine.

I'd begun to picture him as too immature to ever settle down. I'd begun to assume that he didn't want to be with anyone for any length of time at all. I think I had believed in my heart that none of us were meant for him. That I could live with him not wanting to marry me as long as he didn't want to marry anyone. He wasn't wired that way. I think that I had let myself believe this so my heartache could be composed mainly of sadness, that I could be conventionally broken-hearted, to a certain extent. And now it feels as though the plaster has been ripped off and there is nothing conventional, or ordinary, about the rotting mess underneath. He is going to spend the rest of his life with Issy. Issy is the one.

Everybody at work avoids me. They all assume the careful expressions that were reserved for me when he first disappeared after Christmas. When I'm able to leave, I go without a word to anyone. I only just manage to push myself onto the bus. Other commuters, slick with perspiration and bad-temper, must smell my stale bitterness and the fresh panic. All try to move away. I close my eyes. The soreness, the faded imprint of the ache deep in my chest is resurfacing as if no time at all had passed.

By the time I get home, Molly's inbox has been inundated with 'reply alls' from the recipients of Ellen's news, each one more profuse and gushing than the last. I delete Molly's hotmail account. There's a message from Anna to my email that gives me the same news.

From: Anna Stewart [mailto:AnnaStewart@hotmail.com]
Sent: Tuesday 28th February 6:07pm
To: skyegrant@btinternet123.com
Subject:

Hi. I don't know how you're going to take this. You probably won't even believe it – I know I can't. Johnny told me (via text message) that he proposed to Issy and that she said yes. Sorry to tell you, just hope you're OK about it. We'll both have to move onwards and upwards now, eh?

X

I message her mobile. Can we meet tomorrow?

Sorry, really really sorry. Got to go to his for drinks, don't want to but already said I would. He'll think it's odd if I don't go. Sorry.

I stare blankly at the mobile.

I hope that Issy breaks your heart. I hope she is as difficult as Anna says. She must be determined. She has caught you, at any rate. What has she offered you that we did not? Independence? Perhaps she is actually the boss of you, perhaps she is in charge and this is where I went wrong. Perhaps she doesn't flatter you. Perhaps she scoffed when you suggested the two-metre rule. Maybe she even laughed at you. Perhaps she pokes fun at you and her ridicule is what does it for you. Adoration, clearly, did not.

Aside from the snow globe, the only other thing I have to remind me of you is your inhaler, carelessly left with me in Geneva one day. I took it to the theatre to show Ellen and help cement a connection. I throw it away, wondering how Ellen and Andrew are dealing with the fabulous news alongside their own, less fabulous situation? They can't know Issy well. Do they like her at all? Are they putting their marital differences aside in order to celebrate their only son settling down? Can I even be sure that Ellen questioned Andrew about Molly? Perhaps she ignored what I'd told her about Andrew waiting for me. How is all this working in the Strachan household? The silence in my flat begins to fill with them all.

There is no message from you. I shake my snow globe, hard, as if doing so might elicit something, anything from you. There is nothing from you, of course. By now, you are well and truly gone.

44

March

I reach for my heartache in the morning, expecting it wet and leaden on the pillow beside me but at some point in the night it has been replaced with the hard edge of fury. I let the rage simmer; it's certainly easier to focus on that instead of the constantly drip-fed agony I have been living off since Johnny left. I hold on to it. I've had enough. I have let myself be fooled by someone so horribly duplicitous for too long now. And what sort of person can become engaged so quickly after being unfaithful with other women? I realise that finally, this Wednesday morning, I am in the mood for a fight.

It doesn't take me more than twenty minutes to get to Brunswick Street and my anger has deepened by the time I arrive. What an idiot I'd been to go back, more than once. To imagine that I ever meant anything at all to him, to make excuses for myself and to be so unbelievably, completely pathetic. I hit the doorbell of number 15. I had imagined, I don't know why, that he would be alone. Issy Karlsson opens the door.

She is tall and blonde and her blue eyes flicker over me. 'Yes?'

So what. On I go. 'I'm here to see Johnny.'

She doesn't blink. She turns away, yelling, 'Johnny? Someone to see you.' She has a clipped Scandinavian accent.

Johnny looks upset to see me in the door. He's wearing a suit and he has a piece of toast in one hand and a glass of orange juice in the other, (his usual breakfast) but my addition to his Wednesday morning has brought a heavy disappointment to his face. As if I have taken myself off the naughty step without his permission. That, and something else. He looks tired. There are dark circles under slitty eyes.

He glances behind into his hall. 'What are you doing here?'

'Hello again, Johnny. Isn't the question, what's *she* doing here? Or more to the point, what are we *both* doing here, on alternate weeks?'

'Skye,' he says. 'I understand you might want to talk. But not now.' He is weary. I had expected him buoyed up but he is deflated.

I don't care. I don't give a shit. 'Definitely now. Why not now?' I stick my hands in my skirt pockets. 'Where's your girlfriend gone? Sorry, I mean fiancée. Doesn't she want to have a chat too?'

'No. She really doesn't. Please, Skye.'

I ignore him. 'Congratulations really are in order then?'

'Yes. How did you find out?'

'Does it matter?'

'Only that I might have told you myself.' A woeful attempt at sincerity, just to get me to leave.

'Oh, you are so full of it. Bullshit. Anna told me, if you must know. You wouldn't have, not ever.'

He doesn't seem to care that Anna and I are chatting about these things. He just sighs. He just looks uneasy.

'Does she live here now?'

'Who?'

I take a step forward and alarmed, he says hurriedly, 'Oh, Issy. Sort of. Mostly. But not really. We're going to move. We're going to live in Sweden.'

'She obviously has no idea about you, does she. Well, obviously not. As I didn't. As maybe loads of women didn't.'

He speaks very quietly. 'There haven't been loads.'

'You expect me to believe that? I did once, admittedly. You made me believe it was just me once. Then I thought it was Anna. Now I see it was someone else entirely.'

'Skye. Please. I think you should go. I keep telling you that things are complicated.'

'An understatement, don't you think? At least it explains why you couldn't use my wallet.' I grab for this small, physical thing to hold on to. 'Your bloody Christmas present.'

'Can you keep your voice down?' Behind him, Issy's lithe form, now in some sort of stripy leggings and a black sports top moves into the hall. 'I agree we ought to talk. I totally agree. Just not here and not now.' And then, 'Maybe I do use your wallet.'

I shake my head tiredly. 'No, you don't. Were you really with her all along?'

'All along . . . what?' he side-steps.

Issy moves along the hall. 'Who is it, Johnny?'

'Isa. This is Skye. She's from . . . she's someone I know through skiing.'

'It's a little early for a visit, no?' Issy looks at me, race-horse sleek. 'Johnny, my darling. Shall I get ready? And shall we go to work?'

'You don't want me to come in?'

Johnny frowns at me. 'Sadly,' he says, his back to Isa, 'I don't think we've got time.' And then he leans forward and says so only I can hear. 'Could you just fuck off?' His mouth, a pink O when he came to the door, has thinned white with irritation.

'I'm not sure you're listening to me, Johnny. I don't think you ever were.'

'What is all this about, Johnny?' Issy sounds annoyed now.

'Nothing to worry about.'

Fuck you, Johnny. I'm not sure I say this aloud so I repeat it. 'Fuck you,' and I reach forward for his juice and I pluck it from his hand and throw it onto the ground – glass smashing, flying – and then very quickly he is alarmed. The look that settles on his face is one of fear. It gives me the strangest sensation, a deeply foreign one, because I had not foreseen it, and had never predicted this . . . disgust. I feel real disdain for him in the face of his fear. I watch him struggle and the juice drop down the sides of the steps and then I move away.

'Yes, Skye, just go,' he says, through his fear, through his gritted teeth. 'You're making a fool of yourself.' He turns around to Issy. 'She's unhinged. I'm so sorry, angel. An unhinged ex.'

'Shall I call the police?' She says it like she's asking if he wants her to clear his plate.

'No, angel, no need.'

Issy moves out of sight again.

'Please, don't come here again. She won't put up with it. And you've made your point.'

'I won't come again,' I tell him. 'I can't be bothered any more. I'm going to leave you to your miserable lying life. And even wish you luck with it. You'll need it, it won't take Issy long to work you out.'

He doesn't reply. He looks even worse than he did when he opened the door. Oddly thin, drained. He is fading in front of me.

'One thing,' I say. 'One last question. Why did you go after me? Why did you bother at all if none of it meant anything?'

Sensing weakness, Johnny's expression becomes colder. 'You've got to accept that we got carried away. It can happen in a resort like that. It's in the past.'

'Carried away? Is that what you call it? *Carried away?*' I touch my hand to my forehead. 'Oh my God. I wish to God you'd left me alone.'

His eyes widen. '*Me* left *you* alone? It was quite hard to avoid you. Hanging around all the time, tagging along to everything you could. *You* never left *me* alone.'

I stagger back in disbelief.

'You asked for it. You were all over me from day one, and so intense.'

What is he saying? 'You . . . don't mean that,' I manage. He can't mean that. Of all the charges I had planned to lay at his door, this blatant misrepresentation of our time together had not been one I imagined. 'That's a lie, Johnny, and you know it.'

'I don't know it. I know that I'd have been quite happy with just friends. With just a bit of fun. Well, you've put paid to that now, haven't you. I don't want to see you again.'

'You bastard.' I look at the orange juice drip down the steps, the broken glass glinting. And then back at Johnny. 'You bastard. I will get you for that. I will make you sorry for that, if nothing else.'

'Goodbye, Skye,' and he flicks the door shut.

Issy does call the police. This is probably what she is like generally, law-abiding and unwilling to leave things to chance. She wants to nip this in the bud and the police officer who rings me up tells me that whilst no official restraining order is in place, she would advise me to stay away from Brunswick Street. She tells me that I have

262

succeeded in scaring Johnny's fiancée and when I laugh at this absurd idea, she sounds sterner. 'You've been warned,' she tells me. 'Do yourself a favour and stay away from them. You've no idea how many calls we get about this sort of thing and it always ends in trouble. You'll get yourself into a lot of hot water unless you drop it. Move on, because I promise you, experience tells me ten times out of ten they're not worth it.'

She ought to be sheepish. She is bossy. I slam the phone onto the table and Gillian, knowing better than to ask, busies herself with a magazine.

45

Brunswick Street, where I went this morning, where I had spent the night only a few weeks ago: the old bachelor-like seams must be bursting with champagne corks and merriment this evening. Does Issy offer canapés in that pale-pink dress, or is she too busy? Has Ellen prepared something, does she hand round (graciously, with pride) and does Andrew (more biddable than usual) bring the vintage red that has been languishing, waiting for such an occasion? And Anna, my friend Anna, does she put all her feelings aside tonight and manage to be happy for her best mate? It is unbearable to think. I wish Darcy was here.

I open a bottle of wine and sip at it manically. In no time at all there is only a drop left. Now there isn't.

I only have to swing round on my chair to curl up on my bed and later, much later, when the street lights and the people on Dalkeith Road on the other side of the window are just a blur, that's what I do.

I am on my side facing the window when I wake up later that night. The moon is a razor-sharp sliver of light above the patterned pane, a nick in the sky. It's still night-time. My phone is glinting. An empty bottle of red wine is on the window sill.

I pick up my phone and squint at it. It's 00:02. My headache is excruciating. I have two text messages and they are both from Anna. I push myself into a sitting position. She will be messaging with a report of the drinks party. I seem to have had one of my own.

I read Anna's messages. And then think that I have misread them, or that I'm still drunk. I fumble with my bedside light and look again.

I drop my phone and put my head in my hands.

I'd passed out with my clothes on before ten o'clock. It's now midnight and my mouth is dry and cracked. My arm is sore from where I have lain on it, and my fingers are cold. I crawl slowly off the bed and stumble into the bathroom, splashing my face with cold water and drinking huge gulps of it. I retch, but only a mouthful of bile comes up. My brain doesn't seem to be working.

I take off my clothes, leaving them on the floor where they fall, and this time get into bed, under the duvet and pulling the covers up to my chin. It is possible I'm dreaming this – God, please let me be dreaming this – but I also know that I'm not. I shut my eyes. And Anna's texts, hurt and furious, start replaying themselves over and over in my mind. I can hear her low scratchy voice, bewildered as well as angry.

Who the fuck is Molly? And the next: I saw your picture on Ellen's phone. MOLLY.

The best I can hope for is that Anna did not tell the Strachans what I have done and if that is so, I am simply back to where I began – but worse. I had a sort of excitement in the new year when I was tracking Ellen and when I met the Strachans at Abbotsford. It was all wrong of course, it was always messed up, but it didn't feel despairing. It felt as if it was going somewhere. This is going nowhere. This is the full stop. And I've lost Anna as a friend. I pick up my phone again and try to think what I can say to her.

After a while, I let it drop again and when I turn over, it thuds to the floor. There's nothing I can say.

After a few minutes lying there I run back to the bathroom and am sick, red wine and the acid taste of shame and guilt rushing from me.

I ring work on Thursday and tell them I'm ill, but I don't get back into bed. I shower and dress myself and gathering my courage I take the bus to the Princes Street Art Gallery.

I know Anna starts work at nine thirty and I'm waiting for her when she comes towards me down the street. She stops when she sees me.

'Oh no. Look who it is.'

'Anna. I just want to explain.'

'Actually, I'm not sure who it is. Molly?'

'Please. I'm so sorry. Really I am. Would you just let me tell you how this all happened?' Tam's words come back to me now. She had been right – I can't explain this.

Anna folds her arms. 'Well, that would certainly be a story. A fucking weird one. Can you imagine – sitting there in Johnny's kitchen, looking through Ellen's photos for the one of Johnny doing, I can't even remember what now, and I get to you. You in Café Paris with Ellen!'

'I know.' I hang my head.

'You never said you knew her. You always talked about her as if you'd never met her before in your life.'

'I couldn't say. She doesn't know me as Skye . . . did you say anything?'

She looks at me sarcastically. 'I thought you'd be worried about that. As usual, only worried about the bloody Strachans.'

'I don't mean that,' I say hastily. 'Of course I'm just sorry I lied to you and I know how bizarre it seems. I didn't want to lie to you, I promise I didn't. I just also didn't want you to know how I'd been . . . how I behaved after New Year.'

'Try. Explain it, I have no idea what this all means. How did you behave after New Year?'

'I . . . I met Ellen, and Andrew, at a hotel.'

'How? Where?'

'In the Borders. It was a lecture. It was something anyone could go to. I found out she was going via Instagram.'

'Why?' She keeps snapping these questions at me.

'Oh, Anna, I don't know! Because I was determined. Because I wanted to meet her.'

She yawns. 'None of this is good enough.'

'I mean . . . I mean.' I try and gather my thoughts. 'What I mean is that after Johnny and I came back to Scotland and he disappeared, I went a bit too far. I know that. I tracked Ellen and when I'd met her, I had to give her a false name. But do you remember when we were at Nora's? Before supper? And we talked about me not knowing who Johnny was?'

She looks at me warily.

'After he went, I just wanted to get to the truth of it. To find out who he was. It wasn't a deliberate meeting Ellen and Andrew thing, I know it looks like that. But I just wanted the truth about Johnny and it seemed an obvious way to go. They were just . . . there, and once I'd met them, they didn't make it easy to let go of them. They were nice.' I trail off and then try again. 'It didn't seem totally wrong.'

Anna is silent.

'The way Johnny just ignored me, the way he just left. He didn't leave me any answers about anything. He left me with nothing, and he had promised quite a lot. He shut down and Ellen was so open. She was such an easy way in. And I liked her.' My eyes fill with hung-over, self-pitying tears. I ignore them and try to carry on. 'I just wanted to find out things. He'd driven me mad wondering.'

People push around us, darting to work and shops, jostling. I take no notice of any of them. After a moment, Anna sighs. 'It's just insane though. And you obviously kept on seeing her. I can't think how you managed it really. How you didn't get found out.'

'Being Molly was how it worked.' I look away for a second, ashamed. 'And by the way, I nearly did get caught. I went to their house for supper once. It was a silly, dreadful thing to do. I wish I had told you,' and I turn back to face her again, pleadingly.

'You're only saying all this now because you don't want me to tell them.'

'Did you? Tell them?'

'Oh, wouldn't you like to know. Skye, Molly whatever you're called.'

'Please,' I beg. 'Please, Anna. I'm embarrassed. I couldn't bear for them to know.'

'Oh, don't worry,' she says scathingly, in the end. 'I didn't say anything. I didn't give you away.'

I can't help the relief. 'Thank you.'

'Don't thank me. I didn't keep quiet to protect you, I kept quiet because I had to.'

I swallow. 'Yes.'

'Fucking nutcase,' she says.

'Yes.'

'I didn't say anything because I couldn't. With Johnny and Issy holding hands in one corner and Ellen all gooey and emotional in the other. I couldn't say anything then.'

'No,' I say miserably. 'Well, it's over now, Anna. My being friends with them, that is. Johnny's getting married, Ellen doesn't want to know me – it's all over really.'

She doesn't ask what I mean about Ellen. She doesn't care. 'So why are you here?'

'I want to say sorry. I really do. I wish that I'd told you about Molly. About knowing Ellen.'

'So do I,' she says bitterly. 'But you didn't. You've had so much time, including the weekend we spent in Fort William. But you didn't. You're a bloody liar. You sat in the car with me for nearly ten hours and you lied all the way.' And she pushes past me into the gallery, leaving me standing in the street alone.

I only learned to lie after Johnny. Before that, there were just stories, the ones Nora told, the myths and legends of the Highlands. Her favourites were always the ones about the Witch of Gormshuil. I can still hear Mum's voice interrupting these stories, her smiling face reassuring me, telling Nora firmly, 'That's enough,' but her face is always obscured by something in my memory; mist or rain, or maybe just time. I remember hunting for the witch in the hills above the loch, swimming in the Cat Pool with kelpies, skimming stones and expecting a monster to break through the calm waters . . . I suppose my imagination was a sort of salve. But even though Nora's stories had helped make sense of my isolation, of my world, they had frightened me. Mum had seen that and sometimes I had crawled into bed with her and lain as close as I could to her, imagining the witch's fingers tapping at the window, the witch coming to take me away.

The problem is how easy the lies were. They were easy, once I'd decided they were important. Perhaps I should have learned to lie earlier; perhaps if I had, Nora would have liked me more when I had to pack up the stories and take them with my despair down the road to live with her.

The lies were a bit like a walk down the Dark Mile in the winter. It begins with wanting to get away. It's simple; it seems necessary. An assumption about the length of time is made and some sort of idle preparation (it will take this long, I'll need this coat, these provisions) but a long walk in the Highlands never ends as it begins. The route often fails. It's easy to lose track once on the hill. The destination, initially clear, is hidden in a vast swathe of heather and bog. The sly, silky blackness comes down too soon, bad weather blows over the hills from the west, and the myriad paths are muddling; the temperature plummets, a false summit is reached and the next is invisible. Dwarfed by the hill and deep in the middle of nowhere, it's possible to become confused and not a little scared. The mind can start to play tricks on itself. And by the time a mistake, or some wrong decisions have been realised, it is too late. The explorer is lost. Completely and utterly lost.

46

I wake up early. Although that is too simple a notion for a complicated procedure. More accurately: there is a vague feeling some time during the dark hours of an Edinburgh morning (I won't remember it later on in the day, even half an hour later) that I blunder into some sort of consciousness. The transition between sleep and waking is not achieved so much as wandered into. I don't 'wake up', any more than I can just 'fall asleep'. It is more as if I have been stumbling through a dark wood and then there is a gap in the trees, and a sickening feeling. I lie there, trying to find my way back into the woods. I tread through the memories. They rustle and confuse, this ongoing collision of dreams. They are from the lives before.

The muddle of night becomes the dread of day. Perhaps there is some groggy internal dialogue to help the crossover; I didn't sleep well, is that rain on the window, what day is it today, and then everything comes rushing back. Johnny is getting married; his brief reappearance in my life just a forlorn artifice, created by me and unsustainable. Ellen never wants to see me again. And Anna doesn't want to know me.

I know everything has gone wrong, but I find myself really minding about Anna. I mind the memory of her bafflement. I mind that I hadn't realised our friendship was important to her as well as to me, and I mind that I had been as obtuse as Ellen had been. I had been so caught up in telling Ellen the truth about Andrew that I had conveniently forgotten who the liar of the group really was. I realise that Anna had made life more colourful, in a platonic but not dissimilar way to how Johnny had. With her, the padding hadn't felt like padding. It felt like life.

I'm not going to give up. I'm going to make it up to her somehow, and I become increasingly determined. I ring her twice but she doesn't take the calls so I write her an email, telling her again how sorry I am and asking for another chance. I don't get anything back. I chew my nails and when it is quiet at work, I offer to go to the coffee shop to get Gillian's latte for her and whilst I'm in there, I start listening idly to the women in front of me. I can't help overhearing but I'm also listening with a sort of regret and envy because they are like two Annas, all jokey and knowing. They are talking about their boss and one of them says, 'He'll get his comeuppance.'

It triggers something for me and by the time I get home, I know what I'm going to do. Anna won't resist this. I text her saying that I know she doesn't want anything to do with me but I want to tell her something about Johnny. She calls back.

'I'm still angry with you,' she warns. 'Spit it out quick, whatever you've got to say.'

'Thanks for ringing.'

'I don't know why I have. Come on, hurry up.' At least she's talking to me. 'What's it about?'

'It's about last Thursday.'

There's a short pause. 'What about last Thursday?'

'Do you remember telling me that he'd lost his licence? Well, he may have, but it hasn't stopped him driving around. He drove his car to his parents' garage last Thursday and parked it there.'

272

Another silence. 'Then perhaps he just wants it off the road if he's not using it. And anyone could have driven it there for him.'

'Well, yes,' I concede. 'But – it wasn't you, was it? And it usually is, which could suggest that Issy doesn't know about the ban. And if it wasn't Issy, who he didn't see that night, and it wasn't you, it was probably him.'

'Why are you telling me this?'

'Because I want to tell you everything now. Including why Ellen doesn't want to know me any more. And what I found out about Andrew.'

'What about Ellen and Andrew then?'

'I thought Ellen should know that Andrew has been having an affair,' I say. 'I told her.'

'Really?' she says. She sounds amazed and then doubtful. 'Are you sure?'

'Yes, absolutely. He is awful, isn't he?'

'Who with?' says Anna. 'I just can't see it. I know he's lecherous but nothing more.'

'Much more. It's with the pharmacist at the surgery,' and Anna starts laughing down the phone. It is not the reaction I had expected. 'Why are you laughing? What's so funny?'

'What makes you think it's an affair?'

'Because Andrew paid for her to have plastic surgery. Breast implants,' I say, triumphantly. 'There's no other reason he would.'

'Amy Desmond?'

'Yes.'

'There are lots of other reasons. You idiot,' she says, and starts laughing again. 'You idiot.'

'What?' I'm annoyed now.

'She's Andrew's sister.'

Silence.

'And I know her,' Anna continues. 'Her husband works on the same oil rig as one of Mum's boyfriends. She's happily married.' She chortles. 'Probably because they never see each other. She is not having it off with her brother.'

My phone is slippery in my hand. My cheeks are flaming. I can't think straight. Amy and Andrew, sister and brother? More bloody family connections that I don't know anything about?

'Blimey. You great numpty, Skye. She's all right, you know, Amy.'

'Yes, well. I feel more stupid than ever, obviously.' I stare at that crack again in my sitting room, the slight subsidence in the corner. I wish I could crawl inside it. 'Are you sure, Anna?' but I know she is. I remember Ellen had described the business as family-run. It is why Ellen had dismissed me so summarily when I told her about Andrew's infidelity, and been so uninterested in the texts I tried to show her. She had probably not bothered to ask him later about me. Sad, stupid me.

'You know,' Anna is wondering, 'I heard that Amy hadn't been well. I think she had cancer. I wonder if the surgery was necessary for reconstruction, not just a boob job.'

It had never occurred to me that the surgery might have been for medical reasons. I bite down on my lip, hard, trying to remember the paperwork I had read. Some of the medical terms come back to me . . . most of which I had skimmed over. I had been so focused on the fact that Andrew had paid for it. I had just assumed it was female vanity. 'I don't know,' I say stiffly. 'Clearly, I don't know anything.' There had been references to the operation originally scheduled with the NHS and constantly getting delayed. I shut my eyes. The NHS wouldn't offer implants lightly.

Anna gives another shout of laughter. 'And you told Ellen?'

'I thought she should know. Anna, please stop laughing at me.'

She relents. 'OK. Sorry,' and then I think I hear some sympathy for me in her voice. 'Oh, Skye. What was Ellen's reaction?'

I can't bear to think about it. 'She wasn't having any of it.' She had been grossly insulted.

'I don't know why she didn't tell you straight up that Amy was his sister.'

'I expect I had forfeited the right to know anything.' And she had been protective of Amy and her illness. She had not wanted to talk about any of it with me, a blundering, invasive idiot.

'Come on,' she says, coaxing. 'It's all gone a bit wrong, but cheer up. Look, I've got pizza here. Friday night binge. Do you want to come over?'

'Yes, please,' so relieved that she's not angry any more, 'can I?'

'Of course. I promise I won't laugh at you again. We all make mistakes, after all. It's not the end of the world.'

I hadn't known that embarrassment was such a heavy thing. I order a taxi to Dalmeny Street and try to hide in it, feeling so small under the weight of the embarrassment. It feels so leaden and so real it is almost like a third person in the car. As if someone has draped themselves all over me with sweaty body and hot, insistent hands. I turn my face to the window and it all comes too. It won't get off me and I can't get away. It pushes me further into the corner of the car. Had I got everything wrong, all of it, about Andrew? At least we arrive at Anna's quickly and the only comfort is that she feels so sorry for Skye that she forgives Molly.

*

Anna opens the door and ushers me in, saying immediately, 'I've been thinking. Do you remember I said that Johnny had been at my house?'

'Yes. The night he drove his car to St Bernard's Row.'

'Exactly, last Thursday. Come in, by the way. I've left you some pizza. I didn't bother telling you before,' and she sounds a little defensive. 'It didn't seem important. But something had definitely happened, before he arrived.'

'Something happened? Like what?' The pizza looks cold, congealing in the box.

'I'm in my bed, on Thursday night, all tucked up when he rings the doorbell.'

'Go on.' I sit down and eat it anyway.

'I let him in of course. He wasn't making much sense at first, at least none that I could get out of him. He was in a bit of a mess, to be honest.'

'What on earth happened?' I can't imagine the suave Johnny I know like this.

'Well, I don't know. I never did get to the bottom of it. I felt sorry for him and let him stay on the sofa. He wouldn't go back to his.'

'Well,' I say bitterly, chewing the crust with difficulty. 'There was probably another woman involved, don't you think?'

'I don't know,' she says slowly, 'I don't think so. It seems odd to take a risk with a stranger when Issy's in town.'

'He likes taking some risks.' I can still feel the cold stone of the alleyway wall against the back of my head, see the black night behind him. 'Or maybe a fight?'

'No. There were no marks on that pretty face. I've been thinking that it might be something to do with taking the car to his parents.'

'Do you think he dropped the car off before or after his midnight visit to yours?'

She shrugs. 'I don't know for sure but I assume before. He didn't mention the car and it was late. It was getting late.' She turns away. 'Sorry, there's no wine. Do you want the rest of this Coke?'

'Yes please.' I repeat what I know. 'The car is definitely in the Strachans' garage.'

'Andrew brought it up again on Wednesday. He said, "Please can you move that sodding car before you get married." And I think it was odd that Johnny didn't explain to me what was going on with him when he came over.'

'He's got Issy. He doesn't need to tell you things any more.'

She looks at me sharply. 'Or maybe he *couldn't* tell me. Maybe there's a connection between whatever happened to him, because I'm telling you something did, and him taking his car to the garage.'

I shake my head. 'Oh no, come on. Listen to us. This is a bit silly. We're just scrabbling for clues that aren't there.'

'But they are there,' she insists. 'And we know Johnny. I think he's in some sort of trouble and he's not telling anyone. It's typical. And I've got a plan.'

'A plan?'

Anna laughs. 'Isn't this what this is all about? Making a plan?'

'A plan for what?'

'A plan for what,' she echoes mockingly. 'A plan to pay Johnny back, of course. You once said he'd get his comeuppance, and this could be our chance. I thought that's why you rang to tell me he'd been driving even though he's got a ban.'

I'd rung to build bridges with Anna. 'Did I say that? About his comeuppance?' I'm confused. I thought she'd said it.

277

'Look,' she says, suddenly stern. 'I'm not playing games here. I've had it – I'm fed to the teeth with the way he's used us. I'm not waiting around to be made a fool of over and over.' She looks away briefly. 'I've had enough of him. I'd like to see him sorry. I thought you would too.' She drains her Coke. 'If not – fine.'

'We could just tell Issy about him. About him and me.'

'Feeble,' she says. 'Our word – or rather your word, which doesn't mean much – against his.'

She is looking at me as though I were slightly pathetic. And I am pathetic – I feel so ashamed about pretending to be Molly and getting it so wrong about Andrew and Amy. I've looked like such a fool in front of Anna. And I do want Johnny sorry. I look down at my hands wringing between my knees and remember the days following our return to Edinburgh. I remember Johnny on his doorstep telling me I hadn't ever left him alone in Chamonix. That I'd tagged along to everything I could.

'Personally,' she says, 'if I were you, I'd want to stab him through the heart. You really were nothing more than a holiday fling to him.'

A holiday fling? The beginning of the rest of my life? *The snowflakes. La Marlenaz. The two-metre rule. The delayed plane. La Marmot. It was meant to be. We were supposed to spend the rest of our lives with each other. There was so much on the list for us to do.*

Anna is looking at me. Waiting.

'Of course,' she adds, 'you realise that if he is in some kind of trouble with the law, it will finish his relationship with Issy without any nonsense bleating about infidelity. The engagement will be over as quickly as it began. That upstanding lawyer isn't going to have a law-breaker on her hands. She'll be gone in a jiffy.'

'Yes,' I say, my voice coming out croaky. I clear my throat. 'Yes, I do want him sorry. Of course I do.'

'Well then,' she says. 'Let's do it. This is what I suggest. That we go and take a look at that Golf in the garage.'

My mouth falls open. 'No way, Anna. I'm not going creeping round St Bernard's Row.'

'You've done it before,' she says neutrally and I blush.

'Well, what if they catch me?'

'They won't!' she says. 'And anyway, it won't be just you this time. We'll go together. We'll be fine. No one will ever know. Our only problem is how to get in.'

There's a long silence and I look at my hands again, considering. She has completely forgotten my lunacy about everything and moved on. I need to get with the programme, and move on with her. 'The garage door is broken. It's easy to get in.'

She claps her hands. 'Bingo.'

47

Anna picks me up at eleven o'clock the next night in her car and we drive through the night, through the lamp-lit cobbled streets to the bridge in Stockbridge. Neither of us say much.

She parks on a side street near St Bernard's Row and we get out.

'What are we doing?' I ask, feeling ridiculous. 'Look at us.' By accident or design we are both dressed in black. Anna has one of her dark hats pulled low over her head. 'This is stupid. We're no cat burglars. Why aren't we just knocking on the door?'

Anna puts her hands on her hips. 'Skye. We've been over this. Do you want to do that? Do you want to face Ellen? Tell her that the woman who tried to catch her husband cheating on her – with his sister – now thinks her son crashed his car while driving illegally?'

'Nicely put, thank you. No, but—'

'And can she just have a look in her garage? Just to make sure? But – nothing,' she ends firmly. 'We're here now. I agree, we can both hope there's nothing to find, but I want to know. Something happened and I want to know what.'

She starts walking and I wait a little, hesitating, and then run to catch up.

The garages are all opposite the houses in St Bernard's Row and the garage for number 22 is clearly signed. We don't need lights, it isn't too dark and the street lamps make everything visible but at the same time, we are very exposed. There isn't anywhere to hide in this wide street. *There's probably CCTV,* I think, but I haven't any time to consider the foolishness of what we're doing any more. Anna is standing opposite the Strachans' house. All the curtains are drawn and there are no lights on, none that I can see anyway. She runs her hand along the bottom of the garage, finds the handle and pulls. Nothing happens. She pulls again but it's definitely jammed.

'Sssh,' I say panicking.

'Help me,' she hisses and I bend over and she says, 'One . . . two . . .' and we both tug, hard, at the bottom of the door. It makes the most ear-splitting crack and a dog starts barking but it doesn't budge and we both stop immediately. 'Shit,' she whispers but no one comes running, there is nothing to hear apart from the cars on the bridge, and the dog. 'Again,' she orders, and we bend again and yank. Nothing. We look at each other in frustration. 'Harder, come on,' she instructs and we both use all our strength to pull it up again. This time the door snaps free and we are able to pull it up.

'Anna, we've made too much noise,' but she shakes her head.

'Who's going in, you or me?'

'I don't know,' I hiss back and then she stifles a snort of laughter.

'You've got a smaller bottom than me, you go and have a look.'

When there is enough space, enough space to see the boot of Johnny's car, I squeeze in under the door and move down the side of the car, running my hand along the top of it. It's the black Golf that I followed to Arthur's Seat (a lifetime ago). I reach the front, and I haven't felt anything apart from the smooth surface. I back out again.

'Nothing this side,' I say softly and squeeze in again, this time on the right. There is even less room here. I'm not surprised Ellen doesn't bother getting the Volvo in and out of this tiny space, that she has a permit for the road. I inch down towards the end. Johnny has had to fold his wing mirrors in. And there is something wrong with this wing mirror. It is loose, hanging off its hinges. I carry on and near the end of the bonnet my hand touches something rough and splintery.

'Can you see anything?' Anna calls softly.

I pull my phone out of my coat pocket and turn the torch on. I lean over the bonnet, shining the light down into the corner. The bumper has been totally smashed. One of the headlamps is also cracked and damaged. I open my mouth to alert Anna, stop myself and start to back out of the garage.

'Anna, you won't believe this,' I whisper when I am closer. I have to drop to my knees and shuffle out back-wards. 'You were right,' I start saying and I rise and turn to face her. She is not looking at me. She is turning as if to flee. Andrew is watching me emerge from his garage.

'Run,' Anna says over her shoulder, and she is already running, but I am not quick enough. Andrew's bulk steps in front of me, his leg darts out and I fall, hard, over his foot. My chin, or my mouth, hits the ground. I am lying on the road with blood, I think, coming from my lips and Andrew is standing over me.

'You. What the bloody hell are you doing here?' His surprise and dislike fills the deepened lines in his face. 'You've got a bloody nerve.'

I push myself to my feet. 'What are you doing here?'

'No, Molly,' he corrects, 'that's what I'm asking you. I still live here, as far as I'm aware. Despite your best efforts.'

I search desperately down the street for Anna. She shouldn't have run.

'I don't know what you've been playing at. Leaving me stranded at that pub while you tell ridiculous tales to my wife about Amy.'

He leans towards me. I can smell whisky on his breath.

'I don't know why you just didn't mind your own business. But it seems you're not very good at that. You're not minding your own business tonight, are you?'

'I know what it looks like but I'm not doing anything. I know it looks as though I am. I'm not here to steal anything.'

'It certainly does look as though you are. And who was your accomplice?'

I try to think, to get my brain in some sort of order. *I could come clean*, I think, but something tells me Andrew is not in the mood to hear about Anna's and my sleuthing. Our guesswork, which, as it turns out, isn't just guesswork.

'There is an explanation, Andrew,' and at the same time, I back away.

He is too quick for me, and his long arm shoots out and grabs me painfully by the upper arm. He squeezes hard.

'That hurts, don't . . . Andrew.'

His answer is to shove me up against the wall. 'You're not going anywhere. Seeing as you're here, Molly, I think we ought to have a little chat. You can hear a few home truths.'

I try to turn my face away but he grabs my cheek and forces me to look at him. 'You, my dear, are a prick tease. And a marriage wrecker, and as it turns out, some sort of intruder to boot.' His face is close to mine, his mouth open and the whisky foul on his breath. 'That's quite a CV.' I try to wriggle away and I can't escape. I suddenly think how much trouble I could be in. 'I've been waiting to run in to you again. To ask what you've been up to. And after all we've done for you as well.' *After all I've done for you . . . charmed you at the conference . . . driven you all over the city, giving you lifts . . . had you for dinner.* 'Look how you've repaid me.'

'It's bullshit,' I manage. It is. Ellen may have felt sorry for me at Abbotsford but he didn't. Now he is just angry that he has wasted time and sexual interest in me. 'Leave me alone.'

'Leave you alone?' he taunts. 'You haven't left us alone in weeks. You led me on from the start, pretending to be so demure. Suddenly you were everywhere I looked. You kept on throwing yourself in front of us, at me. Ellen thought you were a lesbian,' he adds unnecessarily.

'But you didn't. She was wrong to think I was safe with you, wasn't she?' and Andrew's piggy eyes bulge nastily.

'You don't fool me. Don't turn this on me. Turning up at the surgery like that, pretending to be surprised to see me. Flirting in the car, making eyes over dinner. I know what you wanted.'

I shake my head. 'It wasn't like that. You're wrong.'

'The thing is, you might think you're some sort of femme fatale at the moment, but you aren't getting any younger, are you, Molly? Meals for one, night after night . . .' His hand brushes against my chest, and he pauses, his breath coming a little faster. 'All alone.'

Oh no. Please no. 'Andrew, no. Don't touch me.' There is a look on his face now that there wasn't before. *Anna, where are you?*

He is much stronger than me, and he has my arms trapped by my side so I cannot free them, and his body has me caught against the wall so I can't move my legs. It's no good, I can't get away. Behind him, the street lights seem to be darkening. The midnight sky is pitch black. He is too heavy and too strong and for a moment I think I can't breathe. Then he moves his head to the side and I bite into his neck, hard.

His head snaps back, pain and surprise on his face and then he raises his arm and hits me. It feels as though my head has exploded and it connects with a smack against the concrete. Loud whirring somewhere. Burning face.

He steps away. He is in some sort of daze and he looks at me and then at his hands. 'Jesus Christ.'

I am on my knees in front of him. 'Just let me go,' I manage.

'Jesus,' he says again. 'I didn't mean that. I don't know what happened then. A lot of strain recently,' and then he pulls himself together. 'Don't worry. I'm not interested if you're not. Just go.' He touches the side of his neck gingerly. 'But before you do, tell me what you've been doing here.'

And then, the glorious sound of a car, coming very fast and very loud down St Bernard's Row. Andrew turns to look and in the same second I force myself to my feet and duck past him. I stumble towards the car as fast as I can. Anna puts the brakes on and the door opens and I throw myself through it.

She locks the doors and reverses. I stare at Andrew's receding figure as we drive off, gingerly wiping the stickiness from my raw chin. He is standing at the end of the street, his shoulders sagging, watching us go.

'Are you OK?' Anna's voice is unnaturally shaky.

In the end I just say, 'I'm not sure. Keep driving.'

She takes me back home and we walk up the steps to the flat together. Inside, she finds ice-cubes and I find some gin. Pressing the towel to my face, and with the gin in our hands, we look at each other in disbelief.

'I don't get it,' says Anna, still shaky. 'I would never have thought Andrew was like that. He hit you,' she says wonderingly. 'Jeez.'

'He'd been drinking. He was angry, he caught me snooping in his garage. He's angry that I got it wrong about him and Amy. About everything.'

'I know. But still. Look at your face.'

'Never mind that.'

'Does he know where you live?'

'No. Ellen does, but I don't think he's going to come after us. After me.'

She considers this. 'I suppose he'll be worried you've gone to the police. This is assault.'

I shake my head and then wince. 'Ouch. We can't go to the police. He caught me on his property, breaking and entering. But I think we're OK. I don't think he meant to get so angry. He's not like that, not really.' Even though I had been frightened, I don't think he would have gone any further. He had just wanted to show me who was in charge.

Anna crosses her arms. 'What about the car?'

I put the ice cubes in the towel down and take a slug of gin. 'No doubt about it at all. It's been in an accident. Someone's crashed it.'

Anna looks jubilant and starts pacing round the room. 'I knew it. I had a feeling, didn't I?'

'We don't know anything for sure,' I caution, and she nods.

'Maybe not. But we've got a starting point.' She pours more gin and goes to my computer. 'Can I wake this up?'

I nod, and she says, 'Password?'

'I'll do it,' and I type in Chamonix2. 'What date did he come and see you? It was a Thursday, wasn't it?'

'Yes. Twenty-third of February. Type it all into Google and see what comes up. If anything.'

I put in Edinburgh, I put in the date and add the make of the car and finally the word accident. I press search.

The answer comes back swift and easy and it's so shocking. I put my hand over my mouth.

'What?' says Anna. 'What?'

I can't speak. I move away from the computer and let my head fall into my hands. I am suddenly horribly weary. My head aches and my mouth, where I fell, feels huge and bloody. My left eye is beginning to close.

Anna looks at it for a long time and then she looks back at me. 'This is him, isn't it? This has got to be him, this has got to be him. Oh my God. I didn't imagine this.' She collapses onto the sofa and then immediately gets up again.

I look at her, with doubt and worry. 'Anna, it's awful.'

'Yes,' she says. 'That goes without saying. What I mean is that we've got him. Not even Johnny can magic himself out of this one.'

'I can't think about this now. I think I need to sleep. Can I? Do you mind?'

'No,' she says, concerned again for me. 'No, of course.'

She helps me onto my bed and there is a crash from outside the window in the street below. We look at each other and my heart starts pounding again. Anna peers through it.

'Nothing. Don't worry. A cat. It's nothing.' I start to say something and she nods. 'I'm going to stay. It's OK. I'll be here all night. I've got to leave early but I'll be here all night.'

'There are blankets in that cupboard. And another pillow.'

She clambers onto the bed and lies down. 'We'll think what to do in the morning.' She gives me a reassuring squeeze and I close my eyes.

I'd been thinking along the lines of an accident with . . . another car. Or with a bloody *bollard* or something, a bloody *wall*. I'd been wrong. And now I know, I feel none of Anna's triumph. I feel sick to the stomach and wish beyond all wishing that I didn't know. Johnny hadn't hit an inanimate object. Johnny had hit a child.

48

I dream that I am on the island of Skye with him. We are
walking on the beach near the tideline without speaking
to each other, walking amongst the crusty fishermen's
ropes and the empty blue shells, and then Johnny starts
to run towards a road that looks like the Dark Mile. He
doesn't wait for me, and I couldn't make him hear me,
even though I was shouting with all my might. And when
I look around, the tide is coming for me, the waves, white-
tipped like old man's arms, are grabbing at me. I call for
Mum who is always somewhere in my dreams, but she
is nowhere to be seen, and then as if she knew I needed
her, she materialises. I see Johnny in the distance, getting
into a car with her.

I can't keep up, I can't get there in time. The mist
is coming down and swallowing them and then someone
starts laughing, only I can't tell who. I start to run across
the beach and the laughing morphs into sobbing and then
I get to the end of the beach onto tarmac and there is a
boy lying in the middle of the road, his body impossibly
twisted and the sobbing gets louder. The car, a silver Volvo,
is stationary by the child and I can fling the door open and
get in but Mum and Johnny have put up a glass screen,
like I am a passenger in their taxi and the glass is thick
like ice between us. I bang the screen but I am invisible
to them. I think I scream; it is pointless.

My knuckles feel sore when I wake, and I can smell the sea, the salt-water smell that drenches the beach, and I feel the same desperation and the crying is what wakes me up and I realise that the person crying is me. Crying for everything that might have been and really could never have been; for everything that I once believed might be perfect and so demonstrably wasn't. Crying for the boy in the road and his mother. For what we had to do now.

It doesn't look as though Anna slept much either. She is waiting for me as we'd agreed in Starbucks because she had to get to the gallery to open it for a Sunday exhibition. She has the newspaper open in front of her; last week's.

'I got you a coffee,' she says, and pushes the article over to me.

Police in Edinburgh are still searching for the owner of the car that they believe to be involved in a hit and run at about ten pm on Thursday 23rd February. The victim is a twelve-year-old boy, still in a critical condition, and has been named as Archie Fraser who was bicycling home after a school club that finished late. The car failed to stop at the zebra crossing between Iona and Dickson Street in Leith. A witness believes the car to have been black. Police have set up an incident hotline and are urging members of the public to come forward with any information they may have.

'This is awful,' I say eventually. 'It's so awful. I can't believe Johnny is involved in this.' None of the black and white print of the newspaper feels real or remotely possible.

'Well, yes and no,' Anna says. 'It is awful, obviously, and if the poor boy dies it's a tragedy. But it seems to

290

have Johnny's fingerprints all over it, don't you think? It's exactly the sort of thing that he would try and get away with. It is stupid and irresponsible and it bears all the hallmarks of him.'

'Oh God,' I say miserably. 'Why didn't he just stop?'

'I'm afraid, Skye,' she says briskly, 'that it's not up to us to wonder. Although, I've a pretty good idea why not.' She starts counting on her fingers. 'One, he's not supposed to be driving. Two, he's drunk. Three, he's a lawyer, four, Mummy and Daddy are going to hit the roof and five – he doesn't give a fuck.'

'He would give a fuck about a child on the road,' I say quietly.

'Yes,' she concedes. 'I meant he doesn't feel responsible for anything he does. I can just hear him, can't you? Oh, the brakes don't work, or the road was slippery. And so on. He never deals with the consequences of whatever it is he's done.'

'I know. But surely, what's really most likely is that he wasn't aware of what he'd done. That it happened too quickly or something like that. By the way, how do you know that he was drunk?'

Anna purses her lips and then says shortly, 'He'd been drinking by the time he got to my flat. Anyway, never mind that. You know what he's like. Why is it so difficult for you to blame him for this? Why are you making excuses for him?'

I look at my coffee for a minute. 'I'm not making excuses for him.'

'Well why is it so hard to believe then?'

'My parents,' I say. 'I don't want Johnny to be that man.'

Anna is silent.

'It seems impossible to me that Johnny's the same sort of man. Worse even. This man stopped, you see, when he

291

realised what he'd done. Johnny didn't even stop. How can that be?'

'Skye,' she says, in the sort of voice that won't brook any argument. 'Your parents – this is just an awful coincidence. And neither of us thought Johnny capable of this. But it happened, perhaps unknowingly, and the point is we can't ignore it, now we know what we do. We just can't, and that's nothing to feel guilty about.'

'I don't want to believe it,' I repeat stubbornly. 'If we're wrong, he'll be fired, you know, they'll find out about him not being allowed to drive and he'll lose his job—'

'We're not wrong. You know it and I know it. You know what else I think?'

I look at her questioningly.

'I think it explains the marriage proposal. Why he wants to go and live in flipping Sweden all of a sudden. He would never have proposed to her if he didn't need to. It always felt odd. To me, anyway.'

'Yes. Maybe.' I don't know any more. I can't second-guess him now, if ever I could.

'Issy won't stick by him,' says Anna.

'Probably not.'

'Who would?' and there's a small silence before she carries on. 'Anyway,' and her face hardens. 'It really is nothing less than he deserves.'

'He'll go to prison.'

'And with any luck, rot there.'

'I feel sorry for his mother.'

'I feel sorry for,' Anna glances down at the newspaper, 'Archie Fraser's mother.'

'Yes.'

'I'll call the police now.'

'Will you? Is that OK if you do?' I look up at her.

'More than,' she says grimly and takes out her phone.

It doesn't matter who does it, I think, numbly. *One of us has to. It may as well be her.*

Her call is answered almost immediately and then she's on the phone for twenty minutes or more. She has to repeat it all, over and over. She tells them that she knows someone (Name, Age, Address) with a black Golf (Registration? She looks at me with raised eyebrows and I shake my head), and that she saw it in a garage belonging to Andrew and Ellen Strachan at 22 St Bernard's Row with a smashed bumper and headlamp. She gives a few other details and then she pauses and says, 'Acquaintance.' They take all her details and then she says, 'Is the boy going to be OK?'

She hangs up.

'They say they'll be in touch.' Anna stands up, slinging her bag over her shoulder. 'Right. I've got to get back to work. Call me if you hear anything, and vice versa.'

'What about the boy?'

'They can't say. Family only, which doesn't sound good to me.'

'No.'

'And let's hope that's the end of it for you.'

'What do you mean?'

'Well, you can't have anything more to do with them, can you? Now Andrew caught you in the garage. It's not that far from Molly to Skye when they've got you searching for Johnny's car in between the two. And if they put Molly and Skye together, it will look like you've deliberately engineered the whole thing somehow. You'd better stay away.'

I stare into my coffee. 'I've no reason to go anywhere near them.'

She turns to go. 'Let's speak later. Will you be all right today?'

'Yes. You?'

'Yup. Hug?' She gives me one – 'your poor chin looks as though it's lost a layer of skin' – and dashes out.

I could never have done any of this without Anna. She had what it took, and I didn't. And by admitting that, I'm not saying she was the boss, or was more actively decisive than me (although she might have been), or that she was more culpable somehow. We were both in this together and that's what I liked about it. I know that this is my opportunity to really hurt Johnny. I'm saying that revenge, even when it's right, can feel wrong.

49

I'd been late to bed and so I am still asleep when the sound of my phone ringing wakes me up. It takes me a few seconds to find it amongst the bedcovers. I blink at the name flashing at me and then I sit up. It's Ellen.

I don't want to answer it but I don't want to not answer it and whilst I'm staring at it, it rings off. I lie back down again. I can't call her back. It's likely that Andrew will have told her he found me in their garage.

I'm just about to get up when a message from Anna pings through.

Johnny arrested last night.

I tear out of bed and run to the sink, panic engulfing me. It's all happening too fast. Arrested already, on Sunday evening? What had Ellen wanted? She has put two and two together about Andrew finding me in the garage and Johnny's arrest. She must have. I splash cold water over my face and stand against the basin looking at myself in the mirror. A stranger, with cut lip and purpling eye stares back at me. And then my mobile rings again. 121.

Ellen's message is completely garbled. She is crying uncontrollably, and says that something awful has happened. She says that she knows we argued but there's no one else. She asks me to come over.

I call her back straight away. 'Ellen, please . . . try to calm down. Calm down. What's happened?' I have to ask. I don't need to ask.

'Everything. Everything. The worst. It's Johnny. Can you get here?'

'Yes, immediately. But where is Andrew?' *Has he not told her because he punched me*?

'He's at the police station with Johnny. They're accusing him of something dreadful.'

'Ellen—'

'The police are here too, all over the street, in the house and in the . . . the garage. I don't want to be alone. I can't bear to be alone.'

I was never going to refuse her. There was nothing I would ever have done except say yes. Was there? I don't think there was. I throw on my jeans and a jumper, grab my coat and run out of the door.

Spring is approaching Scotland, gathering momentum as it floods like a river over the border. It emerges majestically from the grips of winter and reaches the Highlands late, a waterfall of promise and colour when English blossom is already beginning to die. But today, in Edinburgh, I catch glimpses of its arrival here, half-noticed in the pink-budded cherry trees in the elegant crescents of New Town, tangible in the March air biting freshly into my face. White crocuses are poking tightly through glistening soil in the park's borders; I run across them. I can see St Bernard's Row from the top of the hill, I know it is St Bernard's because the police cars, although silent, are flashing blue and red into the sky and houses below. I slow down and as I walk over the bridge, over the Water of Leith, I think of the times I have walked here before, innocently hoping for just a glimpse of Ellen.

Ellen hadn't exaggerated, the police are everywhere. I stop at the garage opposite the Strachans', and it is open, and empty. Police tape is across the front. I get to the navy door and have to tell a policewoman that I am a friend before she lets me through.

'Ellen?' I call, shrugging off my coat. I leave it by the door in amongst the debris of their life, the walking sticks and the wellies, and walk down the hall. 'Where are you?'

She is in the kitchen, on the sofa. Her face is puffy and she looks absolutely stunned. More than anything, she looks as though she is in shock. Witchy is on her lap but she leaps away when I come closer.

'Ellen. I'm so sorry, truly I am.'

'Have you heard what's happened?' There is a carton of milk on the sofa leaking into the cushion.

I look at her helplessly. 'Yes . . . I think so.'

'They think Johnny hit a boy on his bike. In his car. Suspicion of drunk-driving.' *Druunk* she says, in a monotone.

I pick up the carton of milk and put it on the island.

'Apparently he wasn't even supposed to be driving. I had no idea. He lost his licence last year.'

'But the boy? He's alive, isn't he?'

Ellen closes her eyes. 'At the moment. We don't know if he'll survive. Not yet, not for sure. They did think it was just concussion at first, but he's not out of the woods.'

Dear God.

'I was about to make some coffee.'

'Shall I?' The carton has toppled over again and a small trickle of milk has started to drip from the island onto the floor.

'I'd read about the hit and run, you know. The mangled bike. I even knew they were looking for a black car. Never,

297

in a million years, would I have thought it was the one in the garage.' Her eyes close briefly. 'I don't know yet how the police tracked it down.'

I'm not looking at Ellen when I say, 'And Johnny? How is he? Has he got some sort of defence?'

Ellen reaches for Witchy again. 'Defence? What sort of defence could he possibly have? It's indefensible, the whole thing. It couldn't be worse.'

'He'll find someone.'

'Who'll take it on, though? A friend, a colleague? I don't think so. Do you want to hear the details?'

I shake my head. 'No.'

'I'll tell you. I don't know what barrister is going to want to be mixed up with this. He wasn't even supposed to be in the damn car,' she says again, her voice rising. 'He was banned. Banned following a speeding conviction last year. He was driving over the limit, banned and he hit a small boy on his bicycle. And he didn't stop. He's a coward.' She pushes her blonde hair from her face defiantly, as if daring me to disagree.

'But he can't have known he'd done it. That he'd hit someone. What does he say?' The awful, treacherous thought that it can't have been totally his fault. That there is something we are all missing, not getting.

'I don't know. I haven't seen him yet. I don't know. They marched in here yesterday, demanded the car and then went to his flat. Andrew is with him and he will call me when he knows anything. But, Molly, I can't bear it. He can't go back to GMT. There will be a trial, press. We will all be smeared in the papers. What will it mean for the practice?'

The vision of Archie Fraser in his hospital bed comes back to me. I don't reply. We both sit there, Ellen looking at me with a sort of sullen dullness, and me looking at the floor. The sounds of the police on the street outside come through to us intermittently, the odd rough shout or slamming of car doors.

Finally, I stir and reach for a cloth. I mop up the milk and then say, 'Let's have that cup of coffee,' and she nods.

'Thank you. Thank you for coming. I know there's nothing anyone can do, not least until we know more, but I couldn't bear to be on my own another second. I didn't really know who else to call. I couldn't think of anyone who would be . . . nice.'

'I'm glad you rang. I'm so sorry for you. It's going to be all right.'

'I'm not so sure,' she says, 'but thank you. You know, last week I was furious with you.' She looks at me properly, perhaps for the first time. 'Molly, something's happened to your face. What's happened?'

'Don't worry about that. It's fine. Last week you were angry with me — rightly so.' I've got my back to her, filling up the kettle, so it's easier. 'I found out how wrong I got it about Amy. I'm so sorry. You must have thought I was mad.'

'Your face,' she says, again.

'I walked into my cupboard last night,' I say shortly.

She seems to accept this. 'It's not really me you owe the apology to, you know. It's Andrew.'

She can't be serious and I turn around to look at her. 'Ellen, please. For some reason you don't want to believe this about Andrew and he's your husband, and I get that. But he's not the man you think he is.'

'Don't start,' she says wearily, getting to her feet. 'Not now. I must lay the table for lunch.'

'I know this isn't the time. I know I was stupid about Amy. But I wasn't lying about the way Andrew was with me.'

Ellen turns her back and starts opening drawers. She pulls a large white tablecloth from one.

'You must see what he's like. You must see he set everything up for us, right from the start at the conference. So he could keep seeing me.'

She shakes it out over the table and for a second she is hidden from me by the billowing linen. And the doorbell rings; the white material settles. Ellen doesn't move, looking at the table.

The bell rings again, shrill in the silence. I look at her expectantly. 'Shall I get that for you?'

'No. I'll go. It'll just be another policeman wanting something,' and she walks into the hall. I hear her open it and then voices coming down the hall and back into the kitchen.

I am standing behind the island, mug in hand, expecting to see uniforms. I see Johnny.

It is Johnny, forlorn, then confused in the doorway.

My first thought is, this isn't the script. This isn't how it's meant to be. I am here with Ellen, consoling her – something has gone wrong somewhere. I am here to help, I am not an imposter on the verge of discovery. This is an interruption, not a denouement. Of all the ways I had imagined I might be caught, this one, in broad daylight, with a family crisis raging, wasn't one of them. This wasn't supposed to be it. Johnny looks at me and I look back at him.

'Skye?'

'Johnny,' I say.

'I've come to see Mum.'

He stands there, not getting it, waiting for me to explain this away. He looks meek, he looks as though he knows he is being slow about something but just doesn't know what. Ellen pushes past him to her armchair.

'Mum,' he says, brokenly, looking after her.

'What did they say?'

'They said . . . they said . . . that, oh God. That the boy had better not die.'

Her face is ashen but steely. 'And where's your father?'

'He won't be long. He went straight back to Amy's to check on her.'

'Yes.' And then, for my benefit, Ellen adds, politely, robotically. 'Amy, Andrew's sister, has had another cancer scare. A setback. He had to go to her house late on Saturday night and hasn't been home since. It's been awful for Andrew. Amy's husband works offshore on an oil rig.'

Andrew has not even seen Ellen since he found me. He has been coping with his sister's illness.

'I got bail, Mum. What's she doing here?'

'She's a friend. She's been keeping me company through this nightmare morning.'

'I'll go now.'

'You've hurt your face,' says Johnny blankly. 'And what does Mum mean, you're a friend? Since when? I don't want her around.'

Ellen looks up. 'Have you met each other?'

'Yes,' says Johnny. 'What's she doing here?'

'Johnny,' I try to find some courage. 'There's something you need to know.'

'You know Johnny?' Ellen to me. 'You never said.'

I don't take my eyes from him. 'Something I was going to tell you. I would have told you.'

He seems older. He's tired. 'I don't get it. You would have told me that you know my mother? How do you?'

'We met her on the train,' explains Ellen. 'On the train coming back from Abbotsford, that political conference there in January.'

'We met at the conference,' I say pointlessly.

'Is now the time to go through this?' asks Ellen. 'Does it matter?'

'Yes, it matters.' Johnny may have been going to say something more but I walk over and stop him.

'Johnny. Please. All you need to know is that I'm sorry, about everything. And that it's over now. I'm going.'

'Sorry about what? I don't understand. My life has just gone down the drain and you're here in Mum's home, talking gibberish . . .'

'Yes,' I nod. 'I know. It started after you went, after you disappeared . . .' And the strange thing is, I remember now. I know why I did it. And I remember how it had never felt wrong, or at least why I had never questioned the ethics of it. Johnny, and finding out about him, staying close to him, was the imperative. It had always been irrelevant that I 'shouldn't' get to know his parents. That I 'shouldn't' be making names up for myself. 'After you disappeared, I wanted to find your parents.' I just had to do it, do something. Anything.

'You arranged to meet my parents?'

'I didn't arrange it, I let it happen.' I remember now, remember what I had been unable to explain to Tam or Anna. I may not be able to justify it to anyone else but at last I know. 'I wanted to keep something of you.'

'Skye, this is really weird.' He is incredulous.

'Why are you calling her Skye?'

Johnny nods in my direction. 'She's Skye. Of course.'

'She's Molly.'

302

'Molly?' Just for a second some of the old glint comes back — 'she's bloody not' — and then dies away again. Johnny shrugs. 'No, she's not.'

'Please listen to me. I wanted to meet Ellen because she is your mother.' Because, short-lived and dispensable — orphaned — I had never been given the chance. 'So I went to the conference.'

'You came deliberately to meet me?' Ellen stands up. 'You were there for that purpose? And what is Johnny calling you?'

'Skye is my name. Molly was because I was in love with Johnny. Because I wanted to keep knowing him. To understand him.'

For a while, there is only the sound of the large black and white clock ticking. Johnny is stock-still.

'You looked so sweet, I thought,' Ellen's voice, after a while. 'At the conference. I thought you seemed so sweet. Wistful, and sad.'

'I was sad.'

'You weren't. You were cunning. You were lying to us. It was all an act, a set-up. You knew Johnny all along.' Ellen's voice sounds strangled. 'How did you even know I was going to be there?'

'I knew you were going because you told the world. On your Instagram.'

She is bewildered, slack-jawed. It doesn't make any sense to her. And then the bafflement clears a little. 'I know your name. I remember it from the waiter at Café Paris, because it was unusual. I told him the credit card wasn't either of ours.' Ellen tries to take a deep breath. 'It was yours.'

'I'm so sorry. It's true, my name is Skye. I know Johnny. I knew him first. I've known him since last year when I met him skiing in France. He was skiing, I wasn't,' I amend, as if it matters. 'I was studying. I was snowshoeing.'

'You've been stalking us,' Ellen says through white lips. How quick she is to name it.

'It wasn't like that.' It hadn't seemed like that.

'You tried to break my marriage up. You tried to use Amy against Andrew and when that backfired, when that didn't work, you tried to use yourself. You were still trying this morning.'

'I made a mistake with Amy,' I cry, 'but it was true about me,' and at the same time, Johnny says, 'Amy? What's poor Amy got to do with this?'

'Exactly,' says Ellen. 'Nothing – except to prove you got yourself mixed up with a fantasist and a liar. I was right not to believe you, *Skye*.'

'I was telling the truth about everything apart from my name,' I say desperately. 'Ellen—' but she shakes her head.

'All for revenge,' she says hoarsely. 'Because you had been scorned, first by my son and then my husband.'

'No. No, it wasn't about that. I didn't want to hurt anyone. I am not a bad person. Johnny, please don't look like that.'

'You went after my parents. My father?' He is revolted.

'I didn't go after them. I just . . . met them. And we were friends! I didn't want to lie to you, Ellen. I often thought about how to tell you the truth. I know it looks odd—'

'Odd? It's not odd, its completely fucking pathological,' sneers Johnny. 'You're a bloody bunny-boiler.'

'I'm not.' I'm not. 'Look. I know you don't care. I know you won't want to see me again but, I just . . . I just.' *Keep it together*. 'I fell in love with somebody for the first time and I didn't want to let you go. I was trying to hold on to you, in a useless way, I know . . .'

304

'I can't believe this. I don't believe it.'

'I'm sorry,' I tell them both. 'I never meant for any of this to happen.' Ellen is beginning to wheeze.

'Sorry?' There is fury now on Johnny's face. His face is coming alive with the energy. 'A drivelling sorry is not going to cut it this time.'

'I'm not drivelling. I'm sorry.'

'I almost thought about giving you another chance.'

'No, you didn't,' and I feel this bitterly. 'You never thought about getting back with me. How could you? You were with Issy all along. You just wanted someone to listen to you blathering on. You just thought, "I know, she's an easy lay, why don't I have my cake and eat it, as long as I possibly can?"'

'I can't believe I'm hearing this. How can you even think about turning this on me?'

'Because of what happened between us, that's why. The way that, after Chamonix, you treated me as though I was something to scrape off your shoes.'

'You're even more mental than I thought. It was over, done with. What did you expect?'

For the hundredth time, I think, *I'm not mental. I'm not bonkers*. I say, simply: 'I expected you.'

And he looks away.

'I expected you, Johnny, and failing that, a conversation. I know I'm not perfect but neither are you. You made mistakes too.'

'I made a mistake with you,' he says, glacial now.

'What you shouldn't have done is gone to Anna's after the accident. She told me.'

Johnny's eyes narrow, the hazel-green eye and the brown eye. 'She told you, did she? About the night I went to hers? A big mistake, obviously. In more ways than one.'

He turns to stare out of the window. 'Some fucking friend she turned out to be.'

'I think she thought the same about you,' but Johnny doesn't answer for a minute. When he turns back from the window, a look of comprehension is dawning on his face.

'Two of you. Mum, what did you say her name was? Molly?'

Ellen nods. 'Johnny, have you got an inhaler?'

'Molly,' he says slowly. 'The name of the woman that Dad says he caught snooping in the garage. With someone else. There were two of them, he said. I'd never heard the name before, I didn't understand why someone called Molly would be looking at my car.'

I can feel the colour draining from my face.

'And I thought, how strange, how weird. I don't even know a Molly. What would a Molly have against me? It can't have been you. Skye, it can't have been.'

I nod, very slowly. 'Both of us.'

'You and Anna,' says Johnny in a deadly calm voice. 'Were you looking for the car?'

I back away then. 'Yes. We found your Golf. All beaten up.'

'But how did you know the car was here?' Ellen asks. She is still wheezing.

'Because you told me.' Ellen falls back into the armchair. 'And then we came to look for ourselves. Because we saw the accident in the news and Anna was suspicious.'

Johnny is shaking his head in disbelief. 'You promised you'd get me. Didn't you. That's why you told the police. This is all happening because of you.'

'It's happening because of you, Johnny.'

'You must have set out from the start to ruin us all.' Ellen's voice is quiet, rasping.

'I did not.'

She ignores me. 'Starting at Abbotsford and ending with your search of our garage. You are only here now to see what you've done to us.'

'I'm here because you asked me. And the garage,' I add desperately, pointing at my face, 'was when Andrew did this.'

'Stop it,' she shouts suddenly. 'Stop lying.' She shakes her head. 'Not the cupboard story then after all? Do you know, I wouldn't believe anything you ever said to me again.'

Johnny is strangely un-emotive now. 'One last thing. Did you call the police about me? Or was it Anna?'

'Does it matter?'

'Yes, it matters to me.'

Just the clock ticking and Ellen's uneven breath. *It matters to me.*

'Anna did.' *It would never have been me.*

Johnny goes back to staring out of the window and then he says, 'We could press charges,' almost conversationally, to no one in particular. 'She can't get away with this.' She? Like the beginning, as on the train journey from Abbotsford. I have lost my identity again. I am nameless again.

'Johnny,' Ellen, who has been leaning back into her chair, speaks in a croaky, jagged voice. 'That's not going to happen. No police. I hardly think more police involvement is going to help the family now. No charges. Wouldn't stick. I don't. Want her. Here. Tell her. To go.'

'Yes,' Johnny says tonelessly. 'You're right. Just go, Skye.' He looks at me, or at least I think he does, but his eyes are so dead. He's looking through me. He has no expression on his face at all. He looks beaten. Blank.

And Ellen clutches her chest. 'Ellen,' I say, and she looks up at me. She can't breathe. She does that thing with her hand and Johnny starts searching his pockets wildly.

'Inhaler. Skye, where's a bloody inhaler?'

Ellen looks at me again, in desperation. 'You have one,' she manages.

'I don't. I'm so sorry. I don't.'

Johnny takes her head in his hands. 'Mum, don't worry, keep calm, breathe . . .' and he's talking to himself, saying 'I didn't bother getting another, why didn't I get another,' cradling her in his arms and I don't know what to do and then I think *dial 999* and I grab Ellen's phone from the island and make an emergency call. Johnny is saying, 'Help is coming, Mum. Help is coming.' The sound of her reaching for air is almost inhuman.

'She has one,' Ellen croaks again and when I shake my head I see real fear on her face.

'Find her doctor's bag, for God's sake, quick. Look in there.'

I stay on the phone and rush into the hall. Ellen's bag isn't there so I go as fast as I can back into the kitchen.

'How long? Mum, the ambulance is on its way.'

'How long?' I repeat, my own voice rising in panic and I repeat to Johnny, 'They're close by. Keep calm, they say keep calm. Is she breathing?'

It must be me speaking but I sound very far away.

'Barely.'

'Not really,' I say, my voice breaking.

The voice on the other end of the mobile intones, 'We're going to talk you through this. Three minutes,' and my own disembodied voice echoes the timing to Johnny.

'Please just hurry. It's the house with the police outside,' and I pass the mobile to Johnny. Where is her damn bag, and I start throwing cushions off the sofa and upturning chairs, rifling under papers on the island and searching behind curtains. I don't give up looking even when the thought of the inhaler in Andrew's coat pocket on the train comes into my mind. I keep looking even when I've remembered that Andrew keeps Ellen's rarely used inhalers with him. Ellen doesn't carry them herself. Ellen needs Andrew. She can't survive, she can't be who she is without him. She can't be anyone at all without him.

She is unmoving on the floor now, and Johnny is bent over her and then I stop looking at them. The scene is personal. I can't watch any more. I go to the front door instead and open it, and immediately get pushed aside by a flurry of paramedics and a policeman. I point down the hallway, the gold bugs on the green wallpaper flying towards the kitchen, as always, showing the way. The policeman must have been on the grass by the garage because he leaves muddy footprints on the white marble slabs. The Sardinian scarf flutters off the banisters in the draught.

50

I meet Anna at the weekend. We walk together all the way down Canongate and I tell her how the Strachans found me out.

'I couldn't not go to Ellen,' I say, trying to sound reasonable and grown-up. 'I had to see if she was OK, and then Johnny came back.'

'Poor you,' she offers, but not entirely as if she means it.

'I don't deserve any sympathy at all. It was my fault.'

'I suppose it doesn't matter any more. It's over now.'

'Yes, and all the lies too. I'm not sorry about that. But the Strachans think I had it in for them from the beginning.'

'Yes,' she agrees and links her arm through mine. 'Do you care?'

'I suppose I shouldn't.'

'Any news on the boy?'

'No. Still the same. It's touch and go.'

Then Anna says, 'I heard the latest on Johnny.'

'Oh?'

'Didn't you?'

'No. I'm not really following it,' I add lamely. Mostly I can't bear to look, although it's hard to avoid. To see his name in print, to see the official charges and the gravity of the crime. It's all over the news and the internet. Someone has shut down his Facebook page because of the abuse.

'They've charged him. Actually, they've thrown the book at him. He's being charged with driving without a licence or insurance. Dangerous driving, failing to stop and report; driving while intoxicated—'

'How can they prove that?'

'Because the original witness who saw a black car has said it was swerving all over the road. And,' she clears her throat, 'because I can testify to him smelling of alcohol that night.'

'Right.'

'Everyone says he's looking at a custodial sentence. Because of all the charges and also because he's a lawyer, the jury will see his dishonesty as a particularly severe crime. I'm amazed he got bail.'

'He'll go to prison then.'

'Looks like it.' She shrugs. 'Lawyers are the public-facing side of justice. It's got to be done. And the best place for him anyway, I say.'

I wait a moment and then I say, 'Anna.'

'Yes?' She turns to look at me, small and determined with her dark hair flying around her face. 'What?'

'What happened with Johnny that night? With you and him, I mean.'

'Why do you ask?' She folds her arms and then is still, staring back at me.

'Something he said. Something to do with that night he came to yours.'

'I don't know what he said. He can go and jump in the river for all I care.' There's a pause, and then she says, almost angrily: 'He can't have meant anything – except that he's uncomfortable with you and me being friends.'

'No.' I shake my head. 'It's more than that. And you hate him. More than me, I think, you're gladder than I am that he's going to prison. That he's being punished.' She doesn't say anything so I soldier on. 'I just wondered if anything had happened that you hadn't told me about.'

'It's not totally about revenge. Why can't it also be that Johnny got found out for once? That instead of getting away with everything like he usually does, he had to face up to what he did. That's how I look at it, anyway.'

I don't know why I can't look at it that way. I guess it all feels too personal. It's all tied up with me and Johnny and I'm so ashamed of feeling guilty and still feeling sad. But I don't say any of this, I say, 'Fine. But I hope you'd tell me if anything happened when he turned up.'

She's quiet for a bit and then she says, 'I really don't want to talk about it.'

After a while we reach Holyrood Palace. Arthur's Seat is above us and the crumbling ruins of St Anthony's chapel. 'Ellen's doing well,' I say.

'Yeah, you said. Have you actually seen her though?'

I tell Anna that I've tried, twice. 'But she doesn't want to see me, not surprisingly.'

And then she wrong-foots me with her next, quick question. 'And Johnny? Have you seen him?'

'Have I seen him? No. How and when would I see him?'

'I don't know,' she answers, looking at her feet. 'Only that I'm never quite sure with you.'

'No more lies,' I say firmly and she nods.

'Yes.' And then, from nowhere, 'In which case, I don't think I can keep this from you after all.' She takes a deep breath. 'Something did happen that night.'

I'm glad we're walking, and the hill is steep. Both of us are looking down, breathing heavily.

She carries on. 'I suppose it doesn't matter any more. But only so you know. I'm not proud of myself. You see, at first, I was pleased. Overjoyed, really. He hadn't come near me for so long.'

I stop then and turn around, keeping my face from her. *He'd been with me, that's why he hadn't been near you, Anna.* I can see the car park down below, and a taxi dropping someone off.

'But I couldn't hide from what was really going on, I couldn't pretend. That he was in a mess, that he didn't really care whose bed he was in.'

He clearly had cared. He'd chosen hers.

'So hardly love's young dream. He left early, as always, before it even got light, and the next thing I know, he's engaged to Issy.'

I don't know what to say, but I know what I mustn't say, what the old me might say. I'm trying to ignore a hot, jealous spark that has flared up.

'It's partly why I wanted to go to his for the drinks that night at his flat, when I should have been with you. I couldn't believe it. I wanted to see him and Issy together for myself and ask him what was going on.'

'Did you?'

'I tried. He managed me though. Made sure I wasn't ever alone with him, kept me at arm's length, that sort of thing. He made me feel about this big. And I hated him for it even more, when the truth came out. He'd hit a child on a bike, hidden the evidence and come straight to me. He just used me.'

The thought of her providing solace. I don't like it at all. But I can keep this away, I must keep this spark small. It's over.

'But I hadn't hesitated. And then, like I say, it got worse. When we found out what he'd done, I felt like some sort of accomplice.' Andrew's word for her and me. It was supposed to be her and me, not her and him. 'He was desperate, and as it turned out, so was I. I think he probably just came to me because I live nearby.'

Maybe. 'You mustn't think like that.' Probably.

'I feel sick when I remember it. I keep imagining there was blood on his shirt.'

'Of course there wasn't.' Every time. Love it.

'Well, you can understand why I want to forget about it.'

'Yes, I suppose so.'

'What do you mean, you suppose so? Talk about a walk of shame. And I've done quite a few. You can't imagine it's a memory to treasure.'

'No, not for a second.' I don't add: he hadn't come to me. He hadn't come the extra few miles to me. He chose Anna. In his hour of crisis, he had not come to me.

Anna and I turn around at the chapel to head back to the city, and before she leaves me at the library, she tells me that she's got a friend looking for someone to rent their spare room. She knows I don't want to live in my flat any more and this is just the sort of thing I'm looking for. I don't want to be on my own. And when Anna has gone, this thought reminds me to put the date into my calendar that Tam and I have arranged supper together on. Then I turn my phone off, and run up the university steps to fill my head with the world of ice.

When I emerge a few hours later, it has started to snow. Huge, oversized flakes are tumbling from the sky and turning the world grey. It feels odd, but it's not uncommon to have spring snow fall. I turn towards the centre of Edinburgh and keep walking through it, down Princes Street, past the Balmoral and the Scott Monument and finally I get to the Water of Leith at Stockbridge. St Bernard's Row is within sight and I rest against the stone in the snow and think about you. Spring flowers are struggling through the snow-spotted earth along with the fag ends and broken bottles of

314

Irn-Bru. I can't do anything about you, or about you and Anna, any more than I can do anything about the weather.

This time, I begin at the end. I think about you likely behind bars in prison soon, perhaps for some time. I think about the boy you almost killed. I think about your car, covered with the fact of your guilt, concealed in the garage nearby. I think about Andrew's genuine horror afterwards, and his face before he had hit me. His sister facing more chemotherapy, and Ellen in hospital. And then I go back to thinking about you, this time in Anna's bed, and Anna comforting you, her giving everything to you, unreservedly, without knowing why you needed her. I would have done the same. I think about that until I can't think about it any more. It's in the past, I tell myself.

And the times I spent as Molly. I think about how I had thought of getting back with you, and wished for it for so long. I think about what I am keeping from Anna, the time after the pub and the times since the pub, when I met you in your flat and in St Bernard's Row. I remember the desperate quality of my life without you, when you left so suddenly and without explanation.

And I think about us in the Alps. You, dragging the sledge behind you up the hill with icy breath and carefree gait. Your hand, outstretched for mine, such a small gesture, received so gratefully and with far more meaning inferred from it than was meant. I never did learn that indifference is still indifference even when so affably displayed. I always mistook you for someone else. It wasn't your fault. I suppose we were doomed from the first moment we spoke, the moment by the automatic doors in the hostel when I was struggling with my boots and I thought I saw something in you. I thought you better than your group of the morning.

You at the bar, undecided as to whether or not you should join me. The tealights and the wine, and your eyes, as ever, absolutely conflicting and in the end, indecipherable. The two-metre rule. *Stay close*. I obeyed you, didn't I, but I have stayed close for too long now. You are going to prison. *No one is leaving*. You will be there, and I will be here. No one else has you. It's over between you and Anna. There is no future that I can see. Perhaps it is time to finally say goodbye, and with this idea, there is a seed of hope. I hold on to this hope, and allow it.

I think about the power of silence and how you had harnessed your power over me incidentally. You were never Machiavellian; there was no endgame for you, and nothing you wanted to achieve other than a departure without fuss. You just didn't want to engage. And I'm tired now, tired of holding on. And glimpsing the idea of life without you is like finally turning away from an infected bite or a lesion that I've been unable to let alone all this time. I clutch at the hope. I'm going to let you go.

Taking the snow globe you gave me out of my rucksack, I shake it once more. I leave it on the bridge, snow falling in the tiny ornament, and snow falling.

Epilogue

Anna

In the end, I couldn't keep what happened from anyone.

It's hot where we are. It's bloody gorgeous too. I think I like it better than Skye does, which isn't really surprising because she doesn't do so well in the sun, being so pale and all that. She burns really easily. But it doesn't matter, she doesn't mind. She pulls her sunbed up into the shade and reads all day looking willowy and elegant and I pull mine down to the sea and listen to music, taking loads of photos and watching the world go by, getting sweatier and browner. Resting. I haven't had a holiday for ages. Since before all this.

That cold, snowy spring, the one when Johnny was charged, seems so long ago. He's still in prison. Archie Fraser, the boy, survived but because Johnny tried to hide the car and because he shouldn't have been driving anyway they gave him three years as an example. He got sent down immediately after the trial finished. He'll be out this summer we think, but struck off the roll of solicitors and fair to say, not many prospects open to him, at least not in Edinburgh. He will need his family then. Issy, as predicted, left and went back to Sweden. GMT fired him, of course, and it all got ugly. The papers followed the trial and people took against him. Ellen came out of hospital and

317

arrived home to find bricks were being thrown through those large posh windows of theirs. They sold the practice and went to live in Oban. I know Andrew misses it and for all his faults, he was pretty committed to running the place. We're going to stay with them next week. It took some time before they forgave me, but they didn't really have a choice in the end.

It wasn't any fun being on the witness stand and testifying that Johnny had come to my flat, and seemed drunk on the night of Thursday 23 February. He had, I wasn't lying about it, only that he seemed so many other things too, things that they weren't interested in. That he'd seemed vulnerable, and scared. Skye didn't come to the trial (ever) and neither did Ellen, at least not on the day I had to. Andrew did, he was there every day without fail. Loyal to the end.

I don't think I told Skye, but I never really blamed her for lying to Ellen about who she was. I would have lied too once upon a time, if I'd thought it would help with Johnny. I would have told the worst lies if I had to. I would have invented disasters of every kind just to try and rouse his interest. But they only had to be small lies. Lies like where I was, and why I was there; they were just to help with the presentation of me. Sometimes he had rung, idle and incurious, to ask what I was up to. It was hard work, it was exhausting being so bloody fun all the time. I would say, I'm just mixing cocktails. Getting ready to go to a party, that sort of thing; the truth was probably having a cup of tea or leaving work. I just wanted to be interesting to him so I used to give him an overload of false information that he didn't really want (he never asked what cocktails or why, or whose party I'd gone to). It took me too long to see that if someone doesn't care, it follows that they don't care what you do or who with, whatever it may be.

And I kept so much of myself hidden from him. To try and keep the distasteful (e.g. smoking) and the unpalatable (e.g. affection) from being discovered. It was exhausting.

I tried (and failed) to make him envious too. I made more of men that came and went than I needed to. But he never showed the slightest trace of jealousy about any of them. I could have, and it often occurred to me to do so, made up countless numbers of them to flaunt in front of him but truthfully, I knew that they wouldn't bother him. In all the time we were friends, we only ever talked about his love-life, and his stuff, endlessly complicated. All his exes, we dissected them all, (with the exception of Issy, who really outlasted everyone) but always jokily because he never took any of them seriously. All of them had in common that they were too . . . something. Excessive in one way or another. Too clever, too tearful, too sporty, too hairy, too smiley. I won't tell her but Skye was a source of amusement for being – too serious. The one he should have taken seriously.

I'd been getting fed up, I'd had enough of him really, but it took becoming friends with Skye for me to fully realise the truth. I knew Johnny didn't care about Skye but she had acted as I used to and it was like looking in a mirror. He didn't care about me either.

He made a fool of us, of all the women unfortunate enough to get in his way. I was glad at the time that we caught him out in the accident. I didn't regret my part in what happened at all. But looking back now: if I had known then that I couldn't ever escape him – would I have done the same?

I glance up towards the shade again.

She is cool as a cucumber, calm and composed. She's such a relief after all the bullshit. She always seems direct and honest, which is why the Molly thing was so weird. She's determined, I suppose. And so together, and totally reliable. She never lets me down; if she says she's going to do something, she will. Her aunt died six months ago. She's on her own now. I don't know what I'd do without her really. I bought her a gift from the market yesterday. I'll give it to her at dinner.

We don't talk about Ellen and Andrew. It's too awkward now because they didn't forgive Skye. But we can't avoid talking about Johnny and sometimes she goes where I can't follow, back to their past. She honestly had no idea that he had a girlfriend when she met him, but she's naive about things like that. I think she thought he was going to propose after that Christmas. He must have laid it on really thick. She kept saying he'd seemed perfect. And she always says that the worst thing was the way he'd ended it, just disappearing and never having the guts to tell her. He's not brave, I told her, and she said, but he could be. She smiled and said in her mysterious way, *Feel the fear and do it anyway*. Jeez, I replied. We've all heard that one before. It was horrid to see the look on her face and, to be honest, I'd rather not talk about all that. I'd rather not go there. But I catch her sometimes, staring into space, her green eyes unreadable. Sometimes she seems miles away and I've no idea what she is thinking.

And sometimes I see a look on her face that worries me. Not worries me exactly, that's going too far. A watchful one. Maybe I'm just reminded that I didn't know her before Johnny and so I can't really tell if she's changed or if she was always so attentive, so sombre. Then a child's cry interrupts my reverie and immediately I am on my feet, running over the sand towards them. But Skye has it under control, Skye is there in that pale-green dress that makes her look like a water nymph or something. Her hair, long and red, is loosely tied back with two tortoiseshell clips on either side (like Ellen's clips, I think suddenly. The way Ellen styles her hair) and, as usual, those two guys from the hotel are staring at her. She has that effect on men.

Fred's floppy blond hair is sticking to his forehead. 'Is he OK?'

'Of course,' Skye says. 'Don't worry,' and she reaches out to tickle Fred under his arm. Immediately he is giggling again, laughing up at her slavishly. 'He's fine. Aren't you, my darling?'

I collapse into the chair next to her and we both watch my little boy with his bricks and the dinosaurs his grand-mother gave him. He is happy to be here in the warm and on the beach, adored by us both. The holiday has been a tonic, a long overdue change of scene. Clever Skye for suggesting and choosing it. Fred and I hadn't been fussed, but she had insisted on Sardinia.

'Maybe he's a little tired,' Skye says after a while. 'I'll put him down if you like. For his nap.'

Fred's head snaps up to us, his smile fading.

'Don't you want a little snooze, darling?' and Fred looks appalled at the idea and I wonder, when Fred is like this, if Skye recognises it too.

'I'll take him,' Skye says, standing up, and now Fred's eyes fill with mutinous tears. One brown and one hazel, filling with the disappointment.

'No,' I decide. 'I've cooked myself in the sun and I'm too hot. I'll go with him and meet you later on for happy hour. Go and chat to those poor sods gawping at you,' and scooping the reluctant Fred into my arms I blow Skye a kiss, and walk with Johnny's son back to our room.

Thank You

My mother and father. Jane, Annabel, Tom and Rosie.

Rollo. Our children, Rory and Isobel.

My classmates on the MA in Creative Writing at Bath Spa. Richard Kerridge, Celia Brayfield, and especially Beatrice Hitchman and Samantha Harvey.

Matilda Forbes Watson and Alina Flint at WME, Harriet Bourton, Olivia Barber and Laura Gerrard at Orion.

Annabel Byng, Joanna Frank and Melanie Golding, for reading the manuscript at various stages.

Emily Bearn, Lucy Burnand, Donald Cameron of Lochiel, Netta Carey, Ant Gordon Lennox, Antonia Howatson, Gillian Johnson, Alan Parker, Adam Polonsky and Nicholas Shakespeare.

And James, with love.

Author's Note

I have moved the locations of the Dark Mile and Caig Falls to where the witch of Moy lived. In reality, both are nearer Achnacarry, the ancestral home of the clan Cameron.